Berkley Prime Crime titles by Sheila Connolly

Orchard Mysteries

ONE BAD APPLE
ROTTEN TO THE CORE
RED DELICIOUS DEATH
A KILLER CROP

Museum Mysteries

FUNDRAISING THE DEAD
LET'S PLAY DEAD

More praise for

FUNDRAISING THE DEAD

"She's smart, she's savvy, and she's sharp enough to spot what really goes on behind the scenes in museum politics. The practical and confident Nell Pratt is exactly the kind of sleuth you want in your corner when the going gets tough. Sheila Connolly serves up a snappy and sophisticated mystery that leaves you lusting for the next witty installment."

—Mary Jane Maffini, author of the Charlotte Adams Mysteries

"*National Treasure* meets *The Philadelphia Story* in this clever, charming, and sophisticated caper. When murder and mayhem become the main attractions at a prestigious museum, its feisty fundraiser goes undercover to prove it's not just the museum's pricey collection that's concealing a hidden history. Secrets, lies, and a delightful revenge conspiracy make this a real page-turner!"

—Hank Phillippi Ryan, Agatha Award–winning author of
Drive Time

"Sheila Connolly's wonderful new series is a witty, engaging blend of history and mystery with a smart sleuth who already feels like a good friend. Like all of Ms. Connolly's books, *Fundraising the Dead* is hard to put down. Her stories always keep me turning pages—often well past my bedtime."

—Julie Hyzy, national bestselling author of
the White House Chef Mysteries

"Old families, old papers, and the old demons of sex and money shape Connolly's cozy series launch, which will appeal to fans of her Orchard and (as Sarah Atwell) Glassblowing mysteries . . . [The] archival milieu and the foibles of the characters are intriguing, and it's refreshing to encounter an FBI man who is human, competent, and essential to the plot." —*Publishers Weekly*

continued . . .

Praise for the Orchard Mysteries

"Sheila Connolly's Orchard Mysteries are some of the most satisfying cozy mysteries I've read . . . Warm and entertaining from the first paragraph to the last. Fans will look forward to the next Orchard Mystery."
—*Lesa's Book Critiques*

"An enjoyable and well written book with some excellent apple recipes at the end."
—*Cozy Library*

"The mystery is intelligent and has an interesting twist . . . *Rotten to the Core* is a fun, quick read with an enjoyable heroine."
—*The Mystery Reader* (four stars)

"Delightful . . . [A] fascinating whodunit filled with surprises."
—*The Mystery Gazette*

"[A] delightful new series."
—*Gumshoe Review*

"The premise and plot are solid, and Meg seems a perfect fit for her role."
—*Publishers Weekly*

"A fresh and appealing sleuth with a bushel full of entertaining problems. *One Bad Apple* is one crisp, delicious read." —Claudia Bishop, author of the Hemlock Falls Mysteries

"A delightful look at small-town New England, with an intriguing puzzle thrown in. And anybody who's ever tended a septic system is going to empathize with amateur detective Meg Corey."
—JoAnna Carl, author of the Chocoholic Mysteries

"A promising new mystery series. Thoroughly enjoyable . . . I can't wait for the next book and a chance to spend more time with Meg and the good people of Granford."
—Sammi Carter, author of the Candy Shop Mysteries

LET'S PLAY DEAD

Sheila Connolly

BERKLEY PRIME CRIME, NEW YORK

THE BERKLEY PUBLISHING GROUP
Published by the Penguin Group
Penguin Group (USA) Inc.
375 Hudson Street, New York, New York 10014, USA
Penguin Group (Canada), 90 Eglinton Avenue East, Suite 700, Toronto, Ontario M4P 2Y3, Canada
(a division of Pearson Penguin Canada Inc.)
Penguin Books Ltd., 80 Strand, London WC2R 0RL, England
Penguin Group Ireland, 25 St. Stephen's Green, Dublin 2, Ireland (a division of Penguin Books Ltd.)
Penguin Group (Australia), 250 Camberwell Road, Camberwell, Victoria 3124, Australia
(a division of Pearson Australia Group Pty. Ltd.)
Penguin Books India Pvt. Ltd., 11 Community Centre, Panchsheel Park, New Delhi—110 017, India
Penguin Group (NZ), 67 Apollo Drive, Rosedale, Auckland 0632, New Zealand
(a division of Pearson New Zealand Ltd.)
Penguin Books (South Africa) (Pty.) Ltd., 24 Sturdee Avenue, Rosebank, Johannesburg 2196,
South Africa

Penguin Books Ltd., Registered Offices: 80 Strand, London WC2R 0RL, England

This is a work of fiction. Names, characters, places, and incidents either are the product of the author's imagination or are used fictitiously, and any resemblance to actual persons, living or dead, business establishments, events, or locales is entirely coincidental. The publisher does not have any control over and does not assume any responsibility for author or third-party websites or their content.

LET'S PLAY DEAD

A Berkley Prime Crime Book / published by arrangement with the author

PRINTING HISTORY
Berkley Prime Crime mass-market edition / July 2011

ISBN: 978-0-425-24220-9

BERKLEY® PRIME CRIME
Berkley Prime Crime Books are published by The Berkley Publishing Group,
a division of Penguin Group (USA) Inc.,
375 Hudson Street, New York, New York 10014.
BERKLEY® PRIME CRIME and the PRIME CRIME logo are trademarks of Penguin Group (USA) Inc.

PRINTED IN THE UNITED STATES OF AMERICA

10 9 8 7 6 5 4 3 2 1

ACKNOWLEDGMENTS

The setting for this book was inspired by Philadelphia's outstanding children's museum, Please Touch, where I worked several years ago. The core philosophy that kids should be free to enjoy the whole museum experience, which means being able to touch and even climb on the exhibits, was and is wonderful. While the physical setting in this book bears no resemblance to the real museum, and none of the characters are based on anyone there, past or present, I did borrow the hands-on spirit.

There is no Harriet the Hedgehog series (although maybe there should be!), and most children's book writers I've met have been delightful people, not prima donnas.

Thanks as always to my perceptive editor, Shannon Jamieson Vazquez, who keeps forcing me to plug those pesky holes in my plot, and to my agent, Jessica Faust of BookEnds, who made this series possible. Thanks also to Carol Kersbergen, who keeps me up to date about goings-on in Philadelphia, and to former colleague Sherrill Joyner, from whom I've shamelessly borrowed a character I'm sure she'll recognize. Paul Garbarczyk provided valuable information on how to electrocute someone (and if there are any errors, they're mine), and thanks to Julie Hyzy for putting me in touch with him. And as always, Sisters in Crime and the Guppies chapter have been there from the beginning to cheer me on.

CHAPTER 1

I wanted to lay my head down on my desk and weep. Or pound my head on it. Neither was appropriate treatment for the lovely eighteenth-century mahogany desk that I had inherited from my recently departed predecessor. Somehow I had ended up with his position, a turn of events that I was still trying to figure out more than two months after it had happened. In a moment of dazzled weakness, I had said yes when the board had asked me to take over as president of the Pennsylvania Antiquarian Society. *Why* they had asked me was another matter altogether. That had been before Thanksgiving, and ever since I had accepted their offer, I'd been running around like a headless chicken trying to keep the Society on course. Luckily nobody had paid much attention during the holidays, but now it was January, a whole new year, and it was time to get things done.

So here I was, trying to wrap my hands and my head around running a historical institution with a creaking hundred-plus-year-old building in Center City Philadelphia, filled with literally millions of priceless objects relating to Pennsylvania history. I'm Nell Pratt, former fundraiser, currently crazy.

My most immediate problem was filling some conspicuously empty staff positions. The president slot was already filled, thanks to me. But that meant I had to find someone to fill my old position, since we couldn't afford to let the pace of fundraising slow if we wanted to keep the lights on, and pay staff salaries, and beef up our security systems, and . . . the list kept going. At least I knew the right questions to ask of applicants for my former job. I was less well prepared to interview applicants for the position of registrar, the person who kept track of what we had and where it was—or was supposed to be, which was not always the same thing. The last registrar had been extremely efficient and meticulous in his record keeping, and finding someone to step into his shoes was not going to be easy, especially since we had difficulty paying competitive salaries at the moment.

And then there was the position of assistant to the president—in other words, the person who was supposed to be handling all the pesky details like scheduling appointments for me.

So, three important jobs to fill. And possibly more to come, if I didn't manage to stabilize operations and convince my long-suffering staff that things were looking up. I wasn't sure they were, but I had to believe that, didn't I?

It was four o'clock in the afternoon. I had conducted six (at least, I think it was six) interviews during the day, and by now I was having trouble remembering my own name, much less what the applicants' names were. I hoped I hadn't insulted anyone, or worse, scared them away by giving them the impression they would end up working for a crazy lady who had no idea what she was doing. That would be me.

I compromised by laying my head on my folded arms, on the desk. No tears: I couldn't afford to mar the original, highly polished finish on the piece. My respite was short-lived, interrupted by a knock at the door. Could I pretend to be asleep? Unlikely, and that would set a very poor example. For the life of me I couldn't remember if I had any more scheduled appointments that day, but I wouldn't put it past me to forget. Yet another reason why I was in desperate need of an assistant.

Reluctantly I sat up and regarded my latest visitor. Female, fiftyish, well put together. Blonde hair pulled back in a ponytail that should have looked dated but worked on her. A smile that was sympathetic rather than smarmy. And most important, she was carrying two large cups from the place around the corner that made dynamite coffee.

"You look like you were rode hard and put away wet," she drawled, a hint of the South in her voice.

"That sounds about right." I smiled. "Do I dare hope that one of those cups is for me?"

"I took a wild guess that you could use some caffeine about now. I brought milk and sugar, too. Can I come in?"

"Of course." At the moment, I would have let in just about anyone who was carrying that large cup of coffee. "Please, sit down. There must be a coaster around here somewhere . . ." I rummaged in my desk drawers, which contained . . . nothing. Apparently my predecessor had existed on air alone.

"Way ahead of you." With a flourish, my guest whipped out some paper napkins.

I was impressed. I took the coffee and inhaled about half of it before I could résumé normal functioning. "Thank you from the bottom of my heart. Now, let's start over. Do we have an appointment?"

"Actually, we do. At least, I made one with your human resources person, Melanie . . . ?"

"Right, Melanie Wilson. She probably told me, but I've had so many interviews lately it's hard to keep straight. Your name is?"

"Shelby Carver. You don't have my résumé handy, do you?"

I looked at the snowdrifts of paper on my desk. "Uh, maybe."

"Well, I'd be happy to make up some good stuff."

I looked dubiously at Shelby, trying to figure out if she was serious. "Why don't you tell me what you think I need to know? Oh, no, wait a sec." With the infusion of caffeine, my brain seemed to be working again. "How did you get up here?" I knew we had security problems at the Society, but letting a stranger just waltz up to the administrative floor was a bit much by any standard.

"You mean, up to this floor? Don't you worry. That nice man at the front desk—Bob, was it?—stopped me, and when I told him I was here for an interview, he called upstairs and talked to Melanie. But she was kind of busy, so she told Bob to just send me right up. He escorted me to the elevator, and I guess he had to use his key to get me up here?"

I groaned inwardly. I didn't want to count the number of things wrong with what Shelby had just told me. One, no outsider should roam unescorted within our building. Melanie should have gone down to the front desk and taken Shelby in hand personally. Two, because Melanie hadn't, Bob had had to leave his post, which left the front door unguarded—which he shouldn't have done. Obviously my message about building security was not getting through. Okay, not many people were going to wander in off the street—well, except for the occasional homeless person looking for warmth and a bathroom—and even fewer would grab a nineteenth-century history of Bucks County from the nearest shelf and make off with it. But someone could easily have hidden somewhere until closing and then rifled the collections at will. Note to self: *Bring this up—again—at the next staff meeting.*

"Did I lose you?" Shelby asked innocently. "Have some more coffee, while I give you the short version. I started out as a social wife and did lots of party planning and schmoozing—that was back when my husband, John, was trying to break into local politics."

"Not around here, I take it?"

"How'd you ever guess?" she said with a smile. "We're both Virginia born and raised, although John's mama's family comes from just outside of Philadelphia. Well, John eventually gave up on that political idea and took up with something else, and our daughter, Melissa, was in college, so I got a real job, raising money for the local historical society back home. If you ever find my résumé, it's all on there."

I knew Melanie had vetted the applicants and had sent through only the ones who actually were qualified. Besides, I wanted to believe Shelby. I liked her. But hiring decisions were supposed to be rational and carefully considered. And I didn't fully trust myself—my instincts had been wrong as often as right recently.

I sighed. "How long have you been in Philadelphia?"

"About two years. John works for a medical group, when he's not building boats—that's his real passion, but it's an expensive hobby."

"You have any background in history?" I asked.

"Sure do: ten years with my local historical society, first as treasurer, then as president. Of course, there were only about twenty members, and half of them were over seventy, so there wasn't a whole lot of excitement going on there."

"You would fit in just fine here. Most of our members won't see sixty again, but since they're mostly retired they have plenty of time to explore our collections." I scrambled for more questions. While I was floundering, Shelby asked, "What do you need here?"

"I'll be frank with you—we're kind of in flux. I've been president for only a couple of months now, although I've worked here for over five years. You'd be taking the job I had until last fall, so at least I could walk you through it, when I have time. If you know Philadelphia, you'll know that this is a combination of historical society, library, and museum, and we've got a lot of collections shoved wherever we can fit them, in an old building that leaks. We've got a board whose average age is seventy, and none of them like change much. None of them have megabucks, either. We have an endowment that is pathetic, and a budget that includes a lot of wishful thinking. I'm also looking for a new registrar, and I desperately need an assistant."

"Sounds like it's been a wild ride. I've seen the job description, of course, but maybe you could tell me what I'd really have to do? *Director of development* sounds so vague."

She was right. Most people didn't have a clue what *development* meant in our context. "Raising money, of course—direct-mail solicitations, grant writing, that kind of thing. Event planning—parties where we try to keep the board and the local people with money happy so they'll keep giving us more donations. I assume you've done all this sort of thing before?"

"Sure have," Shelby replied promptly. "We pulled in some nice historic preservation money for my old historical society, which I swear was about to fall down around our ears. And I just love putting together parties!" She stopped for a moment, then said delicately, "I seem to recall you've had some troubles here lately?"

Of course she would have heard. She *should* have heard if she had any involvement in the Philadelphia cultural community. "They're all behind us, I promise." Well, except for a few missing artifacts, but she didn't need to know about those, or at least, not yet. "But you're smart to ask, because it will make it a bit more challenging to raise money at the moment."

She nodded once. "So you're saying there might be some bumpy spots ahead?"

"There might," I admitted. "Does that bother you? I mean, if you're looking for stability and security at this point in your life, maybe this isn't the place for you."

Shelby laughed. "Shucks, and here I was hoping for a nice boring, repetitive job for my twilight years." She paused and cocked her head, studying me. "Okay, you've been straight with me, so I'll be, too. I think we could work well together. I'm a self-starter, but I know when I need to ask for help. Word on the street is that this is a good place, in spite of your recent problems. I get along well with people, and I know how to wheedle money out of them. Is that good enough?"

"We can't pay a lot," I said dubiously, knowing that might be the deal killer, and I was starting to really, really like Shelby. I mentioned a number that made me cringe.

Sure, it had been *my* salary, but I'd been willing to accept the mediocre pay because I loved the place; I wasn't sure it would be enough to entice someone from outside the institution.

Shelby didn't answer immediately, and I held my breath. "That's about what I figured. Low, but I don't think you're playing games with me—that's what you can afford to pay right now, right?"

"Exactly. And I can't tell you it'll get better anytime soon. I don't want to promise you something I can't deliver."

"You're an honest woman, Nell Pratt, and I appreciate that. I'd be pleased if you'd consider me for the position."

Bells and bluebirds went off in my head. "Can you start tomorrow?" To hell with checking references—just for once, I wanted to go by my gut. "Er, you don't happen to have a criminal record, do you? History of embezzlement? Drug habit?"

"No, ma'am. None of the above. Where's my office?"

A miracle had just occurred: I'd actually filled a position! "Let me give you the grand tour."

I showed her the administrative offices and pointed out the general layout of the place, and we decided to save the areas where the collections were housed for a later date. I made sure to escort her to the door, since the front desk staff had already left for the day. "So I'll see you in the morning, Shelby?"

"Sure will. Thanks, Nell. I'm really looking forward to being here. Bye now!"

I'd barely shut the door when I turned to find Marty Terwilliger standing behind me in the lobby. If I'd had anything to drop, I would have. Not that Marty was frightening—she was a wiry, fifty-something woman from one of Philadelphia's oldest families, and I knew her well, as a board member, ally, and maybe friend. "Hello, Marty, I didn't know you were in the building. Were you looking for me?"

"Not particularly—just working on the Terwilliger Collection. Who was that?"

"That, I hope, is our new director of development. Her name's Shelby Carver."

"Not from Philadelphia, is she?"

"No, Virginia. You have a problem with that? Being born in Philadelphia wasn't one of the job requirements."

"Not if she can get the job done, I don't. You heard from Jimmy lately?" she asked.

Jimmy was a cousin of Marty's—half of the residents of Philadelphia and the surrounding counties were Marty's cousins, and I didn't even try to work out how they all fit together—but more important, Jimmy was also Special Agent James Morrison of the Philadelphia office of the FBI, who was helping us to recover some historical items that had vanished from the Society's collections. He remained cautiously optimistic about their recovery, but we hadn't seen many pieces come back yet.

"No, he hasn't been in touch."

Marty snorted. "I told him he should call you."

"What, socially, you mean? You playing matchmaker now, Marty?" I'd thought there'd been some sparks between us, but when I hadn't heard from him over the holidays, I'd begun to think I'd just imagined it.

Marty grinned at me. "That boy's a little slow. I thought I'd give him a nudge."

"We'll see. Are you on your way out?"

"I'm done for now, but I'll be back in the morning. This Shelby person's coming back, then?"

"I certainly hope so."

"Maybe I'll introduce myself."

"Whatever you do, Marty, don't scare her off." Marty was good-hearted, but could be . . . blunt on occasion.

"Who, me? See you tomorrow, Nell."

CHAPTER 2

Still brimming with glee about having finally crossed one thing off my enormous to-do list, I took the train home to my pleasant and pricey suburb of Bryn Mawr, west of the city. Finally one thing had gone right. Sure, I knew there were a few hundred other things that were still hanging over my head like melting icicles, but I was going to savor my victories where I could. Now if I could only find an assistant, I would be ecstatic.

The name *Bryn Mawr* means "big hill" in Welsh. It was a far more euphonious name than its former one, Humphreysville, which had been deemed too prosaic when the railroad came through in the 1860s. To be fair, there had once been a lot of Welsh settlers in this part of the world—that was one of those facts that, as a manager at an important historical institution, I was expected to know—so the Welsh title had some legitimacy, and it certainly was prettier. I loved the sleepy college town that lay along Route 30 (the old Lancaster Pike that led from Philadelphia to—

surprise—Lancaster), with a convenient train line running alongside. I, and the bank, owned a small, converted carriage house behind what had once been a grand estate, in convenient walking distance to the train station.

And it was all mine: no kith, kin, or even pets, unless you count dust mites.

There are many people who live in Center City who never venture beyond city limits, and many confirmed suburbanites who quail in terror at the very idea of braving the big bad city. The latter had a point: there were some pretty rough areas of the city that lay close to the historic and cultural districts, and one wrong turn could land you in trouble—or in New Jersey. Me, I liked having one foot in each camp. I enjoyed the hustle and bustle of the city, but I also liked to be able to get on the train at the end of the day and make my way to my quiet little town, where I could unwind.

And I did unwind. The last couple of months had been difficult, and had resulted in some major changes both in my life and in that institution where I worked, and my staff and I were struggling to adjust to our new realities. And while I had been in upper management for a while, actually running the place was a whole different kettle of fish—and I'd been thrust into that role with little preparation. So I was improvising, making things up as I went. But, heck, the place had survived for 125 years already, and I didn't think I'd destroy it.

My positive mood carried through to the next day, and was boosted when I arrived early to find Shelby waiting for me on the steps, once again with two cups of coffee.

"I could get used to this," I called out as I climbed the steps.

"Don't—I'm still in the sucking-up stage."

"It's working just fine. Follow me. I'll get you a key of

your own." I opened the heavy metal doors that guarded our precious collections. Front Desk Bob was already in place. "Good morning, Bob. This is Shelby Carver, our newest employee. Please be nice and don't scare her away."

"I'm always nice," Bob said with his usual good cheer. He *was* always nice; he relied on his imposing presence and his experience as a former cop to manage any unruly patrons. "Good to see you again, Ms. Carver."

"Shelby, sir, if you please. I'm happy to be here." She took Bob's outstretched hand and shook firmly.

I led her back through the large catalog room to the elevator. "I need to give you a key for the elevator, too. The public can go up to the second floor, but only staff can go to the third and fourth floors, or to the basement. I'll give you a tour of the stacks when I have time, but it's kind of overwhelming at first. We have a *lot* of stuff here."

The elevator made its dignified way to the third floor and we stepped out. "Maybe we should begin with human resources and get the paperwork started? And then I'll walk you around and introduce you to the staff up here, and then there's the library staff downstairs, and—"

"Nell, will you stop and take a breath? Are you always this manic?"

"No, just the last couple of months, since I ended up with this job and all its baggage. Ah, here we are. This is Melanie Wilson, our human resources coordinator. Melanie, I believe you and Shelby Carver have been in touch. I've offered her the position of development director."

Melanie pushed her glasses up on top of her head. "Oh, wait, right—she came in yesterday, late. I gather everything went well?"

"Unless you tell me that she's wanted in three states for bank robbery."

Melanie looked guilty. "Well, I was just about to check her references . . ."

Shelby laughed. "I can go sit in the hall if y'all want to talk about me. But I don't have a thing to hide—you just go ahead and call whoever you want, Melanie."

Melanie's expression wavered between relief and pique. "I'll do that, just to keep our records up-to-date." She rummaged through a desk drawer, then pulled out a thick folder and handed it to Shelby. "Here's the standard new-hire info package—insurance and all that stuff. Read it, fill out the forms, and get it back to me by the end of the day."

"Yes, ma'am!" Shelby took the packet and tucked it under her arm. "Do I need computer access? And Nell said something about keys?"

"Oh, yeah, right." Melanie opened a different drawer and fished out a box that rattled. She opened it and extracted two keys, a large one and a smaller one. "Front door and elevator," she said, handing them to Shelby. "Don't make any copies. Tell me if you lose one or both. And fill this out." Melanie handed her another piece of paper, and glanced quickly at me. "That's the form acknowledging receipt of the keys and promising you won't copy them. Security, you know."

"Of course." Shelby helped herself to a pen on the desk and quickly scribbled her name, handing the completed form back to Melanie.

Melanie took it and handed Shelby another form. "This is your computer access information, so you can get to the donor files. Once you're on, you can change your password."

"Any luck on the other positions, Melanie?" I asked hopefully.

"Not really. I'm doing what I can. For the registrar position, I've asked that the listing be posted online at a couple of university sites. For your assistant, lots of applicants—I've sent you a few—but most are either unqualified, or they're overqualified but lack the specific skills you need. Unless you really want a middle-aged unemployed mechanical engineer answering your phone?"

"The age doesn't bother me, but I'm not sure engineering talent is required. Keep trying, will you? I really need someone, and fast." The unresolved paperwork was building up to avalanche proportions.

"I'm on it, Nell. Or do you prefer *Madame President* these days?"

I laughed. "Nell is just fine. Shelby, let's go to your office and I'll show you how the computer works. I warn you, it's not exactly new." When I had changed offices, I'd made a point of clearing my own files off of it, leaving only those that were relevant to the development position.

"Lead on, Madame President."

"Stop!"

The office was across the hall from Melanie's, a small room tucked around the corner from Carrie Drexel's desk. Carrie was membership coordinator, and would be working closely with Shelby to keep membership records up-to-date, to generate contribution letters and thank-yous, and to file the paperwork that even the electronic revolution hadn't managed to eliminate. Carrie was just arriving, a few minutes late, and didn't meet my eye as she hung up her coat.

"Sorry, Nell—there was some hang-up in the trains."

That was an excuse I knew only too well, having had to use it many times myself. The regional rails were old—both tracks and cars—and notoriously prone to delays. "Don't worry about it. I wanted you to meet your new boss,

Shelby Carver. She's taking my old job, so break her in easy."

"Hi, Shelby!" Carrie stuck out a hand. "Let me know when you want me to show you the database."

"No rush," Shelby said. "I'm sure you're doing a great job."

Carrie beamed, then turned back to her computer while I led Shelby to her office.

Inside, she cast a critical eye at the peeling paint, shabby filing cabinets, battered chairs, and uninsulated window—I could feel the steady trickle of cool air from where I stood in the doorway. "Nice fireplace," was all she said.

"It is that. It came from somebody or other's mansion—I think there's a plaque there somewhere. It's not connected to anything."

"I didn't think to ask yesterday, but meeting Carrie reminded me—are there other people who I'm supposed to be managing here? And am I going to have any problems with her?"

"You mean, did Carrie want your job? Nope. She's a good kid and she gets the job done, but she doesn't see this as a career path. She's been here a couple of years, but I won't place any bets on how long she'll stay. Anyway, Carrie and our database manager, Daphne Smith, both report to you, and you report to me."

"Got it." Shelby looked around the office. "Well, where do you want me to start?"

"I've give you a little time to familiarize yourself with our records and collections. The only pressing thing is the member newsletter, but Carrie's been handling that. We usually all get together to stuff and seal." I stifled a twinge: the last time we'd done that, it had been to notify our members of an unfortunate death. I hoped this time around the news would be more pleasant.

"How many?"

"A couple of thousand. It takes most of a day. I know—it seems old-fashioned. We're thinking of going to an electronic newsletter, but a lot of our members are older and they still like a paper copy."

Shelby nodded. "I know what you mean. Anyway, I'm a quick study. What say I do some reading and looking through the files this morning, and later you can take me around downstairs, once I figure out what I'm supposed to be seeing? I don't want the library people to think I'm a dithering idiot."

"Don't worry, they're good people," I assured her. "Overworked and underpaid, but they care about what they're doing. I'm sure they'll welcome you. Why don't we plan to have lunch, and then I'll finish the tour?"

"Sounds good. Thanks, Nell. I'll try not to drive you around the bend with dumb questions."

"You're allowed a few. See you later!"

I went back to my office, which I still had trouble treating as mine. I was afraid to mess it up—I was supposed to represent a prestigious institution, and clutter was not the image we wanted to project. Not that I'd had many official visitors yet. Were my peers giving me a little breathing room to get things sorted out, or was the Society so tarnished by recent events that they didn't want to be contaminated? Maybe I should have a "Welcome, Me" reception and invite all my colleagues, and face the issue head-on. Hmm . . . maybe that would be a good dry run for Shelby. Since event planning was part of her job description, putting together a cocktail party for a couple hundred people on short notice would be a good test of her abilities. And at the same time we could prove quite publicly that life was going forward at the Society. I liked it. I'd have to bring up the idea at lunch and see how Shelby reacted.

I could hear a ringing phone. I looked at the one on my desk: yes, a light was flashing. But the ringing came from the phone on the desk of my nonexistent assistant, who was supposed to be screening my calls and keeping track of my interviews and all that good stuff. I needed to remind Melanie to put finding me an assistant at the top of her priority list. Oh, right, the phone. I picked it up on the sixth ring.

"Nell Pratt," I said, more brusquely than I intended.

"Hi, Nell!"

Luckily I recognized the distinctive voice (no caller ID on my aging phone): Arabella Heffernan, the president of Let's Play Children's Museum. "Arabella! How nice to hear from you. Can I do something for you?"

Arabella loosed a peal of silvery laughter. "Oh, no, my dear. I'm fine. I'm so sorry I haven't been in touch sooner about your elevation, but we've been so busy here, trying to put together our next exhibit while keeping the rest of our place open, that I haven't had time to turn around. Congratulations! I'm sure you'll do a wonderful job. I know it's short notice, but how would you like a teeny behind-the-scenes peek at our new exhibit before it opens to the public?"

Let's Play was a children's museum. I had no children. I had no near relatives who had children. In all my years in Philadelphia, I had had few reasons to enter the portals of Let's Play. Arabella was the first person to extend a welcoming hand to me, and it would be rude of me to turn her down. "I'd love to. When did you have in mind?"

"Oh, how grand. Perhaps later today?"

While I didn't know Arabella well, I knew enough to realize that she was a slightly otherworldly person, the kind to whom details like time management were of little importance. I'm sure she never considered that perhaps I might be completely crazed and hip deep in a difficult transition; in her mind she was making a kind gesture, and I appreciated that. "I could probably get away around four. Would that suit you?"

"Perfect! And we can have tea! I'll see you then, my dear." She hung up with no further ado, probably to start brewing tea.

I sat back and smiled. Arabella was a sweet and charming lady—and ran a good institution, much beloved by more than a generation of Philadelphia children and parents. And touring an exhibit aimed at small children would be a welcome change from the very serious documents that the Society housed.

Despite the disruption to my schedule, I found I was already looking forward to that afternoon's excursion.

CHAPTER 3

The next time I looked at the clock (a handsome, Philadelphia-made eighteenth-century number with a rather ominous face that looked disapproving to me), it was well after one, and I remembered that I'd promised Shelby lunch. That was happening more and more often: I kept losing chunks of my day. Too much to do, too little time. I stood up and gathered my coat from the closet outside my office, and went down the hall to retrieve Shelby.

I found her at her desk, file folders covering its entire surface. That made me feel better, since in my day (was it really only two months ago?) it had often looked like that, covered in piles of paperwork. I rapped on the door. "Shelby, are you starving?"

She looked up and slid off a pair of reading glasses. "That time already? My, time flies when you're having fun, doesn't it?"

"It does. Would you rather not interrupt what you're doing?"

She stood up quickly. "No, ma'am! My mama told me never to say no to a free meal."

"What kind of food do you feel like?" I asked as Shelby pulled her jacket from the hook on the back of the door.

"You pick. I don't know this part of town all that well."

I decided on a nice place around the corner. "Since I never saw your résumé," I said as we walked toward the elevator, "where is it you live?"

"Down toward the river. John and I bought a nice little row house when we moved here. I love the neighborhood, and it's convenient. How 'bout you?"

"I live in the burbs—Bryn Mawr. I like to keep work and home separate, and I enjoy the train ride, most of the time. Gives me time to read, or think, without anybody interrupting me."

"I hear you!"

We descended the Society's front steps, and I guided Shelby toward Broad Street, a long block away. The January air was harsh, but I was happy to get out and move, given all the time I spent sitting at my desk, where my major exercise was tearing out my hair. "Are you that busy already?"

Shelby laughed. "Oh, I'm not complaining. A few folks stopped by to introduce themselves—just curious about the new kid. They were all real nice. Maybe if you could point me to an organization chart, I could figure out who's who?"

"Sure. Remind me and I'll email you one when we get back. But it's your own fault, showing up out of the blue yesterday. If we'd known you were coming, we'd have had things sorted out."

"You think I mind? I'm happy to have the job, and these are just little wrinkles that we'll get smoothed out in no time. Is this where we're going?"

I'd stopped in front of one of my favorite local places—good food, and not too expensive. "This is it."

Inside the vestibule, Shelby sniffed appreciatively. "Smells great."

"It is." We followed the hostess to a table for two and settled ourselves. A waiter appeared promptly and handed us menus, and Shelby took no more than two minutes to make up her mind. I ordered what I always did, a chicken Caesar salad. When the waiter had left, I sat back in my chair. "So, any second thoughts yet?"

"Nell, I've been working at the Society a total of four hours. It might take me a little longer to make up my mind about you all."

"Take all the time you want. Was there something you wanted to know? Or maybe the question should be, what *do* you know?"

"You worried about what's been said in the news?"

"What have you heard?" I parried. We'd had some less-than-ideal press recently, and I was reluctant to give away anything I didn't have to.

"I can read between the lines. You've had some problems in-house, but the, uh, judicious relocation of certain individuals has solved a lot of them."

She could be discreet, too—another plus. "And you gleaned all this from reading the paper?"

Shelby shrugged. "I talk to people, who know other people. Don't worry—there are a lot of rumors floating around, but nobody really knows anything. And in a funny way, they want to see you succeed."

Small comfort. But Shelby needed to know some things that would have a major impact on her job. "Thank you for telling me. Cards on the table?" I looked around quickly: well past the peak lunch hour, there were few people in the restaurant to overhear us. "We've had some serious theft issues recently. We believe we've stopped them, but it may be a while before we sort everything out. I tell you this because if the details get out, it would make your job—helping us raise money—a lot harder. But you have a right to know. And if it's any consolation, the FBI is working with us."

Shelby sipped some iced tea before responding. "That's about what I'd figured."

"And all that doesn't bother you?"

"Nope," she said cheerfully. "I'm pretty sure this goes on all the time, only people don't talk about it much. But I figured whatever news had leaked out might scare off other candidates, so I took a chance."

"You must really want this job," I said. "Is there something you haven't told me? You're supporting your aged parents in a nursing home? You have eighteen cats with obscure and expensive medical problems?"

Shelby laughed. "No to both. One, I got bored sitting around after I'd done all the sightseeing I could stomach. Two, my daughter, Melissa, is getting married next year, and unlikely as it sounds, she wants the whole show—train and doves and white horses—and that ain't cheap. Plus, we're helping her pay off her college loans."

Somewhere inside me, I relaxed. Maybe this was going to work out just fine. "So she's already out of college?"

"Graduated last year. She's got a job, but she and Press—that's her fiancé, Preston—really want to get married now and get on with their lives together."

"Well, I'm glad you're on board. Now, let me give you thumbnails on all the board members . . ." We switched seamlessly to shop talk, and lunch flew by.

As we were walking back to the Society, Shelby said,

"Do you want me to nose around, see if I can find you an assistant? I don't want to tread on Melanie's toes, since that's her job, but I might know of a few potential candidates."

"I would be eternally grateful. I do believe Melanie when she says she's had plenty of applicants but none of them right for the position. There are plenty of people looking for work, but that doesn't mean they can do what I need done. Melanie'd probably thank you, too. I'd rather she concentrated on filling the registrar position, and she's got plenty else to keep her busy. But why would you know any likely candidates?"

"The 'old gals' network. Besides, as I said before, I like to talk to people, and I've talked to plenty since I moved to Philadelphia. Give me a day or two and I'll see who I can come up with."

We'd reached our building, and held off on conversation until we'd passed through the lobby and gone up to the third floor. At Shelby's office door, she stopped. "Thanks for the lunch, Nell—and for filling me in. I'm glad that you trust me."

Our lunch, which had stretched well past two, left me with little time to start anything new before I was supposed to leave for Let's Play. No doubt if I had that magical assistant, she—or he—would have a tidy stack of messages waiting for me, arranged in order of importance; would have updated my calendar; and would have left several letters for me to sign before whisking them away to mail. I sighed. I was beginning to fear that this paragon of efficiency was a fairy tale, or at best, a dinosaur well on the way to becoming extinct. Who wanted to be the nameless, faceless assistant to somebody, after all? As a feminist I applauded that: too many capable, talented women in the past had settled for that type of paid servitude. But as the president of a busy institution, I wished I could resurrect just one. I needed help, and I knew it.

So I didn't get much done before I had to leave for my appointment. I didn't even have anyone to tell that I was officially leaving for the day. I stuck my head into Carrie's cubicle. "Carrie, I'm headed out—I'm going to go talk to Arabella Heffernan at Let's Play, and then go home from there."

Carrie's face lit up. "Let's Play? Ooh, I loved that place when I was a kid. My mom used to drag me to all these stuffy museums and I hated those, but sometimes she'd let us go to Let's Play and it was great. Say hi to Furzie."

"Furzie?"

"The big blue bear at the front entrance. Don't worry—he doesn't bite."

"That's good to know. I'll see you tomorrow, then."

It was a fifteen-minute walk to Let's Play, and I knew enough to stick to the smaller streets—if you took the larger ones, it was like walking through a wind tunnel as the tall buildings funneled the gusts at you.

Let's Play was unique in my experience with museums. It occupied a pair of adjacent two-story brick buildings that had begun life in the late nineteenth century as small businesses, or maybe it was factories. Little had been changed structurally, and there were still a lot of exposed beams and naked pipes inside. The city had changed around the buildings, but their location was ideal for visiting parents, since they lay in close proximity to the other child-friendly Philadelphia museums. Parents had to park only once, and then if they wished they could split up, one parent leading the older kids to the science museums to visit dinosaurs, the other heading for Let's Play, where hands-on interaction with the diverse exhibits was not only allowed but actively encouraged. I loved the concept. Why should a museum be a dark and stuffy place where everyone kept telling you "shush" and "don't touch"? Let's Play was the polar opposite: it was welcoming and friendly. I was curious to see what the new exhibit would be like, but I was sure it would be fun, at least if you were a kid.

I walked in and introduced myself at the front desk, shouting to make myself heard over the noise of happy children. I smiled toward Furzie, who beamed benevolently over all comers. There seemed to be kids everywhere—must be some school group here today, or maybe the usual allotment of children had been compressed into a smaller-than-usual space because of the construction Arabella had mentioned. The frazzled young woman at the desk made a call and nodded encouragingly at me, then pointed toward the gift shop off the lobby. I made the assumption that Arabella would meet me there and drifted over.

I love gift shops, and this one made me wish I had kids. Heck, *I* wanted half the things I saw: a menagerie of wind-up animals; prisms; all sorts of wonderful rulers and crayons and erasers. There was nothing battery powered in sight, thank goodness, and everything looked appropriately indestructible. I was contemplating how a large spider embedded in Lucite would look on my desk when Arabella came bustling in, apologizing breathlessly.

"Nell, so good to see you. Sorry to keep you waiting, but things have been so crazy. Of course, that's been true for months—maybe crazy is the new normal. Let me take you upstairs so we can talk."

There was no way to stem her burbling, so I nodded in agreement and followed her back into the melee of the hall, then up a flight of stairs. Things were appreciably quieter on the second floor, and became increasingly so as we went toward the back of the building. When we reached Arabella's office, she pointed me toward an overstuffed armchair upholstered in bright cotton fabric decorated with bunnies. "Sit down, please. I've made tea, and there are cookies!" She beamed at me, obviously pleased with herself.

Arabella was clearly the mother figure of her small museum. I would have said Earth Mother, but Arabella liked nice clothes too well for that, and I knew she was a shrewd manager. But she was short and nicely rounded, partial to flowery prints; her hair sprang out in determined grey curls, and her eyes twinkled.

The teacup had violets on it; the sugar cookies, matching purple sprinkles. Arabella looked so darned happy to see me, and to have the privilege of plying me with tea and cookies, it would've been curmudgeonly of me to decline. Besides, both the tea and the cookies were excellent.

Arabella gave me time to appreciate them, nodding approvingly as I ate. "You poor dear, you've had quite a time of it, haven't you? How are you settling in?"

"It's going well, I hope. It's a little early to say. But I feel honored that the board chose me." Out of desperation, most likely, but I wasn't going to bring that up with Arabella. "You've been running this place for quite a while, haven't you? You must have seen a lot of changes over the years. Do you think kids want different things now, compared to when you started? It seems that everything has to flash and buzz and beep, and it's all electronic these days."

A cloud passed over Arabella's face. "Sadly so. But the younger ones still enjoy it. Sometimes I go down to the exhibits and just watch them playing. They get so excited! And we try to keep things fresh—that's one of the reasons for the new exhibit."

"What is it about? I apologize, but I don't spend much time with children, so I'm kind of out of the loop."

"It's based on the *Harriet the Hedgehog* series, which is aimed at our precise demographic. It's written by Hadley Eastman—she's a local author, which makes a nice tie-in, and her books have sold well, so she's well-known. She's been working with us to develop the exhibit. And I'm so happy to be able to support children's reading—sometimes I think they may never learn how, and then where will we all be?"

"Amen to that." I poured myself another cup of tea—and helped myself to one more sugar cookie. "So tell me, what other kinds of programming do you offer? Do you have any agreement with the school district?"

"Oh, of course . . ." And we were off, talking shop. After a while it was clear to me that Arabella's reputation as a good businesswoman was well deserved. She knew her audience, and what worked. She also knew her limitations, and she was happily settled in her particular niche, with no plans to expand beyond it. In a way it was heartening to me: young children weren't changing much, and they were still enthralled by simple things, bless them.

When I checked my watch again, it was after five. "Heavens, I had no idea it was so late. I don't want to keep you."

"Oh, but you can't leave without seeing the exhibit! A little sneak preview? Once it opens, it will be covered with children—at least, that's what we hope."

"I'd love to see it." I was honestly curious about what she and her staff had done with the exhibit.

"Well, then, come with me. You're in for a treat!"

CHAPTER 4

I followed Arabella from her office to another part of the second floor. It was hidden behind drop cloths decorated with whimsical animals and birds that looked like they'd been hand-painted by preschoolers, which they probably had. Across the top ran a large banner clearly made by somebody a couple of decades older, that proclaimed in big letters, "Harriet's Coming!" Arabella turned to me and her eyes actually sparkled—something that, before this moment, I wouldn't have believed possible. She was so thrilled to be showing off her newest addition, she simply radiated good cheer. She held back one panel of cloth and motioned me inside.

I immediately felt like Gulliver. I had stepped into a miniature world, and I was at least two feet too tall for it. The space must have measured fifty by fifty feet, and it was filled with animals and plants, interspersed with child-size molded chairs and low tables, presumably for craft projects. A case mounted on the wall contained the books in the

Harriet the Hedgehog series, but they definitely took second place to the three-dimensional versions of the characters. The air smelled of clean sawdust and paint, with a whiff of old building. Two workers were painting statues, and the floor around them was strewn with drop cloths. Harriet apparently had a lot of friends: I thought I could identify a frog and what might be a duck or a goose—the latter's identity was questionable since its feathers hadn't been painted yet.

"It's just me!" Arabella called out to the workers. They looked up, and one waved a hand. Then they résuméd painting. "I'd introduce you, but we've got such a tight deadline I'd rather they just keep working. So much to do!"

I noticed that Arabella was much closer to the right size for this exhibit than I was. "This looks wonderful," I said, and meant it. "What's your target age group?"

Arabella looked like a proud mother hen. "Toddlers, up to five. So they can look Harriet here in the eye, you know."

I admired how whoever had crafted this statue had managed to reduce the hedgehog's signature spines to something that wouldn't impale a child climbing on her. The artist had succeeded, though the result was a wee bit lumpy. But safe. In a public institution that needed to be childproof, safety had to trump authenticity.

"Harriet is a delightful character. You'd think a hedgehog's personality would be prickly, with all those spines, but Harriet is a sweetheart," Arabella said. "That's a real teaching opportunity, you know: don't judge someone by her exterior, but take some time to get to know her. And she has such wonderful friends! Mallory Mouse, Barry Bunny. And of course there has to be a bully—there always is—and that's Willy the Weasel. But Hadley has brought him around slowly, over the course of the series.

Willy just wants to make friends, but he doesn't know how to do it."

I had to ask, "Are there any native hedgehogs in Pennsylvania?"

"Good question, dear. No, there aren't, not in any part of America—but they're found in Africa, Eurasia, Asia, Borneo, and parts of Europe," she recited promptly. "Oh, and in New Zealand, but those were introduced there. But there is a very active group in this country promoting hedgehogs as pets. The little things are fairly low maintenance, and they're rather endearing little creatures, aren't they? Do you remember Mrs. Tiggy-Winkle?"

My mind was blank for a moment until a childhood memory surfaced. "Wasn't that a Beatrix Potter character? Oh, right—she was a hedgehog, too."

"Exactly. And a very sweet one. That's the spirit I think the author has captured, although of course Harriet's stories have a more modern feeling."

"If you don't mind my asking, how did you fund the exhibit?" I said.

"I'm sure you're aware that there are grants available for educational purposes, and we tapped into those where we could. After all, this display encourages young readers. Of course, all that happened before so many foundations faced financial difficulties—thank goodness. I doubt we could do it under current conditions. Hadley Eastman's publisher contributed as well—this is excellent publicity for her series. And our board was very supportive. Most of them have young children or grandchildren."

"I wondered about that. Is it a requirement that they have children to join the board?" Not a problem we faced. In fact, children were rarely seen within the Pennsylvania Antiquarian Society, which was just as well, given the delicate nature of our collections. I shuddered at the thought of sticky little fingers on old documents, and games of tag among the shelving.

"We don't require it exactly, but it's strongly supported, and most board members are in complete agreement with the idea. In fact, when we are working on recruiting a new member, we typically ask them to come during the day or on a weekend along with their children, so they can get the full flavor of the place. Not many have been able to resist joining us after that experience."

"Lucky you. I'm guessing the average age of your board members is about half that of ours."

"Now, let me show you . . ."

As we strolled through the still-incomplete exhibit, Arabella identified the individual characters scattered around the room, each within its own little stage set. After a while I realized that the building had quieted. No more babbling of young voices or shrieks of glee from downstairs. I checked my watch: yes, it was close to six. I supposed you would get used to the noise if you worked in a place like this, but I had to admit I preferred the tranquility of our library. And our walls, while roughly the same age, were at least twice as thick, and muffled what little noise there was.

We'd completed the circuit of the room, which didn't take long because the room was geared to children's short legs, and Arabella asked, "Well, what do you think?"

She looked so eager that even if I'd had anything negative to say, which I didn't, I wouldn't have had the heart. "It's marvelous. I can see why children will love it."

Arabella gave a start. "Ooh, you haven't even seen it in action! Have you got another minute?"

"Sure," I said, mystified.

"Jason?" Arabella called out. "Can you switch on the circuit for the active displays?"

"No problem, Mrs. H." One of the painters—the one who'd waved—made his way through the animals and opened a concealed wall panel I hadn't even noticed. I could hear the click of a breaker.

After a few seconds, Arabella called out, "Jason, dear? Nothing is happening." She turned to me. "Harriet's eyes are supposed to light up when the power is on. And then when you pat her, her ears swivel forward, to show that she likes you."

I stared at Harriet, who remained resolutely still. I wondered what hedgehogs really did to show any kind of emotion. The only thing I could recall about them was that they curled up in a ball when they were frightened, leaving their spines facing out to deter their enemies. I kind of envied them: there were days when I would like to do something like that.

Jason was still flipping switches, but nothing was happening. "Maybe the problem is on this end? Could you come take a look?" Arabella asked. "I really want Nell to see what Harriet does."

"Sure thing." Jason ambled toward us. Up close he turned out to be a nice-looking young man—well, young by my standards, which put him in his early twenties. He was wearing stained painter's coveralls, clearly several sizes too big.

"Jason, this is Nell Pratt, from the Pennsylvania Antiquarian Society. Nell, Jason is my daughter Caitlin's boyfriend. He's helping us out here with some of the last-minute things."

Jason nodded to me and said shyly, "Hi." Then he turned his full attention to Harriet, sitting obstinately dark and mute.

Jason got down on his knees to see if the concealed wires were connected. Apparently they were, so he moved on up to Harriet's head, which grinned silently, her ears unmoving. He reached out and patted Harriet's shiny black nose. Nothing happened. Jason looked confused, and Arabella looked crestfallen. I felt sorry for her: she had been so excited about showing off her charming new toy to me, and it appeared to be a dud.

"Jason, dear, could you try Willy? Maybe then we'll know if it's just one of the figures or the whole group."

"Sure, Arabella." Jason straightened up and approached a second figure a few feet away. Taller than Harriet, this one sported a smarmy grin and sprouted a lot of whiskers. He was leaning over with an elbow on an old-fashioned metal gate, which put his head within easy reach of small children. The placement of his body also prevented anyone from climbing on the low gate, which was no doubt the intention of the designer.

"That's Willy the Weasel," Arabella explained. "He's supposed to . . ."

When Jason reached out and tweaked Willy's nose, there was a sharp snap or crackle or pop, and all the lights in the room went out.

"Oh my!" Arabella squeaked. "*That's* not supposed to happen."

It wasn't the only thing that wasn't supposed to happen. Jason had dropped like a stone at Willy's feet, and I crossed the space in a second, kneeling beside him. "Arabella, call 911!" I said. "Does anyone have a flashlight?"

Since I had been closest to Jason, I figured I'd better take charge. I didn't know how Arabella would react in an emergency—for all I knew she might succumb to an attack of the vapors. I felt for Jason's carotid artery. At least, I think I did—I was going solely by what I'd seen on a lot of TV shows. I groped around until I found what I thought— and hoped—was a pulse. I forced myself to take a deep breath and stop shaking. Yes, it was a pulse—faint and thready, but there. Jason wasn't dead, thank God, but I had no idea how close to it he was.

"Has anyone called 911 yet?" I hollered. "Tell them we need an ambulance!'

"They're on their way." The other worker approached, slipping a cell phone back under his coveralls. "What the hell happened? Is he . . . ?"

"He was fiddling with the weasel and something seems to have shorted out." That summed up all I knew.

"And whatever he did completed the circuit," the man said. "I'm an electrician. Joe Murphy. I was just helping out with the painting 'cause the wiring was pretty much done. But I swear to God, we checked out all the connections, up one side and down the other! No way this should have happened. He gonna be all right?"

How was I supposed to know? Jason didn't look any better: he was pale and breathing shallowly, and showed no signs of waking up.

I was startled when Arabella said, "Don't touch anything," in a calm, clear voice. "We don't know if the circuit's still live. You, too, Joe—just leave it alone until we can figure out what happened. Luckily Jason fell clear of it, or you might have been shocked, too, Nell."

I hadn't even considered that, in my hurry to reach Jason, but she was right. I sat back on my heels. "Should we cover him or something?"

"Good idea. If he's in shock he'll be losing body heat. Hand me one of those tarps, will you, Joe?"

Joe swooped down and bundled up a tarp. He and Arabella together laid it carefully over Jason's nearly still form.

"Is the power out throughout the building?" I asked. I thought I could see lights coming from the open stairwell.

"Shouldn't be," Arabella said. "We installed a separate circuit for the exhibition this time around, since we had the walls open anyway, and we knew the electrified animals would draw a lot of power. But we went over the plans more times than I can count! There should have been no way that this could happen. The codes for this sort of exhibit are very strict, and of course we've had every inspection the city requires. It would be devastating if anything happened to a child. Not that it should happen to anyone."

I felt a sense of relief. Gone was the fluffy Arabella, replaced by a competent leader, and I was happy to let her take charge.

"Mother, are you up here?" A female voice drifted from the front of the building. "What's going on with the lights?"

Arabella stood up abruptly and headed for the sheeting that hid the exhibit. "Darling, don't . . ." She was too late to intercept the young woman, who pushed the sheets aside and then shoved past her mother. "What . . . ?" She took in the scene—me squatting next to prostrate Jason, Joe standing anxiously behind, all of us in the dark—and then she wailed, "Oh, no! No! Jason!" Despite her mother's restraining hand, she rushed over to Jason and knelt down beside me. She reached out to touch him—his face, not his pulse. "Jason, wake up, please!" Then she looked at me, her eyes filled with tears. "Is he . . . ?"

"I think he's had a bad electrical shock, but he's breathing," I said. "We've called for an ambulance."

She kept her hand on Jason. "Who are you? Do I know you?"

"I'm Nell Pratt, from the Pennsylvania Antiquarian Society. You're Arabella's daughter?" When she nodded, I explained, "Your mother invited me to preview the exhibit."

"Oh." She lost interest in me and turned back to Jason.

Arabella had caught up with her, and laid a hand on her shoulder. "Caitlin, darling, come away. Help is coming."

Once again Caitlin threw off her mother's hand. "No. I'm staying with Jason. I want to be sure he's all right. What happened?" Her gaze swiveled wildly between her mother, me, and Joe.

Arabella and I exchanged a glance. I wasn't sure that Jason was going to be all right—shouldn't he be conscious by now? But I wasn't going to say anything to make this situation any worse. I was relieved to hear the sound of an approaching siren.

"We don't know yet, Caitlin. Joe, can you go down and let them in, and bring them up here, please?" Arabella asked.

Joe, looking relieved at having something to do, said, "Sure," and headed quickly for the stairs.

I stood up, since Caitlin had taken over the task of watching Jason breathe.

Arabella noticed my movement. "You don't have to stay, Nell," she said.

"Maybe I should, since I was here when this happened," I told her. "In case the police have any questions."

Arabella looked bewildered. "Why would the police have any questions? Something must have gone wrong with the wiring. It was an accident."

Was it? Any hint of carelessness could do serious damage to the reputation of Let's Play. What if it was something worse than carelessness? No, I was probably just being paranoid. First, see that Jason got to a hospital and, God willing, recovered. Then, make sure all the wiring was checked out—and then checked again. And pray that it was no more than an accident.

We sat frozen for long minutes, awaiting the arrival of the EMTs. I could track their progress aurally: the siren swelled in volume, then stopped abruptly when they arrived in front of the museum. There was commotion at the front door; Joe directed them up the stairs, and I heard their equipment clanging as they made their way up. Someone called out from the head of the stairs, and Arabella replied, "In here! Behind the plastic."

Finally the EMTs appeared. Arabella tugged her daughter away from Jason's still form. Caitlin came reluctantly, and Arabella wrapped an arm around her shoulders—or at least she tried, since she was at least six inches shorter than the younger woman. I wondered irreverently how such a short round woman could have produced such a tall willowy child. The EMTs set to work with grim efficiency. They managed to work and spit out questions at the same time. "What's his name?"

"Jason Miller," Arabella responded.

"What was he doing here?"

"He works here. He's been painting part of the exhibit."

"What happened? He fall?"

"No, we were having trouble making the electronic weasel work. Jason just touched it, and something went wrong."

"It looked like he was hit with an electrical shock," I volunteered. "He touched something, then he fell down all at once, and he hasn't been conscious since. The lights up here went out at the same time."

The EMTs exchanged a glance, then looked at Arabella. "You been working on the wiring lately?"

"Yes. But we've passed all our inspections, and everything was fine. The exhibit's complete except for some painting and touching up. And the other figures were working fine yesterday. I tried them out myself."

Arabella had been answering the questions with admirable calm, all the while holding on to her daughter—or maybe holding her up. Caitlin hadn't said a word since her first outburst, and she was deathly pale, twisting her hands together. Hadn't Arabella said Jason was Caitlin's boyfriend? She certainly looked upset, maybe more so than Arabella. I felt like a fifth wheel, watching the professionals at work. What had happened here? Arabella had just said that the animals in the exhibit had been working fine yesterday, and today obviously they weren't. What had changed? And why?

The EMTs straightened and extended the legs of their gurney. "Elevator?" one barked.

"I'll show you," Arabella said.

"I want to come with Jason," Caitlin said abruptly.

"You a relative?"

"He's my . . . fiancé," Caitlin said defiantly. Arabella shot her a startled glance but said nothing.

"You can't ride with us. You can follow if you want, but you may have to wait awhile."

"Okay. Will he be all right?"

"Can't say."

Can't, or won't? I wondered. Jason wasn't dead, but he didn't look very alive, either. I wished I knew more about massive electrical shock. My closest experience was when I had stuck a fork into a toaster some thirty years ago, an experience I made sure never to repeat. But while it had been unpleasant, I hadn't blacked out. How much stronger was the current that coursed through Willy the Weasel?

I realized I was still standing in the same place, as though rooted to the spot, when Arabella returned from directing the EMTs. "Nell, I'm going to take Caitlin and follow the ambulance over to the hospital. I'm so sorry you had to be here to see this."

I shook myself. "Arabella, don't apologize. You do what you have to—I'll follow you out. And please let me know how Jason is, as soon as you know anything."

"I'll do that."

There seemed to be nothing else to say, so we filed out the front door in silent procession. Arabella took her daughter's limp arm, and after speaking briefly to Joe, who was still standing sentinel at the front door, led her around toward the back of the building, where I assumed she was parked. Joe and I watched as the ambulance pulled away.

"Hey, you okay? You look kind of shook up," Joe said.

I turned to look at him, truly seeing him for the first time. Maybe thirty-five, a bit younger than me. Tall. Curly dark hair, and blue eyes with lashes that no man deserved. Muscled like he worked out, but not too much. At another time and place I might have admired such a fine specimen of manhood, but he was right—I was shaken up.

"Can I give you a lift somewhere?"

He was actually trying hard to be helpful, and I had to admit I didn't feel ready to face a crowded train. "No, but maybe we could sit down and have a cup of coffee or something?"

"Sure. There's a shop on the next street, and I know they're open late. Come on."

I followed meekly as he led me to what would once have been called a greasy spoon, but at least it was warm, and it smelled of good food. Joe held the door for me and waited courteously until I slid into a booth. The proprietor came over and handed us menus, nodding at Joe. I was surprised that despite what I had just seen, I was hungry. Maybe it was reaction, or maybe I just wanted a distraction. I realized that Joe was watching me with those disconcerting blue eyes.

"I guess we never got properly introduced. I'm Nell Pratt—I run the Pennsylvania Antiquarian Society. Arabella invited me by for a sneak preview of the exhibit."

"Hi, Nell. I'm Joe Murphy. So, not quite the show you were expecting, I'd wager."

"Not at all. You said you're an electrician?" When he nodded, I asked, "Do you have any idea how that could have happened?"

The proprietor arrived, pad in hand, and we ordered coffee and sandwiches. Joe waited until he had left before he replied. "I know that part of the building like the back of my hand, and of course we've been extra careful because of the kids and all. No way it should have happened like that, unless somebody's been messing with the wiring."

The coffee arrived, and I wrapped my hands around the thick white mug, mostly to stop their shaking. "Why would anyone do that? Everybody loves Let's Play, as far as I know."

"That they do," Joe said. "I really couldn't say who'd want to do the place harm. Lucky thing the circuit was a new one—the breaker cut off fast. Maybe Jason hit his head when he fell?"

"Could be. I was looking at Willy when it happened, not Jason." I realized I preferred that explanation over a booby-trapped weasel. I took a deep breath and changed the subject. "So, are you from Philadelphia, Joe?"

"Born and raised," he replied, and I steered the conversation toward safer topics. The food arrived and was surprisingly good, and after devouring the sandwich, I felt much better. When it was gone, I checked my watch: ten minutes until the next train, and they didn't run too often after rush hour.

"I need to get going. Thanks for suggesting this, Joe—I guess I was a little rocky after all. Let me get the tab."

"Glad to help," Joe said, standing up.

I noticed he didn't counter my offer to pay, so I left some bills on the table. "I've got to go catch my train. Nice to meet you, Joe."

I left him at the booth and went back out into the dark and chilly night. The train stop was only a few blocks away, and I had to hurry a bit, but I managed to arrive just as the train was pulling up at the platform. I slumped into a seat, hoping that there would be good news in the morning.

CHAPTER 5

Jason Miller was still on my mind as I walked from the station to the Society the next morning. What could have happened? Was he all right? I hadn't heard a word from Arabella Heffernan, but we weren't exactly close, and I doubted that she had my home number. Nor did I have hers, and even if I had, I was reluctant to call only to hear bad news. I'd had trouble erasing the image of Jason's still form on the floor, so out of place among the bright and gaudy cartoon animals. And even if all was well, her daughter, Caitlin, had looked very distressed, and Arabella might have had her hands full comforting her.

I was knee-deep in paperwork at my desk an hour or so later when Front Desk Bob called. "There's a Ms. Heffernan here to see you. Can I send her up?"

Arabella had come all the way here, in person? That was kind. I sighed, wishing I had that elusive assistant to send downstairs and escort Arabella up to my office, according to protocol. "Please see her to the elevator, Bob, and I'll meet her on this end."

"Will do," Bob said, and hung up.

I swept the papers into a sort of neat pile, checked to make sure that my guest chair was clear, and walked down the hall to the elevator. I arrived before it had creaked its way up the two stories. When the doors opened, there was Arabella, looking far more cheerful than she had the evening before, and all but hidden behind a large basket filled with flowers and cookies. My mouth started watering immediately, even though I'd eaten breakfast.

"Nell, I wanted to bring you this as an apology for yesterday. What an awful thing! I'm so sorry you had to be there. What must you think of us!"

"Please don't worry about me, Arabella. Is Jason all right?"

"Thank goodness, yes. That's why I wanted to see you. I was sure you would be worried, though you were so calm yesterday!"

Arabella had done pretty well herself, taking charge and doing what had to be done. I'd been impressed: her warm and cuddly exterior hid a solid core. "Why don't we go to my office?"

"Wonderful," Arabella said.

I led the way, catching a few curious glances directed more at the large basket of goodies than at me. Once in my office, I set the basket on my credenza, then gestured toward the chair. "Please sit down. I was going to call you, but I didn't want to bother you this morning."

"Well, Jason's going to be just fine. He woke up in the ambulance and he was talking. He wanted to go home last night, but the doctors thought he should stay overnight for observation, just in case."

"That's great news. Oh, where are my manners? Can I get you some coffee? It won't be as good as your tea, though." What I really wanted was an excuse to dig into the cookies. "Unless you have to get back to work right away?"

"Coffee would be lovely. And I'm not in a hurry. I thought I'd treat myself to a little time off, after all the stress of yesterday. And of course the electrical inspectors are back, and I'm sure they don't want me hovering over them."

"You didn't think you should close the museum, at least until they had checked things out?"

"The exhibit has its own independent wiring—we added all that recently. That area's off-limits to the public anyway, until we open the exhibit, but just in case I asked one of our staff to stay and make sure nobody strays."

"I'm glad to hear that. Let me get you that coffee. I'll be right back!" I ducked down the hall to the staff room, praying that there was something in the pot, and that it wasn't sludge. For once I was lucky. I rinsed out two cups and filled them, then headed back down the hall.

By the time I returned, Arabella had already laid out some of the cookies (from a local bakery, not a package) for us on pretty matching napkins. This was one very organized lady. I set a mug of coffee in front of her, then went around the desk and sat with my own mug. "That looks lovely."

"Thank you. Your office is quite impressive."

"It is that. I still feel as though I don't belong here, and someone's going to come along and throw me out."

"Oh, pshaw! You'll be fine. As I'm sure you've discovered, this kind of position takes a strong sense of organization combined with an ability to size up people quickly and schmooze them. And I've seen you do those quite well. Don't underestimate yourself."

I laughed. "I think you've nailed the job description, and thank you for the kind words. How long have you been at Let's Play?"

Arabella fluttered an airy hand. "Forever, it seems. I came up through the ranks, so to speak. I started out as a docent when my daughter, Caitlin, was young—I saw how much she and the other children loved it, and I wanted to be part of it. And things just sort of grew from there! I've been president for ten years now, and I still love it. And I seem to have passed my love of it on to Caitlin—she's our exhibits coordinator. She's been working with me at Let's Play for a couple of years now, since she graduated from college, but the *Harriet the Hedgehog* exhibit is her first solo project."

"I know how much time it takes to get things right, whether it's fragile documents or plastic animals. She must have had to work long hours." So Caitlin worked with her mother. I wondered how that had come about—had they avoided any whiff of nepotism?

"Oh yes, she's spent quite a bit of time working on the exhibit. It's a shame she lives in Camden now; I tried to get her to stay with me in the city—I've been in the same house since Caitlin was young, and when my husband . . . left"—a brief cloud passed across her face, and I wondered what the story was—"it was easiest to stay on, since she was settled in school and had friends there. And it was so convenient! Most of the time I walk to work."

"I can see that. I live in the suburbs myself."

"Well, that's nice, too. So it's just you?" Arabella nibbled at a cookie, much like a dormouse.

"It is. I own a house in Bryn Mawr, and I take the train in."

"It's so pretty out there!"

"I think so," I said, sipping bad coffee and compensating for it with a good cookie. "Caitlin and Jason are engaged?"

"If Caitlin says so, I suppose they are. She hasn't shared the details with me, but they've been living together for a while. I can't run a children's museum and broadcast that. But I like Jason—he's a sweet boy. Actually he's a graduate student at Penn, but he's been moonlighting with us because we're behind schedule with the painting, and he can use the money. I'm sure you know how that goes—nothing is ever done on time, or you find something unexpected that has to be fixed before you can move forward."

I had to laugh. "I know exactly what you mean, especially when you're working with an older building."

Arabella nodded. "Anyway, he's Caitlin's first real boyfriend, but they're *so* good together! That's why she was still around yesterday—she was waiting so they could go home together."

"Poor Jason—he was definitely in the wrong place at the wrong time. I'm glad he'll be all right. Caitlin seemed so upset."

"Oh, she was. I practically had to drag her home with me last night, once we knew Jason would be fine. I volunteered to pay all his medical expenses. He's got only minimal coverage through his graduate program."

"Do you know what happened? Was it a wiring problem?"

"I still don't know. I'm having the original contractor come in and check it out this morning. We've been very careful, you know. He couldn't understand what had gone wrong—everything looked correct to him. I've also asked someone else to check it out, too, just to be sure."

"Yes, you said you'd had all the inspections." Which

made it odd that something so obvious would short out—assuming that was what had happened. But I was far from an expert on things electrical, and I knew how often older buildings were plagued by jerry-rigged systems, especially if they'd been around for a hundred or so years. That was a problem we battled with at the Society every time we tried to install something. "Well, I hope whatever it was, it's simple to fix, and I'm very glad that Jason's going to be all right. Have you ever visited the Society? I'd love to show you what we've got. We may even have a collection of children's books printed in Philadelphia—if I can find it."

Arabella clapped her hands. "Ooh, I'd love to see. It's so much fun to take a peek at what goes on behind the scenes."

I stood up. "Then I'll be happy to show you."

I loved showing off our collections, although to an outsider they didn't look like much: rows of old metal shelving holding books and documents, mainly. But once you opened a book or a file, there were all sorts of treasures. I could tell that Arabella was sincere in her appreciation, particularly when I showed her the business records for a long-gone Philadelphia manufacturer of carousel animals.

"Wouldn't it be fun to do something with this?" she said wistfully. "Not with the original pieces, of course, but something derived from those wonderful old animals. Something that the children could actually sit on?"

"I'd love to work with you—maybe we could do a joint exhibit? We could showcase the antique images and the carousel company here, and you could do something updated at your place?" I did in fact like the idea, since it wouldn't take much on our part—we had all the materials on hand.

"Oh, could we?" Arabella clapped her hands with excitement. "It would have to be scheduled for a year or two out, since the *Harriet* exhibit will be up through next year. But it would take that long to plan anyway, wouldn't it?"

"So I gather, although exhibit planning is not my area of expertise. And it would be nice to find some funding for it. Speaking of which, I just hired a development director. Would you like to meet her?"

"I'd be delighted."

We wrapped up the tour quickly, and I led her past Shelby's desk. "Shelby, this is—"

She interrupted me before I could finish. "Arabella Heffernan. Of course! We used to visit Let's Play years ago, when my daughter, Melissa, was young and we were visiting my husband John's family. I've always had a soft spot for your museum."

"Well, isn't that nice? I take it your daughter is grown now? Any grandbabies?"

"Not yet, but she is getting married next summer, so I can hope."

I broke in, "We were just kicking around ideas for some sort of joint exhibit on carousel animals, and were wondering about finding some grant support for it. Maybe you could do a little digging?"

"Happy to! I can see that would be a lot of fun to plan."

"No rush, but it would be good to know what resources are available. Can I see you out, Arabella?"

"You mean you want to get some work done, dear. Of course. I'm so glad we had a chance to talk, and let's keep in touch. Shelby, nice to meet you."

"You, too, Arabella."

I took Arabella back downstairs. In the elevator she turned to me. "Nell, could I ask one more favor?"

"Sure. What is it?"

"I know you must be swamped, with your new position,

but would you mind talking to Caitlin? We're short-staffed, and she's been handling PR for Let's Play. Jason will be fine, but I thought maybe you could walk Caitlin through how to handle . . . difficult situations with the press and donors."

Because I had so much experience dealing with rather public institutional crises? Sadly it was true. "Sure, I can give her some pointers."

"Oh, thank you! Could I send her over this afternoon? Just in case there's any leak about Jason's mishap, I want her to be ready."

Apparently I wasn't going to get much paperwork done today. "Of course, send her over."

"I really do appreciate it, Nell, and I'm sure Caitlin will, too."

The elevator reached the ground floor and I saw Arabella off, then wandered back to my desk. Was it lunchtime yet? Could I skip lunch and just eat those lovely cookies? I had barely settled myself when Shelby appeared and dropped into the chair in front of me. "Aren't you going to offer me a cookie?"

"No, I want to keep them all to myself!" I smiled and offered her the basket.

"I bet you do. You didn't happen to catch the name of the bakery, did you? These are wonderful." Shelby munched blissfully. "What brought Arabella here?"

"There was an unfortunate incident yesterday, while I was at Let's Play—something went wrong with one of the exhibits they're installing, a worker got a bad shock, and they took him off to the hospital. Arabella came by to tell me he's going to be fine. The cookies were compensation for whatever upset I might have suffered from witnessing what happened. I'm just glad it wasn't any worse."

"Amen to that! That was nice of her. And I like that idea for a joint project—collaborative efforts sell well to funders, don't you think?"

"I do. And it would be an interesting alliance, given how different our audiences are. Great crossover potential. I was surprised, though, that you knew Arabella, and Let's Play. You weren't just being polite, were you?"

"Not at all! I do remember it, from years back. It was always a little shabby, but my daughter loved it."

"Still true. So do your in-laws still live around here? Would I know them?"

Shelby laughed. "I doubt it—they don't like to part with a nickel, so they wouldn't be on your fundraising radar. So help me, they had a stick up their you-know-whats, one and all. We visited for holidays when Melissa was young, but after a while even she didn't want to come. They retired to Florida several years ago, and I don't see much of them these days, at least since Melissa left home. Doesn't exactly break my heart." Shelby helped herself to another cookie.

"Did you need me for something?" I prompted her, before she ate all my goodies.

"Oh—yes. I've got someone I'd like you to talk to about your assistant position."

"That was fast. Does Melanie approve?"

"Sure does. I gave her his résumé this morning."

"His?"

Shelby arched one eyebrow at me. "You're not going to go all sexist about this?"

"Of course not. If he can do the job, I'll be happy to talk to him. When can he come in?"

"Would this afternoon work for you? He's temping at the moment, but he's between jobs."

"Bring him on in—I'll make time for him."

"OK, I'll give him a call." She stood up. "I'll let you go back to work now—if you'll bribe me with one more cookie."

"Done." Regretfully I handed her one, refusing to count how many—or how few—remained. "Now shoo."

CHAPTER 6

Fortified by the cookies, I decided to work through the lunch hour. Unfortunately, fifteen minutes later Front Desk Bob called up to say that there was a Caitlin Treacy to see me. "Send her up," I told Bob. "I'll meet her at the elevator."

I'd only seen Caitlin as she had rushed to Jason's side the day before, and I wouldn't have recognized the slender young woman who emerged from the elevator. She was taller than Arabella, and I wondered briefly what her father had looked like, since she bore little resemblance to her smaller, rounder mother. "Thank you for seeing me on such short notice, Ms. Pratt."

"Nell, please," I said absently. "No problem. As your mother may have told you, I know a bit about the situation you're in, and I'm happy to help. How's Jason?" I asked as I led her down the hall to my office.

"He's good, or so the doctors say. They wouldn't let me

stay overnight at the hospital, so I spent the night at Mother's."

We walked in silence until reaching my office, where I gestured her toward a chair. "She mentioned that. So you and Jason live in Camden?"

Caitlin was studying my office, taking in the details—or avoiding my eyes? "Yes. We live together. He's a graduate student so he doesn't have a lot of money, and rents are cheap there compared to here. I could live with my mother, but I'd rather live with Jason."

Well, that was direct, at least. "Does he remember much about what happened?"

"No." She didn't elaborate.

It seemed to me that I was doing a lot of the work to keep this conversation going, which was annoying because she was the one who wanted something from me. "What can I do for you? Do you have questions?"

"Mother thought I should talk to you. Look, my job is exhibits management, not public relations, so I don't really know what to do. Mother said you had something awful happen here, so she thought you could help me with what to say. Or not say. If the press comes around."

Based on her awkwardness, I could see why Caitlin wasn't up to handling public relations. I wondered if she was capable of talking to people at all. She was an attractive young woman but definitely short on charm.

"There's no one else at your place who handles the press?" I hoped there was someone who could bail her out.

"Nope, the person who usually would is out on maternity leave. Bad timing, with the exhibit happening just now." She said abruptly, "You know it takes years to put together an exhibit, right?"

"Yes," I said. I'd been involved in raising money for

more than one at the Society, although luckily we had nothing in the works at the moment.

"And now it's just a couple of weeks before we're supposed to open. It's all set up, and the publicity for it went out long ago. And now this thing with Jason happened. So far nobody's paid it any attention, and he's not going to stir anything up, that's for sure. I mean, like suing or anything. But say somebody at the hospital talks—what do I do then?"

I felt for her. I'd learned the hard way how fragile an institution's reputation was, and one wrong step could do a lot of harm to it. Of course, identifying the cause would go a long way toward easing visitors' minds. "The most important thing you can do is reassure the public that Let's Play is safe for their children. That what happened to Jason was a simple accident, and that you've had everything checked out by experts who have assured you that the wiring is safe. That is, only if this leaks out."

"But it *was* an accident. The wiring is fine."

I was a bit surprised at her almost flippant attitude. "Caitlin, you may know that, but what you have to do is make sure the public does, too—and believes it. Forgive me for saying so, but I think your mother's a much better spokesperson than you are, if it comes to that."

"I know," Caitlin said. "I'm not good with people, and I hate sucking up. I'm a lot happier dealing with paperwork and planning. I think the exhibit is great. Don't you?"

"It looked charming, though I didn't really get to see it working before the accident. I imagine that children will love it. But to get back to the point, do you have any connections in city government? A friend at the *Inquirer*, maybe? Can you invite the mayor to the opening? How about a buddy at a local radio or television station who can help you get the word out?"

Caitlin shrugged—again. I couldn't believe how uninterested she appeared in this conversation. "I don't know. I'll have to check the files, when I get time."

"Make the time," I said firmly. "It's important to keep the press on your side, just in case things like this happen. That means you have to cultivate relationships with them—all the time, not just when you need them. You have to manage all your relationships in this town. People can really pull together and help you, but only if you've laid the groundwork first. And right now, if I were you, I'd brainstorm with the rest of your staff and try to figure out what your strongest contact is and use that." I stared at her. She stared back, her expression blank. Was I getting through to her? I doubted it. I thought for another moment. "Be prepared for quick turnaround—keep ahead of the story. Could Hadley Eastman and her publicity people pull any strings?"

Caitlin grimaced. "I think they'd be happy to wash their hands of this whole mess, including Hadley. All she does is whine."

I wasn't getting a much better impression of Caitlin, frankly. I stood up. "I hope I've helped you, Caitlin. Now I'm afraid that I've got a lot to get finished today. I'll see you out."

Caitlin followed my lead and stood. "Thank you for talking with me, Nell. I appreciate your time." She said it as if by rote. Could anyone be that clueless, even in her twenties? Daughter or not, Arabella would do well to find someone more sympathetic to handle the local media, because Caitlin did not seem to have the necessary skills—or tact. Well, she was Arabella's problem, not mine, and I'd done what I could. I took her back to the lobby and trudged back up the stairs to my desk.

CHAPTER 7

At four o'clock Shelby proudly escorted her candidate for my much-needed assistant into my office. He was a slender young man with a sweep of silky blond hair that kept falling across his forehead. "Eric, this is Ms. Pratt. Nell, meet Eric Marston. Don't bite his head off." Eric gave her a look, and she held up her hands in surrender. "All right, I'm going." She backed out quickly.

Eric walked across the room and extended his hand. "Pleased to meet you, Miz Pratt."

"Let me guess—you're also from the South, like Shelby?" The accent combined with his manners gave him away.

"That I am, ma'am. May I sit down?"

"Oh, please do." Once again, I was in the dark: the résumé Melanie had passed on to me was short and bland, so I had little to go on. "Tell me something about yourself."

"I'm twenty-three, ma'am. College graduate, William and Mary. Been in Philadelphia 'bout a year now. I don't have a whole lot of work experience, but I helped put myself through school by working in some of the offices on campus, and I've been doin' a lot of temp work since I got here. I keyboard one hundred words per minute, and I file like nobody's business. Can you tell me what you're looking for?"

"Well, Eric, I need someone to organize my life here. I haven't been in this position long, but I've worked here for a while. What I need is someone to answer phones, type up letters and reports for me, manage my schedule, take notes at board meetings, and make my life easier. I don't expect you to pick up my dry cleaning, or bring me coffee, unless you're getting some from yourself. Have I scared you off yet?"

"No, ma'am. I appreciate your honesty."

"Well, that's good, because I don't have time to play games. Why do you want this job?"

He smiled shyly. "Well, for a start, I need a job, like a lot of other people these days. This city's not a cheap place to live, you know. I like working with people, and I like organizing things—you should see my closet. I'm punctual, thrifty, neat, and friendly. That's what you need, right?"

"How about tough, like with people who insist they need to talk with me immediately and won't take no for an answer?"

He gave me a bigger smile this time. "Well, I'll just have to turn the charm on until they go away, won't I?"

I laughed. "How do you feel about history?"

I was pleased to see that his eyes lit up. "I truly love it, ma'am. I was an economics major in college, but I focused on the late-nineteenth-century reconstruction of the South, so I know about research and original sources and all. And Philadelphia's where so much of it began, right? Even though Massachusetts claims a lot of the credit."

Could lightning strike twice? Shelby had walked in out of nowhere, and I'd hired her on the spot. Eric seemed too perfect to be true; my luck was never this good. "Eric, how about this? I need someone desperately, like yesterday. Why don't I give you a trial period, say two weeks? We'd pay for your time, at whatever the going temp rate is, and if everything works out by the end of that time, you've got the job. If not, we'll part ways with no hard feelings. Does that seem fair?"

"More than fair, ma'am. When should I start?"

"Can you come in tomorrow morning? And please drop the *ma'am*. I'm Nell."

"Eight thirty okay, Nell?"

"Eight thirty's fine, Eric. I'll meet you in front and we can sort out keys and stuff. You want to stop by Shelby's office and give her the good news?"

"I'd sure appreciate that."

I came around the desk and led him back down the hall. "Shelby, I said I'd give Eric here a trial run."

"That's terrific, Nell. And Eric, you be good or I'll whup your ass. Got it?"

He bobbed his head. "Sure do, Shelby. I'll do you proud, don't worry."

"Well, I'll let you two chat—I've got work to do." I ducked out and headed back to my office. I amused myself by wondering how our patrons and board members would react to a Southern accent—and a male one at that—when they phoned me, but I thought Eric had the right idea: charm conquers all, or at least a whole lot. And I had me an assistant, at least for a while.

And cookies. Things were definitely looking up.

Things got even better when I grabbed my phone just before five. "Nell Pratt," I said crisply.

"James Morrison," said the voice on the phone, matching my tone.

I stifled an inappropriate giggle. Marty had told her cousin Jimmy to call me, and presto, he called—despite the fact that he was a senior FBI agent. And James Morrison, special agent, looked every inch the FBI agent. When we'd first met, I'd wondered if there was a style sheet for agents, because he fit it to a T: conservative suit, polished shoes, regulation haircut. I happened to know he was an all-around good guy, but the immediate question was whether he was calling for personal or professional reasons. I decided not to make it easy for him.

"Why, James, how nice to hear from you! Do you have news about our missing collection items?"

"Uh, no."

He didn't add anything immediately, but I let him dangle. Finally he said, "I know it's short notice, but are you doing anything tonight?"

I pretended to riffle through my calendar. "No, I don't have any plans."

"Would you like to, uh, have dinner with me?"

I didn't really have to think about that. "That would be delightful. Do you want to meet somewhere?"

"You know that new bistro near City Hall, on Broad Street?"

Of course I did. I walked past it almost daily, and I often drooled over the menu they posted. "I do. What time?"

"How about seven?"

"Seven's great. See you then." I hung up quickly, but not before I heard what I thought was a sigh of relief.

I left the office shortly before seven, but James had arrived at the restaurant before me and was seated at a table that was just right—not too public, not too intimate. He rose as he saw me exchange a word with the maitre d' and waited until I approached. "Nell, it's good to see you. Is the new job agreeing with you?" He held out my chair for me. One of the last gentlemen.

"I think so," I said. "I can't believe it's been a couple of months already. I'm up to my neck in trying to keep the day-to-day stuff moving forward, without even thinking about any major changes."

He sat down across from me. "Do you plan any changes?"

"You know the problems we have, but I don't see what I can do about them without a big cash infusion. We've beefed up the front-desk procedures, but it's really hard to know whether that helps. We'll see. Any further word about our artifacts?"

"Not much, I'm afraid. These things take time, and you know you can't count on a high success rate. I wish I had better news, but we're actively working on it. And of course you know Marty's on the case, and she's a bulldog."

He had that right. At least Marty had a strong moral compass to go with her determination. "That's what I assumed when I didn't hear from you. And I'm not surprised. I'm just pleased—and grateful—that we didn't get much negative publicity out of it all." All right, this was silly: I couldn't relax until I knew why he and I were here. "Funny thing—I saw Marty just yesterday. She mentioned you." I waited to hear how he would respond to that.

His mouth twitched. "That would account for her phone call last night. She suggested that I might want to get together with you. I believe this is what's known as a date. Although I may be out of step with the times."

"Oh, is that what this is? You don't have some nefarious scheme to reveal to me? You don't want me to spy on someone for you?" It was kind of fun to tease him.

"No to both. I thought we, uh, had some interesting interactions the last time we met, and I wanted to see you under less, uh, stressful circumstances. Do you want to leave now? I'd hate to keep you here under false pretenses."

"Why would I do that?" An attractive, intelligent man with a steady job—and one who actually knew something about my patchy romantic history—might be interested in pursuing a nonprofessional relationship with me! I could get excited about that—if I had any energy left after trying to keep a financially challenged institution afloat, with no training or preparation for the job. I would definitely consider it. After all, I'd said yes to the president's job with equally little notice. Why not to dating an FBI agent? "I'm happy to have dinner with you. And right now I could use a glass of wine and some food, if you don't mind."

"I think I can handle that." He made an almost imperceptible gesture and a waiter appeared with oversize menus, which he presented with a flourish.

"Chardonnay?" James asked.

"Yes, please." He'd remembered—a point for him.

While we studied the menu, I checked my inner thermostat. I hadn't had the time or the energy to play games for the last couple of months, what with everything that had fallen on my head, but I wasn't about to pass up an invitation from an attractive man—I could make time for James.

We ordered, and once the waiter had left, I realized how out of practice I was at this dating thing. "If this is a social occasion, is this the point where we're supposed to exchange life histories? Oh, wait—you probably have an extensive dossier on me. Right?"

He smiled. "You'd have to file a formal request in writing to find that out. Why don't we just start back at the beginning?"

I laughed. "Okay, I'll go first. I'm single, gainfully employed, and have no criminal records or vices that could result in same at some unspecified future date. No secret children. No history of insanity in the family. Are we good so far?"

He nodded, clearly amused. I pressed on. "I have a job I think I like—although check back with me in another couple of months on that. I own my own home, I have a middle-aged car, and no debt beyond my mortgage. And I still have all my own teeth and my vital organs."

James grinned. "Ditto, except I own a condo in University City."

"Nice short commute," I said, sipping my water. "Any siblings?"

"Two. One brother, one sister. Neither lives nearby."

"I've got one brother who works in Texas, for reasons that mystify me. You weren't born in Texas, were you?"

"No."

"Then I'll feel free to say disparaging things about the place."

"Go right ahead," he said, then asked, his tone neutral, "You were married once, weren't you?"

"Yes, a long time ago. It didn't work out, but we parted on good terms. You?"

"Never got that far."

I bit back a snappy response. He was a good catch, so why was he unattached at his age? Did his job turn women off, or just leave him with too little time to deal with outside relationships? These were questions I didn't think I had any right to ask—at least, not on a first date. Maybe a second date, if there was one.

Our drinks appeared, followed in short order by our appetizers. That effectively ended Speed Dating, Round One. The food lived up to the media hype it had received, and I was happy to see that James gave it the attention it deserved. I wasn't sure I wanted to get involved with someone who didn't appreciate the subtleties of fine cuisine—one of my guilty pleasures, when I could afford it.

"How are things going at the Society?" he asked.

"Well, nothing's disappeared lately, which is good. I'm trying to fill in staff to replace the people we lost. I may have managed to fill my old position. After the recent press we've gotten, I'm not in any hurry to start asking people for money again."

"Memories are short. As soon as the next big scandal comes along, people will forget about the Society's problems," James said.

I wasn't sure I agreed with him. After all, we were in the business of preserving history—and memories. It would be a big plus if we could recover some or all of the lost artifacts, but I had little control over that. James, however, did. "Do you think we'll get anything back?"

He looked down at the table and lined up the remaining silverware. "Let's say I still hold out hope. I can tell you that a lot of people who acquire items they suspect may be illicitly obtained, do so not for any financial reasons but because they really want the items. So they may not have gone far."

"Let's hope. Speaking of problems, I was over at Let's Play yesterday." When he looked blank, I explained. "The children's museum? They had a small problem with the wiring, and somebody received a nasty electrical shock. He'll be all right, but I'm beginning to wonder if I attract disasters."

"It wasn't a criminal act, was it?" James asked.

"I don't think so. Just a fault in the new wiring, apparently. I'm sure they're careful there, because they're dealing with a lot of children. It would be disastrous to their reputation if something happened to a child." We at the Society had had enough trouble dealing with theft—which reflected badly on our stewardship of our historical collections—but if a child were injured or worse . . . I didn't want to think about it.

My expression must have given me away, because James was watching me sympathetically. "I don't think you had anything to do with that, unless you've been moonlighting as an electrician."

I appreciated his effort to lighten the mood. "Not me—I have trouble changing a lightbulb." And our talk drifted to other topics over dessert and coffee.

It was past ten when I looked at my watch and realized I should get moving if I wanted to get the last train. "I'm sorry, but I need to catch a train."

"I could drive you home?" James volunteered.

It was tempting, but I didn't want to rush things. "No, it's all right—I go home late a lot of the time. If your car's nearby you could drop me at Thirtieth Street, though."

"Certainly." He paid the bill in record time and escorted me outside. It had to be well below freezing, and I was glad not to have to walk to the train. The drive to the station took only a few minutes, and James pulled up in front and stopped. I felt a pang of concern: had he done this only to get Marty off his back? Would he consider his duty done and disappear again?

"Nell," he began.

I held my breath.

"I really enjoyed this evening. I hope we can do it again, and sooner than two months."

I exhaled. "I'd like that." But I couldn't resist adding, "Do you want me to report back to Marty?"

He laughed. "Let's keep her guessing. Good night, Nell."

CHAPTER 8

The next morning I boarded my train and unfurled my *Philadelphia Inquirer.* I'm old-fashioned, in keeping with my job: I refuse to read a newspaper online, and the paper version is just long enough to occupy me during my trip to Center City. I liked to know what had happened since the day before, and what was going to happen, in my city. Sometimes events of the day even had an impact on my work, and I read the "Social Circuit" column to see what our board members or patrons were doing.

I dutifully read the national news before flipping to the local section, and stopped in horror: the banner headline read, "Tragic Accident at Museum." Above the fold. After my heart started again, once I determined that it wasn't the Society they were talking about, I realized the grainy picture showed the front of Let's Play, alongside a studio photo of Arabella, taken at least ten years ago. Wait—she had told me that Jason was fine and was ready to be sent home. Had he taken a turn for the worse?

Oh, no. It was a second accident. And this time someone had died.

I read on, my feelings a messy mix of ghoulish curiosity and dismay. Thirty-five-year-old electrician Joseph Murphy had been fatally electrocuted while putting the finishing touches on a newly installed exhibit at a local children's museum, blah, blah, blah.

I had to stop reading to collect myself. Not Joe! Joe, who had been so kind to me after Jason's accident? Had he been working again on the wiring? Arabella had definitely said yesterday that she had other people checking it out.

I shook myself and résuméd reading. Joe had met his end while working on a large animal figure representing Willy the Weasel, a character in the popular children's book series *Harriet the Hedgehog*. The photographer had graciously spared readers the sight of poor Joe collapsed at the feet of Willy; there was, instead, a floodlit view of a covered gurney emerging from the building. The body had been discovered about nine o'clock the prior night, when the electrical incident had triggered an alarm. Alarm? Nothing had gone off when I witnessed Jason's event. Was that new?

There was no mention in the article about Jason's accident.

I laid the paper carefully on my lap and thought. Jason had received a shock only two days ago, but had survived. Apparently that first accident still wasn't public knowledge. Who had checked out the wiring, and had that person found anything out of the ordinary? Or any cause at all for Jason's accident? Or Joe's? Who had installed the alarm?

And now that a death had occurred, the question had to arise: was Jason's mishap an accident, or had it just been a dry run? *Wait, Nell—a dry run for what?* Clearly there was something wrong with the wiring at Let's Play, or at least the new wiring for the exhibit, but that didn't mean anyone had evil intentions. Accidents happen, especially in old buildings—or so I had told myself following Jason's accident. But twice in the space of two days? Something was not right.

I debated my options. I could do nothing. Or I could contact Arabella and see who she had talked to and what she had told them. Or I could be proactive and contact the police myself to let them know what I'd seen when Jason was injured; when they hadn't contacted me, I had just assumed they had written it off as an accident, if they even knew about it. I didn't like option one and wasn't happy with option three, since my last dealings with the Philadelphia Police Department had been barely cordial, especially after I'd proved them wrong. Poor Arabella—she must be devastated. She cared so much for her museum, and this kind of publicity could be very damaging, as I knew too well. I decided on option two: I'd see if I could reach her first and then decide about talking to the police.

I was still lost in thought when I arrived at the Society to find Eric waiting for me on the steps—as had been the case with Shelby, it had been too late the previous day to get him set up with keys and such. He looked young and eager, and was clutching a cardboard box from which I could see protruding a blooming African violet.

"I hope you don't mind—I brought some things to brighten up the outer office," he said.

"No problem, as long as you don't spill water all over the antiques." I unlocked the door and held it for him, then led him to the elevator. "You'll need to get a key to go to the administrative floor and the stacks. Security reasons."

"Got it. You don't want people just wandering around

the building. At least, not ones who aren't supposed to be here."

"Exactly." We reached the president's suite, which was a rather grand name for the two rooms. "I don't know what there is in your desk—the last assistant left rather hurriedly, and someone boxed up her personal possessions, but I hope they left the office supplies. If you need stuff, the supply room is right around the corner, and it doubles as the coat closet."

"What about the coffee room? Oh, and bathroom?"

I had to laugh at myself. "I'm doing a lousy job of getting you settled, aren't I? Coffee room's the end of that hall there"—I pointed—"near the staff staircase, and bathroom is right next to the stairs. Look, why don't I let you look around a bit, and then we can do the paperwork and meet the rest of the staff?" I knew I was doing a poor job of easing him into the job, but I was still rattled by the news of Joe's death.

"Sounds good to me." The phone on his desk rang. He smiled quickly at me. "Let me get that." He picked it up and said, "President's office," in an appropriately professional tone. Then his expression changed. "Just a moment, please." Unfamiliar with the phone and its Hold button, he covered the receiver with his hand and said in a loud whisper, "It's a Detective Hrivnak with the Philadelphia Police. Do you want to take it?"

Oh, damn. This was not the way I wanted to start the day. "I guess I'd better. I can pick it up in my office—wait until I've got it and you can hang up."

I walked the few feet to my office, stripped off my coat and hung it carefully on the back of the door, then sat down behind my desk. The last few conversations I'd had with the detective had not been happy ones, and I'd hoped we were done with each other. Apparently not. After taking a deep breath, I picked up the phone, pushed the button to connect it, and said, "This is Nell Pratt."

Detective Hrivnak, whose first name, if she had one, I'd never heard, said abruptly, "You were at Let's Play when Jason Miller was involved in an electrical accident. You heard about the second one?"

"I read about it in the paper this morning. Since you're calling me, you think it wasn't just an accident?" Detective Hrivnak *was* a homicide detective, after all, as I knew only too well.

She ignored my question. "Can you come in and talk to me, say, eleven?"

At least she'd asked rather than ordered. "I'll be there." She hung up before I could say anything more, like ask her where the heck her office was. Luckily I know how to use my computer, and I quickly verified my first guess: Homicide Unit, Police Headquarters. Walking distance.

I looked up to find Eric hovering in the doorway. "Everything all right?" he said anxiously.

"You mean, will I be arrested before your first day is over? Don't worry. This is about an electrical accident that happened at the Let's Play Museum—it was in the paper this morning. There was a minor one when I was there earlier this week, but this time someone died."

"Oh no! How awful—for them and for you! Can I get you anything?"

Tea and sympathy? "I'm okay. But the detective wants to talk to me at eleven. You can put that on my calendar—if you can find it."

"I'm guessing it's on the computer, wherever that is."

Oh . . . sugar. The last computer used by the president's assistant had . . . well, the bottom line was, it was gone and

I didn't think it would be coming back anytime soon. And there were no electronic records for Eric to go through and familiarize himself with, although I assumed they were all backed up somewhere and therefore retrievable. Of course, there were always the paper copies. "I'll talk to human resources about getting you set up with something."

"Hey, if it's a problem, I can bring my laptop from home," Eric offered.

"Wait until I see if we've got anything you can use. We'll have to replace that one anyway. Why don't you go through the paper files and see if you can get a sense of what goes on here?"

"I'll do that. You sure I can't get you something? A cup of coffee?"

Poor boy, he really was trying hard. "Sure, and get yourself some, too. It's an honor system, a quarter a cup, just so we get something slightly better than swill." As he bounded off toward the break room, I tried to gather my scattered thoughts. So much for the morning—I hadn't counted on a trip to the police station. I wondered if I should try to call Arabella as I had planned, but then decided she was probably besieged at the moment.

The phone rang again, and since Eric was still fetching coffee, I picked up. "Nell Pratt."

To my surprise, it was Arabella. "Oh, Nell, I'm so sorry to have to call you like this. You've heard?"

"Yes, I read about it in the paper this morning. What happened?"

"I can't really talk now, but I wanted to apologize. You shouldn't find yourself in the middle of our mess. But the police said they might want to talk to you, since you were there when Jason . . ."

"Yes, they've already called, and I'll be talking to them

this morning. It was a homicide detective who called. Does that mean they don't think this second event was an accident?"

"I don't know, Nell. But they talked to poor Jason this morning, and his head is still kind of fuzzy. I don't think he remembers much about what happened."

"Arabella, I hate to ask, but didn't you tell me that you'd had someone look at the wiring?"

"Of course," she said indignantly. "And not just the person who's been doing the installation for us—I got in touch with a friend of mine who has his own company, and he's all properly licensed and approved and whatever. He said he didn't see anything wrong. I made sure that he looked at all the animal figures, too, just in case. And he said they were fine!"

"When did you talk to him?"

"Yesterday, in the early afternoon. He did me a big favor, coming over on short notice, but I didn't want anything else to go wrong. But it did anyway." She ended with what sounded like a sob. "What am I going to do, Nell? The police said we can't open today. The children will be so disappointed."

That was the least of Arabella's problems. "That's terrible, but you know the police have to do it. Just take it one step at a time. Find out what happened last night first, and then you can figure out what to do next."

"You're so calm," Arabella sniffed. "I guess I'll have to be, too."

"Arabella, you've done all the right things," I said firmly. "I'm sure no one will blame you." Although I wasn't sure I believed that—but Arabella needed to hear it.

"You'll let me know if the police tell you anything?"

"Of course. I'm sure this will all be sorted out in no

time. Take care." I rang off. I didn't need to share with Arabella my lack of confidence in the local police, after seeing how they'd dismissed my concerns the last time we'd met, just a couple of months ago. But they were certainly better equipped than I was to investigate whatever had gone wrong at Let's Play, accidental or . . . planned?

I checked my watch: less than two hours before I'd have to leave to meet Detective Hrivnak, and who knew how long that conversation would take. What could I do to fill that time usefully?

Eric appeared, cradling a mug of coffee. "Sorry it took so long—I made a fresh pot. The old stuff looked nasty."

I accepted the mug happily. "That happens a lot. People will leave a quarter inch in the bottom of the pot, just so they can claim it wasn't empty."

Eric shook his head. "You look like you need that coffee. Is there anything else I can do to help?"

"Not unless you know something about wiring and/or criminal investigations," I said glumly. I tried the coffee: at least Eric had made it strong enough for my taste.

"Negative on both counts, I'm afraid."

"Then this will have to do. Thank you. Why don't you start by finding a manual for the phone, so at least you know how to transfer calls?"

"No problem about the phone. I've been temping long enough that I've probably seen every model on the market—and quite a few that aren't even sold anymore. I'll also see what office supplies I can scrounge up. Do you know if you have anything else scheduled for today, apart from that police person?"

I racked my brain and came up empty. A million little things, but no big thing. "Not that I know of."

The phone rang again, and Eric dashed to his desk to

pick it up. He came back in a moment, apparently having mastered the Hold button, and said in a bewildered voice, "It's an Agent Morrison from the FBI?"

"I'll take it, Eric." I picked up the phone. "This is Nell Pratt," I said. I wasn't sure whether this call was official or personal.

"Ms. Pratt," Special Agent James Morrison replied. "You've heard about the death at the Let's Play Children's Museum?"

So this was an official call. I wasn't surprised, but I'll admit to being a little disappointed. "I have. I told you I was there earlier this week when a similar but nonfatal event occurred. But isn't this kind of thing outside of the FBI's jurisdiction?"

He hesitated a fraction of a second before answering. "It is." He lowered his voice. "Are you okay?"

The icy block that had formed in my stomach when I'd read the paper melted just a little. "I think so. Except I have an appointment to meet with our friend Detective Hrivnak in a couple of hours. James—does that mean it's homicide? She wouldn't tell me."

He sighed. "Probably. Once is an accident; twice, it may well be deliberate. I'm sorry you have to be involved."

You and me both. "Thank you. I really don't know a lot, but I'll do whatever I can to help." I paused before adding, "I'm glad you called."

"I was worried. We can talk later." He hung up.

Eric appeared in the doorway, looking concerned. "Everything all right?"

"Just fine. Don't worry—I don't usually get calls from the police and the FBI in the same day."

"I'm very glad to hear that."

CHAPTER 9

After clearing a few of the more pressing items on my desk, I emerged from my office to find that Eric had taken care of all the paperwork for human resources and located at least the minimal office supplies, including stapler, tape, notepads, and a pencil holder. Too bad it wasn't as easy to find him a computer. "Want to take a walk around the building and meet some people?"

He stood up quickly. "I'd be happy to."

"How much do you know about the Pennsylvania Antiquarian Society?" I asked as we headed toward the collections management area to the rear of the building.

"Just what Shelby's told me. I haven't visited many of the museums around here."

"How is it you know Shelby?" I asked.

"I knew her daughter, Melissa, in school in Virginia, and we've sort of kept in touch—we're Facebook friends. She's the one who told me her mama lived up here now."

"You said you'd been living in Philadelphia for over a year now?"

"Yes, I have."

"What's your impression of our city?" I was honestly curious. He was young and from a different part of the country, and I wondered what had drawn him here.

"I like it. I thought about moving to Baltimore or Atlanta, but then I figured I should go someplace really different, at least for a while. Since I didn't have any attachments or anything."

"Have you been looking for a full-time job?"

"Yes and no. I kind of liked temping, at least at first—I got to see a lot of different places, sort of like a job sampler. Although if something had opened up when I was at any one place, I'd have considered it. But I get by."

We'd reached Latoya Anderson's office, down the hall from mine. She looked up from her desk when I knocked on the open door. "Latoya, I'd like you to meet Eric Marston. Eric, this is Latoya Anderson, our vice president of collections. Eric's auditioning for the role of my assistant."

Latoya didn't get my joke but extended a hand anyway. "Welcome, Eric. I'm sure Nell can use your help."

"I'm pleased to meet you, ma'am."

Latoya quirked an eyebrow at the *ma'am* but rallied. "I hope you'll enjoy working here. It's an interesting place." She turned her attention to me. "Nell, when you have a few minutes free, can we talk?"

"It'll have to be after lunch. Say, two, in my office?"

"That's fine. Nice to meet you, Eric."

We were dismissed. Latoya and I were still working out the wrinkles in our professional relationship, and her basic personality was a bit peremptory even on a good day, but I needed her in the job. Up until a couple of months ago I had been lower down the staff ladder than Latoya was, and as a vice president she'd had the ear of the president, which meant I was seldom the first to hear collections news. Now our roles were reversed and I was her boss. Still, I didn't want to alienate any staff members right now, and I did respect her abilities. I wondered what she wanted to talk about. "Let's go, Eric—there are more people to meet."

I made the circuit of the third floor: personnel, finance, and my old stomping ground, development, where we waved briefly at Shelby. Carrie, the membership coordinator, was clearly happy to see someone close to her age, and welcomed Eric warmly. "Hey, you want to have lunch today? And I'll see if maybe Rich is free, too."

Eric looked at me. "Well, sure, that'd be great, unless you need me, Nell?" I shook my head. "And you can show me where to eat around here. Who's Rich?"

It was becoming easier to forget that Eric had only just arrived. "Rich Girard is a grant-funded cataloger," I told him, "just out of college, so about your age. He's a nice guy."

"I'd love to meet him, too, then, if he's free. I'll come by about twelve, Carrie. Nice to meet you!"

Back in the hall, as we waited for the elevator so we could go downstairs, Eric asked anxiously, "Are you sure you don't need me to man the phone over lunch?"

I laughed. "Of course not. I think you'll find we're not a terribly formal place, and there are some really great people here. Carrie's sweet—she used to work for me. Well, I guess she still does, but now she reports to Shelby. I'll have to find you an organization chart so you can see who's who."

We rode the elevator down to the ground floor. "So this is the catalog room, and the big room next door is the reading room. You can probably guess what they're used for. There's another reading room upstairs. Let me introduce you to our librarians."

We stopped and chatted with all the staff members we encountered, who all seemed charmed by Eric's good manners and eagerness. I was encouraged to see that he was fitting in so well, although I hadn't really seen him do any work. Of course, to be fair, I hadn't exactly given him any assignments yet, either—or a computer, for that matter.

When we'd made the rounds, I checked my watch. I still had a few minutes. "Are you overwhelmed yet, or do you want to see the stacks?"

"Stacks?" Eric looked bewildered.

"The storage areas, where all the collections are. I don't have time to show you everything right now, but I can get you started, and you can browse a bit on your own—I don't want you to feel chained to your desk. It's important that you understand what we do here."

"That sounds great to me, Nell."

We went back to the third floor, and I fished out my keys and let him in by the door at the rear, past the elevator. Once inside, we paused for a moment. I always enjoyed prowling in the stacks, although I had less and less time to do it—and less reason now that I wasn't writing grant proposals. I hoped Shelby would enjoy that part of her job as much as I had.

The stacks occupied the upper half of the building, with some overflow in the basement, where less fragile items were kept. The ceilings in that part of the building were high, the windows painted over (too much light could damage old books and documents), and ranks of sturdy metal shelves marched off in all directions. The air smelled of old paper and leather. Apparently no one was shelving or retrieving documents at the moment, so it was very quiet. I sneaked a look at Eric and saw that his eyes were shining.

"May I?" he asked.

"Touch them? Of course—that's what they're here for. Just don't take them out of the building—and don't remove them from the stacks without signing a slip. There's a pile of slips on that shelf there." I pointed. I'd been guilty of forgetting that myself on more than one occasion, but I was trying to mend my ways. "There's some wonderful stuff here, both famous names and ordinary documents about daily life. I love coming in here."

Eric slid out a volume at random—early nineteenth century, by my semi-educated guess—and opened it reverently, cradling its spine and leafing through the yellowed pages with a cautious finger. Watching him, I felt something inside me relax: he was showing all the signs of a true believer. Not that it was essential in an administrative position, but it certainly helped if you cared about history and preserving it.

It was close to ten thirty when we tore ourselves away from the stacks, but I had a date to keep, and I didn't want to tick off Detective Hrivnak by being late. I escorted Eric back to his desk and retrieved my coat and bag. "Look, Eric, I probably won't be back before you leave for lunch, but you don't have to rush. Not today, at least. I can't promise you any long lunches when things get busy, but I'm not a clock-watcher."

"Thank you, ma'am. You can trust me." He smiled, showing dimples. "I'd say, have a nice time, but I don't think that applies to police interviews, now, does it?"

"Not likely!" I laughed. "See you later."

In Philadelphia, the police headquarters building is known as the Roundhouse, because, well, it's round. As a local historian, I also knew that the Philadelphia Police Department was the oldest municipal police agency in the country (founded 1751, or so their PR materials said), and the fourth largest. Luckily I had never had occasion to enter the building before, although I had walked past it plenty of times since it was close to Independence Hall. Homicide, as I understood it, was a special unit. I entered the building, submitted to a search of my bag (physical) and person (electronic), and found my way up to Detective Hrivnak's office. As it turned out, she did possess a first name: Meredith, according to the plaque beside her door. Not a good fit, but what did parents know?

She kept me waiting, but only fifteen minutes. She came out to escort me into her inner sanctum, pointed to a battered wooden chair, then settled into her chair behind an equally scarred desk. She stared at me wordlessly for several seconds. I couldn't think of any good opening line, so I returned her stare with as much composure as I could. After all, this time she had called me.

"Jason Miller," she said at last.

"Yes," I said intelligently.

"You were there when he was zapped, right?"

"I was."

"Why?"

"I've met Arabella Heffernan a few times, so she'd called up to welcome me to the upper ranks and invited me to preview her new exhibit. I assume you've talked to Jason?"

Detective Hrivnak shrugged. "He couldn't remember much. He touched something, then blam, he was knocked out. Or so he says."

"Will he be all right?"

"Yeah, sure. No permanent damage. Now, Joe Murphy, on the other hand . . ."

"That was a terrible thing. I assume that's why I'm here? Do you think his death was deliberate?"

She ignored my questions. "Run me through the time line of your visit, will you?"

I did, from Arabella's spontaneous invitation until the time I left with Joe, followed by Arabella's visit to the Society the next morning. I watched the detective make a few notes, but not many. "That's really all I can tell you."

Detective Hrivnak sat back in her creaking chair. "So you knew the dead guy?"

"I wouldn't say I knew him. I'd never met him before that day, but he saw that I was upset and we had coffee after . . . Jason's accident."

"He have any ideas about what happened?"

"No. He told me he was an electrician, and he'd been working on the wiring, but he had no idea how it could have happened. He told me everything had been thoroughly checked."

Detective Hrivnak changed topics abruptly. "What's Heffernan's reputation like?"

Did that mean my part in the investigation of Joe's death was over? "You mean in the arts community?" When she nodded, I went on. "I've never heard anyone say a bad word about her. Let's Play means everything to her, and I think she's done a great job keeping it child friendly. It must be a temptation these days to throw in trendy electronic games and such, but she's kept the exhibits and the programs simple and educational at the same time. I admire her. I like her, too." I took a deep breath. "Was the wiring tampered with, with the intent to do harm?"

"That's the question, isn't it? You got any ideas?"

That was a surprise: she was asking me for my opinion? "Me? No. Since two different people working there were hurt, it doesn't seem likely that it was specifically directed toward either of them. Heck, *I* could have been the one to touch the weasel, as easily as Jason or Joe. Or maybe somebody assumed that Arabella would do the honors. Or maybe it was someone who was willing to hurt any random person, even a child, just to do harm to the place. But for the life of me I can't see why anyone would want to."

"Uh-huh," Detective Hrivnak said noncommittally. She stood up abruptly. "Thanks for coming by."

Apparently the meeting was over. I felt deflated. I'm not sure what my talk could have added to the detective's information, other than confirming the time line she already had. I'd never pretended to have any piercing insights into what had happened, or why, or how. Was it even possible to rig up a major electrical shock that would act selectively? Definitely not my area of expertise.

I made my way back to the Society in a distracted mood, stopping to pick up a sandwich and coffee along the way. Eric was seated at his desk when I walked in, a neat stack of pink phone messages lined up in front of him.

He gave me a big grin. "So they didn't arrest you?"

"No, not even close. Did you get out to eat?"

"Sure did. But I wanted to be here when you came back."

"Trying to impress the boss? You're doing a fine job—keep it up. I'll take those messages. Anything urgent I need to deal with?"

"No, ma'am. Everything's under control."

I had my doubts, but I didn't want to disillusion him. I retreated to my office to return some phone calls.

Latoya appeared at two, and I gestured to her to sit. "You wanted to talk to me?"

She nodded. "Yes. I thought I'd let things shake out for a bit, but now I feel we need to talk."

"I agree. I'm sorry I've been so busy, but it's been a rocky transition. And an unusual one, given the circumstances. But then, you know that." I was curious as to why she had asked for this meeting. I hoped it wasn't to tell me that she was leaving—I didn't want to have to try to replace a senior position at the moment.

As if reading my thoughts, she said, "I'm not quitting, if that's what you think." She gave me a perfunctory smile. "I know I haven't been very good at communicating with you in the past, and I want that to change."

I nodded. "I appreciate your saying that, because, frankly, I need you. But only if you want to be here. Things are difficult right now, but I want to know that you're totally committed to working through this."

"I am. What I really wanted to do was update you on what's happening with Alfred's position."

Alfred Findley had been the Society's registrar, which meant that he'd been in charge of keeping track of what we had and where we had last stowed it, which was not an easy job. His death had thrown us all for a loop, and I'd been praying that he had left his computer records in a form that someone else—either his former boss Latoya, or a new hire—could understand.

"I've installed his tracking program on my own computer and uploaded his files," Latoya began. "I think I have things pretty well figured out, or at least well enough to explain to whoever we hire to replace him." I breathed an internal sigh of relief—that was welcome news. "You saw the job description I drafted? Melanie's posted that to the online sites, and it has or will appear in several of the print media shortly. Since our acquisitions are currently on hold, we're not losing any ground. There have been a few responses, and Melanie has given me a couple of résumés, but I'm not going to hurry this, and in any case it's a slow time of year."

"Fair enough. I'm happy to let you handle that, since you know what qualifications are needed, better than I do, at any rate. Is there anything you would change about the position?"

She considered briefly. "Not really. It requires someone who is systematic and thorough, and has at least some knowledge of historic items so that he or she can describe them accurately. Those are my top priorities."

I wondered if I should add something to her description of the position. Latoya was by no means a tyrant, but she did need to find someone who could stand up to her. Alfred had never learned how to do that. But then, Alfred had never stood up to anyone, as far as I could tell. Still, I wasn't going to interfere. Either I trusted Latoya to do her job or I didn't. Right now I needed to trust her. "That sounds good. Let me know if you want me to talk to any of your picks, but I trust your judgment."

"Thank you, Nell. I won't let you down." She stood up to leave. At the doorway she said, "Sad thing, that accident at Let's Play, isn't it? Maybe we should check our records to see if we've ever used the same electricians. I know we had some work done on the fourth floor when we had to replace part of the roof a few years ago. See you later."

After she'd left, I considered what she'd said. Should I check our own records? Although I was pretty sure that if an electrician looked at what we had in place, he'd run screaming . . . straight to the city's building inspectors. One more problem I did not need.

CHAPTER 10

I hauled myself away from my office at quarter to seven. I'd sent Eric home before six, although he'd volunteered to stay if I needed him. I didn't, but I appreciated his offer. He seemed like a sweet kid, but before I made him an offer of long-term employment I wanted to observe his organizational and administrative skills, and those hadn't really been tested yet. At the same time, I wasn't going to insist on a fat résumé and years of experience if it turned out that he could do the job. In any case, that was a decision that I did not have to make right this minute, unlike a long list of other items.

When I let myself out the front door, I found James on the front steps. "Were you waiting for me?" I asked. "You could have come inside."

"I didn't want to upset anyone. People see an FBI agent, they get concerned." He smiled. "You have time for a drink? The Doubletree?"

Twice in one week. My, my, things were heating up. "Sure."

James escorted me the block to the hotel on the corner of Broad Street and found us a quiet table. We ordered drinks, and when we were settled, I decided to jump-start the conversation. "Listen, this kerfuffle at the Let's Play Museum—that doesn't fall anywhere in your jurisdiction, does it?"

"Kerfuffle? I don't know if that's a legal term. You mean the suspicious death last night? No, that's within the purview of the local police. They wouldn't welcome us sticking our noses in, unless it was an incidence of domestic terrorism. Is it?" he joked.

"I hadn't thought of that, but it's not a bad idea," I retorted. "Attack our treasured local institutions, starting with children's museums, and undermine American society. Good plan, but it might take a while before anyone noticed. If I were planning such a thing, I'd go after something a little more impressive, like planting a bomb at the Philadelphia Art Museum."

He leaned forward conspiratorially. "I wouldn't mention the word *bomb* in the presence of an FBI agent—it makes us nervous." He sat back. "You want to talk about it?"

"The, uh, suspicious death? Yes, I suppose I do, as long as I'm not violating any laws or procedures."

"Let me worry about that."

I smiled at him. "Look, I'm not a crime groupie, if that's what you're wondering. It's just that I know and like Arabella Heffernan, and as I told you, I was there when another employee was jolted in much the same way, a day earlier. So you'd have to say I'm kind of involved, whether I like it or not."

His expression was appropriately serious now. "I'm sorry. That can't have been pleasant for you. How did your talk with the police go?"

I nodded. "About as well as I could have hoped. Our favorite detective is on the job, although I couldn't tell her much. How do you read this?"

"You really are a romantic. I ask you out for a drink and you want to talk about electrocution." He gave a mock sigh. "All right. I don't have all the facts, but we know there was an electrical accident two days ago, which wasn't fatal—and you were a witness. Then there was a second electrical accident last night, which *did* prove fatal. No witnesses. Either somebody working at Let's Play is one lousy electrician, or at least one if not both of those events was deliberate. Is that what you mean?"

I nodded. "Exactly. Arabella assured me that she'd had all the wiring checked by two different people the morning after the first incident. She was horrified at the idea that something could happen to a child, and she wanted to be sure the exhibit was safe. I believe her. That means if it wasn't purely accidental, that someone had to tamper with the wiring after it was looked over in the morning and before the body was found last night."

"What kind of security is there?"

"I'd say it's laughable—but that's not surprising, because there's not much to steal from a children's museum. There's a cash register at the front desk for patrons, and one more in the gift shop, period. They've presumably had a lot of workmen coming through, finished up the new exhibit that's supposed to open soon. I'd bet that if anybody walked in wearing coveralls and carrying a tool chest or paint cans and smiled at the receptionist, they'd be allowed upstairs without any question. So there are plenty of opportunities." I took a sip of my wine. "Listen, can we talk about motive?"

"We haven't exactly exhausted the *how* part."

"I know that, but I don't know enough about wiring to guess what kind of knowledge would be required, or how long it would take to rig things. Besides, I really do like to know the *why* of things."

"Okay, I'll play. Who or what was the target? Assuming we've eliminated terrorism."

"Have we? But in any case . . ." I ticked off the possibilities on my fingers. "One, the trap may have been directed at Joe, the guy who died, and Jason's earlier event was just a trial. Or, two, maybe it was meant for Jason, but the culprit screwed up the first time around. However, Jason is just a moonlighting graduate student, I can't imagine why anybody would want to harm him—and anyway, he wasn't around to set it up the second time. Although if Arabella thought he wasn't right for her daughter . . ." I shook myself: I was definitely headed toward the absurd. "I'm sure the police are looking into both Jason and Joe anyway. Three, it could have been directed at Hadley Eastman—she's the writer of the *Harriet the Hedgehog* books that inspired the exhibit."

"You mean there's somebody who doesn't like hedgehogs?" James asked with a half smile.

"Or doesn't like the author, I guess. I haven't met her *or* read the books. But I'm not done. Four, it might not have been directed at anyone in particular, and the perpetrator just figured a fatal accident would hurt the museum's reputation, or Arabella personally."

"I'd say that about covers all the bases, unless you want to throw in Martians. Seriously, don't you think the police will be asking the same questions?"

"Of course they will, and they have the resources to follow up. But as I've no doubt said before, they are somewhat lacking in their understanding of how institutions of this kind operate. The reputation of a museum is a fragile thing, particularly in this case, where children's safety is involved. This could do irreparable harm to Let's Play, and I'd hate to see that. Besides, if it was a generalized booby trap, it could have been me. I take that personally."

We both paused to take a sip of our drinks. I was happy to find that putting my thoughts into words for him had helped me organize them. The problem was, I didn't have enough information to point in any one direction.

"Should I assume that this is more than an academic exercise?" James said, his eyes on me.

"What do you mean? Do I plan to do something about it? I really hadn't thought that far." That was the truth: I had more than enough to do without involving myself in Arabella's problems. Although she had asked for my help . . . "I'm just an innocent bystander—unless you want to think that Arabella is a devious plotter and invited me there to act as a witness."

"Do you believe that?"

"She'd have to be a really good actress, although I have to say I don't know her well enough to judge. I've never heard anyone say anything bad about her or the place. Everyone around here loves it."

"You know anything about their finances?" James asked.

"No. I haven't heard any rumors that they're having problems. Are you wondering about insurance?"

"Just throwing it out there, but I can't see how that would benefit anyone. Nell, I don't think there's much you can do. And if the police think you're interfering, they won't be happy."

He was right on both counts and I knew it. But at the same time, I felt I was already involved: I liked Arabella and wanted to help her if I could, and on a wider professional scale, any attack against a local museum threatened us all. We institutions needed all the goodwill we could garner if we wanted the public to continue to visit us, and for that to happen people had to feel safe. That made this both personal *and* professional.

I looked up to see James watching me. "What?"

"You don't want to let this go, do you?"

"Am I that obvious? No, I don't. But I agree with you—I'm not sure what I can do. Maybe Marty will have more insight. I need to talk to her anyway."

"Mm-hmm." He sounded skeptical. He knew his cousin Marty well.

I checked my watch. "Shoot—I've got to rush if I want to catch my train."

"You sure I can't offer you dinner?"

"That's sweet, but not tonight. Rain check?"

"Sure." He stood up, then added, "Nell, be careful. Someone is dead, and it's up to the police to find out how and why. Period."

I sighed. "I know. I'm just saddened that something like this has happened again. And surprised that I was anywhere near it." Time to change gears and take the bull by the horns—a nicely muddled metaphor. "Thank you for, well, worrying about me, James."

"You're welcome." He smiled, then his expression turned sober. "I'll call you if there are any further developments. I don't know what my schedule is like over the next couple of weeks."

"You can call me with or without developments. But I know what my schedule is like: jammed. See you."

CHAPTER 11

Friday passed without any additional crises, thank goodness, and I was happy to watch Eric as he settled into his new position quietly and efficiently. I left for the weekend feeling pleased with myself.

I am a self-proclaimed workaholic, which is most likely the reason I have no life outside of work. I have had the occasional romantic relationship that occupied an afternoon or evening now and then, but the last one had left a bad taste in my mouth, and I was determined to take things slow with James. Every now and then I noticed that I seemed to have no friends beyond those at the Society, and I had few people just to get together with. But I spent so much time dealing with other people at work, it was nice to have no one but myself to answer to on weekends.

Of course, since I owned my own home, there was always plenty there to keep me busy on any given weekend. There was always something that needed fixing or sprucing. And of course there was cleaning. I deferred the basic stuff as long as I could, until the dust bunnies started repro-ducing in the corners and chasing me around, and then I tended to do it all at once, so I could try to forget about it for another few weeks. Or months. The forgetting part was easier to do during the winter months, when it was near dark when I left in the morning and definitely dark when I arrived home at night.

I sighed and tracked down my trusty vintage vacuum. At least housecleaning left my mind free to roam, as long as I didn't have to wrestle with such weighty problems as which cleaning agent would best remove the sticky stain I couldn't remember making. That involved close reading of the fine print on package labels, which these days were far too small and loaded with dire warnings. But the basic stuff, like dusting and vacuuming, used only a percent or two of my consciousness, and I applied the rest to the rid-dle of the hazardous Willy the Weasel. Thus went my inner dialogue on Saturday:

Why would anybody wire an animated weasel at a chil-dren's museum to hurt someone?

I don't know.

Who was the intended victim?

I don't know.

Who had both access to the building and the skills to do it?

I don't know.

What was I going to do about it?

I don't know.

Why was I involved in this at all?

I really *don't know.*

But I was already in the thick of the matter, unfortunately—through no fault of my own!—and I knew myself well enough to know that I couldn't just walk away now. Besides, from all I knew and had heard from others, Arabella didn't deserve this kind of trouble. Based on personal experience, I knew all too well the spot she was in, and I also knew that when it had happened to me, I wouldn't have been able to sort things out without some significant help, sometimes from unexpected sources. I wanted to help Arabella as sort of cosmic payback. Or pay it forward. Whatever. I chased down another clump of something fuzzy under my couch with the skinny end of the vacuum hose.

But I had pitifully little to go on, and the delightful homicide detective Meredith Hrivnak was not likely to share much with me. She was probably still peeved that I'd done more than she had to wrap up the recent incident at the Society. James wasn't going to be able to help, either. He wasn't even involved in the case. And I had so, so much else I should be doing for the Society. When did I have time to look into this?

Thinking of things I didn't have time for, I also amused myself by dissecting my date with James. Had there been any chemistry between us? I'd have to say yes. But James and I were both grown-ups with busy lives, so where that chemistry might take us was anybody's guess. When would we find the time to explore the possibilities? Most of my free time had evaporated when I took the job of president, and I didn't see it coming back for a while. And now with Arabella's problems . . .

I went round and round with the whole mess in my head as I scrubbed and polished, and by the end of the afternoon I had a very clean house and no resolution. I took myself to the nearest market and bought fresh supplies for a sumptuous dinner for one, which I prepared, enjoyed, and cleaned up after, feeling very virtuous. Then I watched a movie on television, got bored in the middle, and went to bed.

Sunday morning I knew I couldn't spend another day of the same. The choices were (a) go into work, or (b) find something more distracting to do. I really couldn't face going into work—I had to maintain some perspective and allow myself a few breaks from it, or the job would overwhelm me. What would be a good distraction?

In the end, after an indulgent breakfast, I decided to take a drive. It almost didn't matter where, but I found myself drifting toward Chester County and the Brandywine River: Andrew Wyeth country. I bypassed the lovely museum in Chadd's Ford but turned north and followed the Brandywine River, along the narrow, twisting road that headed toward West Chester. Luckily there were few other people on the road today, a chilly Sunday in January. As I passed it, I saluted the Wyeth farm, familiar from so many paintings.

I had almost forgotten about the Book Barn that lay on this road, since I rarely went roaming the back roads around there, but on a whim I pulled into the near-empty graveled lot in front. Happily it was open, and I tugged open the creaky wooden door to be greeted by a scent of wood smoke and the gaze of a sleepy cat in a battered chair close to a cast-iron stove. I raised a hand to the woman behind the desk and commenced wandering through the many disjointed floors of used books, leafing through old volumes as the spirit moved me. I loved books, both old and new, but the space limitations of my tiny house imposed their own restrictions, so I had to ration myself strictly when it came to buying still more books. But there were always treasures to be found, too irresistible to pass up. I took a quick peek at the children's book section to see if there were any examples of *Harriet the Hedgehog* but came up dry. I drifted through the cookbook section—I probably spent far more time reading cookbooks than cooking from them, but it was a simple pleasure. I poked among the mysteries, but nothing caught my fancy. Then I turned to the home improvement area, and a little lightbulb went on: maybe I could find something simple that would explain to me just how wiring and electricity worked, so I'd have better insight into the accident at Let's Play.

Hmm . . . no *Wiring for Dummies*. The *Simplified Wiring* looked like it required an engineering degree. Now, I'm not stupid, and I've been dealing the structural problems with my own house for a decade, but even I know my limitations, and I'd left the wiring issues to professionals. All I really wanted was a basic explanation of how an electrical system worked—and what things to watch out for if you didn't want to electrocute someone. Which might lead to what things you should do if you *did* want to electrocute someone. But that would be a different book.

In the end I walked out with several books, as usual. I paid, stroked the still-sleeping cat, and climbed back into my car to head back to Route 30, the slow road home to Bryn Mawr. I arrived home before dark despite a quick stop at the decadent French bakery in Wayne, and reheated a plate of yesterday's ample leftovers, then found an old afghan and curled up with my new old copy of *Step-by-Step Home Wiring*.

Two hours later I was still confused, despite the clear language and cute line drawings in the book. Clearly there was a reason I had majored in English rather than something practical: I had no aptitude for anything mechanical. Putting it in the simplest possible terms, electricity flowed into, say, my house, and then it flowed out again. Along the way it passed through my appliances and lamps and whatnot, if the switch was opened to allow that. Or did I mean closed? If the switch wasn't open, the current ignored that detour and kept right on going. That much I understood.

I lay back and reviewed what I had seen of the exhibit at Let's Play. Admittedly my memories were a bit jumbled; Jason getting zapped had driven a lot of other details right out of my mind. But I grasped the basic principles: each of the animals was, well, animated. You—or an eager child—touched them or moved a piece, and they responded with lights or movements or sound, each requiring that an electrical connection be activated by the motion. Presumably this was a simple process, and the installation also had to be both safe and sturdy—I had no doubt that an excited child would want to repeat the process over and over, and might well whack the animal if it didn't respond fast enough. This much was obvious even to me. So what had gone wrong?

As I understood it, the only way the electricity could pass through an innocent bystander was if he or she actually completed the circuit, diverting the current from where it was supposed to go to a different path—that is, through the person instead of the wiring. But unlike metal objects, people were not good conductors of electricity. The current really, really had to want to follow the metal, and even then in most cases the current would not be strong enough to do more than give someone a nasty shock. Of course, that alone could be enough to do serious harm to a small child or an elderly grandparent, both of whom were primary customers of Let's Play.

But the conclusion I had to draw, even in my state of near ignorance, was that a simple mistake would not be enough to cause major harm. Ergo, someone with malicious intent had to have altered the exhibit, for unknown purposes. At least one circuit breaker had blown out the first time, when Jason was shocked. Had it the second time? I had no answers.

So I decided to eat dessert. Buttercream is very soothing.

CHAPTER 12

On the ride to work on Monday, I decided that I didn't have time to worry about poor dead Joe. No, that sounded harsh. As a veteran of a previous murder investigation, I could provide emotional support and guidance to Arabella as needed, but as James had pointed out, there wasn't much more I could do. And I had a museum of my own to run, which was more than enough to keep me busy.

I stopped at Shelby's office on the way to my own and was happy to find her already at her desk.

"Hey, lady," she said as I walked in. "How's our boy Eric doing?"

"Great, so far, but I haven't asked him for much. I'm letting him ease into the job. How is it you know him?"

"I know his mama, back home. And he went to school with my daughter."

"And mama asked you to keep an eye on her baby?"

Shelby grimaced. "Not exactly. She'd rather not talk

about him, since he's made it clear that . . . he's not going to be giving her any grandchildren."

I caught her drift. "Her loss," I said firmly. "How's he been handling the big city? It can be kind of scary."

"He's had a few rough patches, but I'd say he's pretty well grounded. I hope things work out for him here at the Society, but if they don't, you do what you have to do. I don't expect any special favors for him."

"Don't worry, I will. I need someone who can handle the job. That position can be a sensitive one, and Eric's kind of young for it. But he's been handling things well so far. How about you? Are you getting a feel for things?"

"Piece of cake. At least you left your files in good order, and Carrie's been a big help. She's got something going with Rich?"

"My, you do catch on fast. Yes, she does, but I don't have a problem with that, as long as they do their jobs. And Rich's position isn't permanent at the moment—although maybe you can find funding to extend it, if that's what he wants. Among all your other tasks. Oh, and would you please nose around and see what kind of money is available for collaborative ventures with an educational component?"

"You thinking about that carousel project with Let's Play?"

"I am, or something like it. Once they get past this mess." There had been nothing new about Joe or Let's Play in the paper, and other, more urgent news had banished it from the front pages.

"Sad thing, that. I do hope they find out what happened soon."

"So do I. Well, I'd better get down to business. Give me a shout if you need anything. Also, there's an all-hands staff meeting on Friday at nine, before we open. Can you send out a staff email to remind everybody? Eric doesn't have a computer yet, or I'd ask him to do it." One more thing I needed to follow up on.

"Will do."

I made my way down the hall toward my office. Eric was already in place, his desk gleaming, notepads neatly lined up. I could swear he had even buffed the old telephone. His African violet was ensconced on the windowsill behind him, adding a bright touch of color. He smiled happily when he saw me. "Good morning, Nell! Can I get you a cup of coffee? I brought in a new variety to try out."

I hated the stereotype of a secretary—a word now apparently banned from employer vocabulary—who fetched coffee for the boss, but I really did want a cup of coffee. "Thank you, Eric. Just remember, you don't have to make a habit of it."

"Don't you worry—I like to help." He bounded out of his seat and vanished down the hall.

Moving more slowly, I hung up my coat and went to my own desk, where Eric had lined up a few pink message slips. So early? I leafed through them. One was from Marty Terwilliger, who had said she wanted to stop by for a moment. Not seconds later, I looked up to find her, as if by magic, standing at my office door watching me. I shouldn't have been surprised, since she had keys to every door in the place, and came and went at will. She walked in without waiting for an invitation—typical Marty.

"You know, you look right at home in this office," she said, making herself comfortable in a chair.

"Please, come in, sit down." I gestured grandly, after the fact.

She tsk-tsked. "Come off it—I've never stood on ceremony and you know it."

"I do. To what do I owe the honor of this visit? Business or personal?"

"Some of each. Can you do lunch?"

"I guess." I had no idea if I had anything scheduled. Did she want to pump me about my date with James?

"Great. I've got some research to do, but I'll head back up here about noon. Hello!"

Eric had appeared in the doorway, cradling a mug of coffee. Intent upon not spilling it, he hadn't noticed Marty. "Oh, excuse me—I didn't know you had a guest. I'll get right out of your way." He carefully set my coffee on a coaster I didn't even know I had, then backed away.

"Hold on, Eric. Am I free for lunch today?"

"Yes, ma'am," he said promptly, without consulting a calendar. "Is there anything else you need?"

"Nope, I'm good," I said.

When Eric had retreated to his desk, Marty raised a quizzical eyebrow. "Who's that?"

"My new assistant, Eric—I'm trying him out."

"He's a lot cuter than Doris. Well, you can fill me in at lunch. See you!" She breezed out as quickly as she had appeared.

When she was out of earshot, I called out, "Eric?"

He returned with lightning speed. "I'm sorry," he began.

"Don't be. That's Marty Terwilliger—she's a board member, but she kind of feels she owns the place, since both her grandfather and her father were board members, too. And she's also a friend. You'll be seeing a lot of her because she spends a lot of time here, including downstairs in the library and in the stacks."

Eric nodded. "That's good to know. Anybody else I need to know about?"

I sighed. "I'll find you a board list, and we can go over it—you'll no doubt be fielding a lot of calls from them, and I can tell you in advance which ones need special handling. And someday, all things willing, there'll be files on your computer—as soon as there is a computer. When you have spare time, that will let you review our donor list, or if someone calls, you can check that list quickly."

"Got it. Thanks."

"And it appears I'm having lunch with Marty today, so you can put that on your nonexistent calendar," I called out after him.

Before I tackled the next item on my never-ending to-do list, I thought I should touch base with Arabella and see how she was holding up. She was such a sweet person, and seemed so ill-prepared for this kind of trouble. I was surprised to be put through immediately.

"Oh, Nell, how nice of you to call!" she said when she picked up. "I was afraid it was another annoying person from the newspaper. Or the police."

"I just wanted to be sure you were all right. You've talked to the police again?"

It sounded as though Arabella swallowed a sob before answering. "Yes. They keep asking the same questions. *Do I have any enemies? Is there someone with a grudge against Let's Play?* I don't, Nell, I swear. This is a children's museum, and I thought everyone loved us. Do you think they believe this was deliberate? Because they won't come straight out and tell me anything."

"The police have to look at all angles, Arabella. Don't take it personally. For that matter, it could be directed at someone else, like Hadley Eastman. Or someone who thinks you're exploiting hedgehogs. Or even someone who simply likes to stir up trouble."

"Do you really think so? Because I've been going over and over this in my head all weekend, and I can't see why anyone would want to hurt us."

At least Arabella sounded a little less depressed, so I said, "I can't, either. Let the police do their job, and I'm sure they'll get to the bottom of this." I debated about crossing my fingers to cover the white lie, but my goal was to reassure Arabella. "Have they let you reopen?"

"Tomorrow, they said." Arabella sighed. "Thank you for calling, Nell. It's nice to know I'm not alone in all this."

"Let me know if I can do anything to help, Arabella." We rang off. I hoped I'd succeeded in cheering Arabella up, because she sounded as though she needed it. At the same time, I was troubled: the police seemed to be edging up on labeling this a murder, and that wasn't a good thing for Let's Play.

True to her word, Marty reappeared promptly at noon. I smiled to myself when I heard Eric address her by name and send her directly in. He learned fast.

"You ready to go?" Marty asked, leaning against the doorjamb. She was dressed for research: since our stacks were more than a bit dusty, that meant jeans and sneakers.

"I guess. Where did you want to go?"

"How about that Israeli place around the corner?"

"Sounds good to me," I said, gathering up my coat. But then, almost any restaurant usually sounded good to me.

"So, what's up?" I asked once we were settled at one of the restaurant's small tables. "How's the hunt for Major Jonathan's documents going?" Marty spent most of her time at the Society working on the Terwilliger Collection, a massive but disorganized collection of items bequeathed by her family. A number of documents that had belonged to Major Jonathan Terwilliger—Revolutionary War hero, colleague of George Washington, friend to most of the country's founders, and Marty's lineal ancestor—had been removed—or rather, stolen—from the Society's collections, and we were still hoping to get them back.

Diverse expressions raced across Marty's face: anger, regret, determination. "So-so. The Feebs are on it, as I'm sure you know, but I know the missing items better. We're still working on it."

"Speaking of the FBI, I had drinks with your cousin James the other day."

That pleased her. "Good! Did Jimmy ask you, or the other way around?"

"He called me, on short notice. We had a nice time, we may see each other again, and that's the end of the story."

"I won't pry. But do remember I'm kinda fond of him, so if it doesn't work out, let him down gently, will you?"

"What, you aren't worried about *my* tender feelings?"

"You can take care of yourself. What should we order?"

Scanning the menu before the harried young waitress appeared occupied the next couple of minutes. When we had placed our orders, I asked Marty, "You heard about the death at Let's Play?"

"I did. Too bad—they're good people there."

"Do you know Arabella Heffernan?"

"We've met. You know I don't have kids, so I don't get in there very often. But my former brother-in-law was on the board for a while."

"During Arabella's tenure?"

"Sure. She's been there at least a decade."

"What was his opinion of the place?"

"He liked it, but then, he had young kids at that time. When they graduated to more serious stuff, he kind of lost interest and moved on. I think he said he was sometimes frustrated because Arabella wasn't very interested in the financial bottom line. She was all about the displays and the programs, and left it to the board to find the money. She's got vision, I'll give you that. You have to believe she actually thinks like a child, and it works. Sometimes she got overextended and had to be reined in. But she means well, from what I understand."

"You think the death this week was accidental?"

She sat back in her chair and took a hard look at me. "I assume you're asking because you don't?"

I looked around carefully. Nobody in earshot seemed even slightly interested in our conversation. I leaned forward. "Normally I would say it was just a tragic accident, but as it happens I was there when a similar event happened a day earlier. Luckily that guy didn't die, but I thought it was odd that the same thing happened twice in two days."

"Huh. That first one didn't make the paper. What did the police say?"

"I was summoned before our dear friend Detective Hrivnak, but she didn't tell me anything. At least they're looking this time around. Arabella told me she thought they hinted that it was more than an accident, the last time she talked to them."

"Poor Arabella," Marty said, then fixed me with a critical eye. "Are you asking if I might know some dirt that would point to why this is happening?"

The short answer was yes. Marty knew everyone in Philadelphia and the surrounding counties, and could tell you who their great-grandparents were, too. Thank goodness Marty was smart, which was why we worked well together: I didn't have to explain. "Exactly. Right now I'm just collecting information. From all I've heard, everybody and his sister loves Let's Play and would have absolutely no reason to do it harm. I don't know Arabella well, though—is she hiding some deep, dark secret? Did she used to run a brothel or sell drugs out of the gift shop?"

Marty snorted. "Not hardly. Believe it or not, she's exactly what she appears to be: a really sweet person who happens to be a decent administrator. There was kind of a stink when her husband left her, oh, twenty years ago, and she struggled for a while. But she seems to have come out of it well."

I debated asking Marty for details about the husband but decided that I didn't need to dig up decades-old gossip. I hadn't been around Philadelphia then, and I hadn't known the parties involved. And would this husband have waited twenty years to act, if he had a grudge against his ex?

"James and I were kicking around possibilities." Okay, so now I'd gone and brought up James again.

Marty gave a short laugh. "Sounds like a great date—discussing motives for murder. He have anything useful to say?"

"It was helpful to me to have to put my ideas into words. But there are a lot of possibilities, unfortunately. What I can't figure out is—assuming it's not an accident—was the target the place or a person? Arabella's a sweetheart, and Let's Play is a real favorite around here. Was it meant to harm Joe, the guy who died? If not, who else could it be?"

"Isn't there a new exhibit?"

"Yes, based on the *Harriet the Hedgehog* series. The writer's—"

"Hadley Eastman. I've got a couple of grandnieces who beg for her stuff, like the day the new book comes out."

"Do you know her?"

Marty shook her head. "I gather she lives out in one of

the burbs. That's more your territory. And she wasn't raised around here."

Unless Hadley's family had lived in the state for a couple of centuries, Marty probably wouldn't consider her local. "I gather she's done well with the books. It's not easy these days—lots of competition in that market. Or so I'm told." I had no direct experience with the popularity of current children's books. "So who benefits most from this exhibit? The museum or the author?"

Marty took a sip of water before answering. "It's a coup for the museum to get Hadley Eastman—although I hear that her star is waning. You know how long the lead time is for exhibit planning, so maybe things were different when they signed. I wonder what kind of a deal they cut. But Hadley stands to lose, too, if her name—or do I mean Harriet's?—is linked to a death. Although, what's the saying? No publicity is bad publicity?"

"I refuse to consider murder a publicity stunt for anyone," I said firmly.

Marty eyed me. "Amen. But you don't need to get involved. You've got plenty on your plate as it is."

"Are you saying that as a board member?"

"And as a friend, Nell. Your first couple of months are important—you need to show you've got a handle on the Society and that you've moved beyond what happened. Both you and the Society are under a lot of scrutiny right now. That's got to be your first priority."

"I know." It would be easier to follow Marty's good advice if I hadn't known what Arabella must be going through. It was too easy for me to imagine just how she felt.

I was interrupted in my musings when Marty asked, "So, how are things going?" And we were off. Marty was, for me, an invaluable resource, because she knew everyone and everything there was to know about the place. In fact, since her father and grandfather had been on the board, she probably had hereditary knowledge. And she was one of my staunchest supporters: she had, in fact, engineered my rapid and unexpected ascent to its leadership. Since I'd been foolish enough to say yes, I was grateful that she was willing to help me. Of course, we did share a common goal: keeping the Society afloat financially, in the near term, and polishing it until it shone like the gem of American and local historical information that it deserved to be, in the longer term. I hoped I lived long enough to see that.

Lunch arrived promptly, and we consumed it quickly, then split the tab and emerged into the cool November afternoon. "You seem to be hiring staff nicely," Marty said as we turned our steps back toward the Society.

"They've kind of fallen into my lap, but so far so good, knock on wood. We're still working on filling Alfred's position, but I want to be sure we get someone qualified, and who really cares about the place, not just the job. So far that one hasn't crawled out of the woodwork."

"I don't have any candidates in mind, but I'll keep my ears open. It's just as well to let things quiet down a bit, anyway. And the collections have been sitting there for years without a whole lot of oversight, and after your recent improvements, I don't think they're going anywhere soon. So take your time and choose wisely."

"That's what I had in mind."

As long as other things, like murder, didn't distract me.

CHAPTER 13

By the next morning, Eric and I were already settling into our own pattern, alternating who got the coffee, each time going through a polite ritual. Shall I? Will you? The quality of the coffee continued to improve, which seemed reason enough to keep Eric around. Although he definitely had other much-needed skills—my phone messages were neatly recorded and appeared on my desk in a timely fashion, and what projects I gave him, he executed quickly and accurately. He was almost too good to be true, but at the moment I was not going to look a gift horse in the mouth.

I was reviewing the agenda for the next Executive Committee meeting of the Society's board when Eric answered the phone, then stuck his head in my office. "There's a Hadley Eastman downstairs to see you?"

It took me a moment to remember who Hadley Eastman was: the author of the *Harriet the Hedgehog* series. Why on earth would she want to see me? "Could you go down and escort her upstairs, please?"

"Will do." He darted down the hall. I stacked up my papers and put them back in their folder, and mentally reviewed what I knew about Hadley Eastman, which was essentially nothing other than what Marty and Arabella had told me. I didn't spend a lot of time around children, and while I enjoyed browsing in bookstores, I seldom strayed to the children's section. I put on a cheerful smile in preparation for my unexpected guest.

Who stormed in, with poor Eric trailing in her wake. He sent me an apologetic glance and retreated quickly. I had a quick impression of a fashionably thin and carefully made-up woman in her middle decades before she turned around and barked an order. "Chloe, wait for me there." Chloe, a wispy young blonde clutching several bags, looked wildly around for a seat, which Eric pointed out for her. She sat down like a well-trained dog.

My guest turned the full glare of her attention to me and launched into a harangue. "What the hell do you mean, telling Arabella that this death is my fault?" Hadley Eastman demanded, leaning on my desk, braced on both arms.

Getting in my face was not the best way to introduce herself. I counted to three, internally, before saying, "Excuse me?"

"At Let's Play. You gave Arabella Heffernan the idea that this stupid accident was directed at me."

At first I didn't remember saying any such thing, and then I recalled that when I'd talked to Arabella on Monday, I'd suggested a number of alternative scenarios. Apparently Arabella, faced with a belligerent Hadley, had tried to deflect her by pointing out that she could have been the target—and she hadn't taken it well. "Why don't we start over here? Welcome to the Society. I'm Nell Pratt, the president. Won't you please sit down? Would you like a cup of coffee?" I had to grit my teeth to get this out, but at least one of us had to take the high road.

"No, you're not going to distract me with coffee and showing off your historic stuff. I want to know what you said to Arabella. And to the police, who showed up at my door yesterday."

"Then you'd better sit down," I said, with more steel in my voice. "This is, after all, my office."

For a moment it looked as though she was going to balk, but then she grudgingly dropped into a chair and glared at me. "So?"

Hadley Eastman did not exactly correspond to my mental image of a children's book writer. Arabella came a lot closer—warm and friendly and happy. Hadley was coming across as a harridan, at least so far.

"Tell me, why are you here?" I asked in what I hoped was a reasonably calm tone.

Hadley tossed her artfully colored hair behind her shoulders. "I had a very unpleasant interview with a police officer yesterday, about this accident at Let's Play."

So the police were still calling it an accident? Or was that Hadley's label?

"You mean that tragic event that resulted in someone's death? That the police are investigating?"

I enjoyed watching Hadley trying to mold her face into an appropriately sympathetic expression—not very successfully.

Hadley went on. "They wanted to know if I had any enemies, anyone who would like to destroy my reputation."

"Do you?" It wouldn't surprise me, given what I'd seen of her so far.

"Well, of course there are those who envy my success. I can name quite a few writers in my genre who would love to see me brought down. Getting published in children's fiction is brutal."

"I don't doubt it." That at least squared with what little I knew about the publishing business. "But how far would they go?"

The flush on Hadley's cheeks was receding. "How should I know? I try to stay away from them. I don't do signings anymore—too many sticky-fingered kids whining. I go to a few conferences and make nice at the cocktail parties, and that's it. I don't need to suck up to the masses at this point in my career."

A children's author who didn't tolerate children? "You're saying you're that successful?"

She stared at me. "You *do* know who I am?"

"Yes. You write the *Harriet the Hedgehog* series."

"*New York Times* best seller, six times over. Millions of books sold. Harriet is an icon of contemporary society, at least among the under-five demographic."

"I see." What I actually saw was a vitriolic stick of a woman who was older than she wanted to appear— probably a good ten years my senior. "Do you have children of your own?"

"What's that got to do with anything?"

"Just wondering," I said mildly. I was beginning to enjoy this dialogue. "I don't know your books, but I thought the exhibit at Let's Play was charming—until someone died. Certainly the police have to look at all angles. Do *you* think you might've been the target, rather than the museum or someone there?"

"I . . . don't know." She looked momentarily deflated, then rallied. "If there's any hate mail, my publicist would have it. I get lots of mail, you know, from children and their parents, but that goes through my publisher, and they forward it to my assistant." She waved vaguely at Chloe in the outer office. "I told the police to talk to her. I certainly couldn't tell them anything."

"But you do think it's possible?"

"Well, of course. For anyone of my stature, it's certainly possible. There are some rather sick people out there, who hate anyone who does well."

"You've spoken with Arabella since this happened?" I asked.

"Of course I have. I *am* involved, after all—through no fault of my own. My participation in this exhibition was a *huge* favor to her, and one that I'm beginning to regret."

Hadley certainly was self-centered. She might be a successful author, but Let's Play was also a consistently popular museum. The advantages were clearly mutual, and Hadley stood to receive some nice publicity from the event—at least, she would've until the death. She'd still get publicity now, but not the kind she had hoped for. Presumably. "I'm sure she appreciated it. And it does look charming. Why do you think anyone pointed a finger at you?"

Hadley sniffed. "If you know Arabella, you know she seldom takes responsibility for anything. And she'll say almost anything to deflect attention from her and her precious little museum. Nothing is ever her fault. So she said that she'd talked with you, and you had suggested that I might have been the target, rather than Arabella or that place she runs."

If true, this was a side of Arabella I hadn't seen. But my initial impression was that she was a sincerely sweet person. Plus, she'd managed her institution successfully for over twenty years. To do that, you had to accept responsibility and take the bad along with the good. Still, I could see Arabella quailing in the face of a rant from Hadley and grasping at any excuse to end the confrontation, including redirecting her my way. Hadley could have construed Arabella's flustered defense as an attack on her—since apparently everything came back to Hadley. I wondered what Arabella's description of Hadley would be.

Actually, I'd be happy to end this interview sooner rather than later, so I cut to the chase. "Again, what is it you want from me, Hadley?"

"I want you to stop bad-mouthing me to other people. Unfortunately, after that last little mess you landed in, the police and other people might actually listen to you."

I wouldn't say that my comment to Arabella could be called bad-mouthing, and I didn't like the idea that my brush with crime had actually penetrated Hadley's protective veil of self-interest. "I would never make an unsubstantiated accusation about anyone," I said neutrally. Actually, now that I'd met her, it would be a pleasure to fling some mud at Hadley and let her worm her way out of it. But I was a better person than that—I hoped. "Let the police do their job. If you're not involved, I'm sure the police will clear you."

"I should hope so. And if things get any worse, I'll sue . . . somebody for libel or defamation of character or whatever. Or my publisher will—they've got a lot of clout."

I was rapidly tiring of Hadley Eastman. Luckily I was rescued by Shelby's appearance.

"Did I hear that Hadley Eastman was here?" Shelby walked into the office, wreathed in smiles. "It *is* you! This is such a pleasure! Do you know, my little nieces and nephews just adore your books? That Harriet—she's *such* a sweetie!" Shelby's southern accent had mysteriously grown thicker—and dripped sugar.

I watched with amusement as Hadley switched gears to

gracious-author mode. "Why, aren't you sweet? It's *so* nice of you to say so. Which one is their favorite?"

Shelby beamed. "Why, they just love them all!" While Hadley wasn't looking, Shelby winked at me. I'd bet money Shelby couldn't name a single one of the books.

"Let me sign a copy for you, then." Hadley reached into her very large purse and extricated several books. "How many would you like? And to whom should I make them out?"

Shelby looked momentarily baffled but bounced back quickly. "I'm sure they've got all of them back home. Why don't you just sign a copy of the first book? It's such a classic!"

"I'd be delighted. Chloe!" she yelled. I jumped. Chloe didn't respond, and I didn't see her in her seat. "Damn, where is that girl? Where are the rest of the books?" Hadley muttered under her breath, and she rose and stalked out to the jumble of bags Chloe had left by the chair. She rifled through them and pulled out a book, opened it to the title page, and signed it with a flourish. Then she held it out to Shelby. "There you are. That'll be twelve dollars."

I fought hard against the urge to giggle. Hadley definitely had nerve to spare. "Let me get that for you, Shelby." I fished in my purse and handed over the money to Hadley—exact change. I wondered if there was some way I could count this as a professional expense. In any case, it would be a small price to pay to get Hadley out of my office.

Shelby took the book and clasped it to her chest. "Thank you so much. You're just too kind! May I walk you out?"

Hadley shot a hostile glance toward me. "That would be nice of you." She stood up. "Nell, I hope you won't continue to spread this nonsense about me having anything to do with this whole mess. Remember what I said." She turned and stamped out the door, trailed by Shelby. Chloe had returned, looking like a scared rabbit. "Chloe, where were you? Never mind. Call for the car—now!"

Chloe fished a cell phone from her purse and issued an order to someone to bring Hadley's car around immediately, while Hadley disappeared into the hall, followed by Shelby. I was pleased to see that she had seized the opportunity to escort Hadley out of the building.

Shelby was back within three minutes and threw herself into the chair Hadley had vacated. "Saints alive, but that woman is a piece of work! Thinks the sun rises and sets from her, um, posterior. How'd she ever get to be so popular?"

"Got me. I'd bet she's got handlers who make sure her public appearances are strictly limited. They wouldn't want her to reduce a child to tears, which I'll bet she could do in under a minute."

"I hear you. What on earth did she want with you?"

"She thinks I persuaded Arabella that the events at Let's Play were somehow connected to Hadley—like a crazy stalker or something. I never did anything of the kind, except to suggest to Arabella that there were possible motives that didn't involve her or Let's Play. But Hadley wasn't happy when the police showed up at her place, asking questions."

"You think she's involved in some way?"

"Before now, I thought it was just one rather remote possibility, but having met her, it seems a whole lot more likely than I previously thought. Do you really want that book of hers?"

"I thought maybe I'd donate it to my church—they're having a rummage sale soon."

"That sounds about right to me. Poor Chloe. I can't imagine working for someone like Hadley."

"What, you never had a boss from hell?" Shelby asked.

"I've worked for some rather, uh, challenging people, and they weren't always pleasant, but I've never taken that kind of abuse from anyone, and I wouldn't stand for it. How about you?"

"There've been a few interesting interactions. But not with you, of course—you're a peach."

"Of course I am." I grinned at her. "But you have my permission to swat me if I start showing signs of morphing into a Hadley. Her take on Arabella was interesting, though. I may be way off base, but I think Arabella is exactly what she seems to be—a very sweet woman, who loves children and loves making her museum welcoming. Whereas Hadley is a crass and pushy, uh, dame who oozes insincerity. I'll take Arabella any day."

Shelby stood up. "Well, if the excitement's over, I'll get back to work."

"Oh, Shelby? Thanks for interrupting us. I might have said something regrettable if you hadn't walked in."

"That's about what I figured. I thought I'd lay on a little southern sweetness and save you from Hadley—and yourself."

Eric hovered uncertainly near my door, and Shelby smiled at him as she passed by. I gestured to him to come in. "Did you want to say something?"

"I feel bad that I distracted Chloe. She looked like she wanted to burst into tears, so I took her down the hall for some coffee. But I probably made things worse, because then Miss Hadley was annoyed at her."

"Don't worry about it, Eric. I gather Hadley is annoyed at everybody, all the time. I wonder how Chloe stands it."

"She needs the job. She told me that it sounded so perfect when she saw the ad. I guess Hadley can turn on the charm when she wants to, long enough to hire someone, but it didn't last."

"Did Chloe say how long she's been working for her?"

"Six months, maybe? But I'd bet it won't be for much longer. Chloe's already taking antianxiety medication, and she says she'd rather do anything else than work for that woman any longer. Chloe was an English major, which is why she thought working for an author would be so cool."

I felt an immediate pang of sympathy. As a former English major myself, I knew how bleak the prospects were outside of academia. "Let me talk to Melanie. Maybe we have an opening here where she'd fit. You know, you learned quite a bit about Chloe in a short time."

"She looked like she needed a friend. I know what that feels like," Eric said simply.

"Good job, Eric."

CHAPTER 14

The next morning I woke up thinking about electricity again. I needed more information, and I didn't think the kind of questions I had could be resolved by reading a short publication or even by a quick Internet search. I had reviewed the basic concept of electricity, but I couldn't even say whether ordinary current—as opposed to high-voltage wiring—was enough to kill someone. The big question was: how *do* you electrocute someone?

I was troubled. When I had mentioned to James that the victim at Let's Play could just as easily have been me, I hadn't been joking. In fact, I'd already found out that I didn't know enough to guess whether the flaw in Willy's wiring had been set to shock indiscriminately— that is, whoever was first to touch it would be zapped—or targeted to a specific person. And the timing was odd. If someone had wanted to do harm to a random patron, wouldn't they have waited until the exhibit was open? Maybe the culprit hadn't wanted to risk harming a child? I shuddered at the very thought of a child getting hurt.

My next question was, who could have rigged this up? Not me, and I figured I represented an average person. An electrician could have, sure. But was there someone who fell between ignorant me and a trained professional, who would know how to manage it? And how would that person have gained access to the wiring for the *Harriet* exhibit? That might have been the easiest part: as I had told James, plenty of construction people had been wandering in and out of Let's Play lately, and it was unlikely that anyone would challenge their right to be there—which suggested slack security or a charming naiveté among the staff of the museum.

But that was outside my purview. However, I was the president of an institution that occupied an aging building, and who knew how many electrical problems were just waiting to happen to us as well? I recalled that we'd had the building assessed a few years earlier, in contemplation of a renovation project that had withered for lack of serious funding. I could dig out those records and see what the results had been. Luckily, as the new kid, I was entitled to take a fresh look at our problems in that area—as long as it didn't cost the Society anything. I could probably locate the person who had done the original evaluation and have him walk me through the reports, if I asked nicely. I could inquire about what wiring changes we might need for modern surveillance systems and computer connections, as we hoped to improve our security. We might be able to afford those things someday, and I would look responsible if I investigated them now, rather than waiting. And I could ask all sorts of dumb questions about wiring along the way. It was a plan.

My enthusiasm carried me through breakfast and the train ride to the city, and into work. Once again Eric was at his desk waiting for me, looking like an eager puppy.

"Mornin', Nell. Great day, isn't it?"

"I hope so. Hey, I've got a challenge for you." I could have sworn his ears pricked up, and if he'd had a tail he would have wagged it. "A couple of years ago, or less than five, anyway, the Society commissioned a structural evaluation of this building, to see what we needed to fix and how much that would cost, and to put together a wish list of smaller construction projects that we could undertake if we ever found the money. We called it something like *The Ten Year Plan*. Do you think you could track that down for me?"

"I'd be happy to. Uh, where do you think I should start?"

"Why don't you and Shelby work together to find it? I'm pretty sure that I remember reviewing some portions, looking for text that I could lift for grant proposals, so there's probably a copy somewhere in the development office."

"I'll get right on it. Oh, did you want coffee first?"

"I'll get my own. Do you want some?"

He dimpled. "Why, thank you, ma'am. I'd truly appreciate that."

I hung up my coat and set off for the coffee room, where I found it unusually tidy—I suspected Eric. I really didn't expect this initial enthusiasm to persist, but it was lovely while it lasted. I made a pot of coffee and watched it percolate, my mind wandering.

Felicity Soames, our long-term head librarian and queen of the reading room, came in just as the coffeemaker finished gurgling and dribbling. "Good morning, Nell. How's the new boy working out?"

"He does seem like a boy, doesn't he? He's survived living alone in Philadelphia, and it barely seems to have touched him. But to answer your question, fine, so far. And he makes good coffee."

"I thought I detected someone else's hand in yesterday's brew. That'll get him my vote any day." She lowered her voice. "Awful thing about Let's Play, isn't it? They really don't need this kind of trouble."

"I agree." After a moment, I decided I might as well launch my inquiry into our own electrical state now. "I've decided to check our own electrical specs—anytime you've got an old building like this, there are bound to be patches and quick fixes, and I'm pretty sure we're pushing our load limits, or whatever you call them. Perish the thought that we should ever try to add more lines."

"Or a security system?" Felicity added wryly. "Good idea, and it will make us look good, being proactive. But if whoever looks finds something that's not up to code, we might find ourselves having to do some tap dancing to fix things up. It'll cost money."

She was right, and she would know—she'd been here longer than anyone else in the building, as far as I knew. "Doesn't everything? But some things we can't afford to put off. We've got a building full of paper and other flammable objects here, and an electrical fire would be devastating."

We were both silent for a moment, contemplating the unthinkable horror of such a thing. Then Felicity shook herself and stepped forward to pour a cup of coffee. "I'd better enjoy this while I can—it wouldn't do to set a bad example for our patrons. No food or drink in the reading room!"

"I hear you." I filled two mugs and carried them back to

my office. Eric wasn't at his desk, and I wondered if he had gone off hunting for documents already. I'd leave him to it and see how he did.

He was back before his coffee cooled, clutching a thick folder. "You were right—there was a file in development." He deposited it on my desk with a flourish. "But like you said, what's in there is mostly descriptive. I'll go through the files out here and see if there's any more detail. Or would the business manager have them, do you know?"

"You're amazing. But drink your coffee first. And he might—you can ask him."

"I'm on it!"

I sat back with my coffee and contemplated the weighty, battered folder in front of me. It dated from two presidents back—an individual with grand schemes and little fund-raising prowess. I was glad the document existed, but saddened by the sheer volume of things that we should be doing, that we couldn't possibly do. At least, not now. Maybe in a few years. I opened the folder and riffled through the pages until I came to something that looked vaguely like a wiring study—one that was less than complimentary about the status quo, which hadn't changed since the document was written. Again, I had to wonder if we would trigger any official attention—like citations for egregious code violations—if I asked someone to look at the wiring again. All I really wanted, right now, was someone to explain to me what I was looking at in the report, and whom I could pump discreetly for information along the way. But I had no electrical connections—I smiled at my own pun—in the city and only a vague knowledge of how the city's licensing and oversight agencies operated. I needed a consultant.

"Eric?" I called out. "You know any electricians?"

He came and stood in the doorway. "No, ma'am, I do not. I live in an apartment, so I don't have any call for one. But I'll see what I can find out. Do we have a wiring problem?"

"Not yet, but I'd like to keep it that way."

"Amen!"

My thought exactly. "Why don't you get in touch with the company that did the last review and see what they'll tell you?"

"Right away."

Eric came back a few minutes later, looking troubled. "Problems already?" I asked.

"Well, no, or maybe not. I called that company, and they said they'd be happy to come on over and tell you what they said—for a fee. And they won't tell you anything about the state of things now, because they'd have to start all over again and look at the wiring. I figured maybe you didn't want to go that far right now."

I sighed—so much for the easy route. Eric was right, of course. I couldn't throw money at this casually, even if it was for a good reason. And we weren't anywhere near ready to do a complete review at the moment, even if we could afford it. "Thanks, Eric. I'm not surprised. And you're right—I didn't want to run up any bills for it right now. Thanks for checking, though."

"You don't have any friends in the construction trades, in Philadelphia?"

I shook my head. "Nope, I live in the suburbs, and I think the rules are different here, plus this is a public building, not a home. So anyone I do know would probably be useless to me. I'll ask around, though."

Poor Eric looked disappointed that he hadn't been able to help. His shoulders drooped as he headed back to his desk. I tried to think of who might know someone I could talk to. Most of our staff members were not particularly skilled at the construction arts: give them an old book and they were in heaven, but give them a hammer and they were clueless.

Shelby knocked on my door frame. "You look like somebody's rained on your parade."

"Just thinking. You wouldn't happen to know any Philadelphia electricians, would you?"

"Of course I do. When John and I moved into our little town house, the wiring was a mess, so we had the whole place redone. You looking for an electrician? Eric said something about that."

"I just want to make sure we're not at risk for any unfortunate accidents. We can't do a whole reevaluation right now."

Shelby lowered her voice. "This wouldn't have anything to do with Arabella's little problem, now, would it?"

"Yes and no," I admitted. "As the president of the Society, I have primary responsibility to make sure that our building is safe and our treasures properly protected. As witness to Jason's mishap the other day, I'd really like to know how that could happen. You can draw whatever conclusion you like."

"I'll go find that guy's business card. If I lay it on thick, he might do me a favor. He wasn't cheap, but he did good work. At least, all the lights are still working at my place."

"Thanks, Shelby." One more small task I could check off my list. I dove back into the several dozen others.

I looked up what seemed like mere minutes later to find it was after three o'clock, and Shelby was standing in the doorway once again. "You have time to talk to Barney around five? He's got a job in the neighborhood and said he could swing by."

Barney, Barney . . . did I know any Barney?

"Barney Hogan, my electrician pal," Shelby prodded.

"Oh, right. That was fast! You didn't promise him anything, did you?"

"Well, maybe a quick look at some early Philadelphia sports memorabilia, if that's not too much trouble. He's a lifelong fan of Philadelphia baseball."

Interesting system—bartering our information in return for other information. I'd have to think about broader applications. "Seems fair enough. Of course, I don't know a whole lot about sports, but maybe he can tell me what he's looking for. Five o'clock, you said?"

"Yup. Want me to hang around?"

"At least long enough to introduce us, please. You're welcome to stay if you want—two ears are often better than one, particularly when it's all Greek to me."

"Not a problem. I'll bring him up when he gets here."

CHAPTER 15

Shortly past five I could hear Shelby's laughter and the deeper rumblings of a second voice approaching. Eric snapped to attention at his desk. Shelby played right along with him. "Eric, this is Barney Hogan. I believe Nell is expecting us."

They waited as Eric knocked on my half-closed door and then popped his head in. "The electrician is here, Nell."

I suppressed a smile—I wasn't used to all this formality. "Send him right in, Eric. And thank you."

Shelby entered first, then stood aside as Barney extended a hand, and I stood to shake it. He was a paunchy, sixtyish guy, wearing work clothes, and he looked a bit battered by the years. "Barney Hogan. Shelby tells me you've got some questions about the wiring here?"

"I'm Nell Pratt. Yes, she's right. You've heard about the accident at Let's Play? In light of that, I thought I should make sure nothing like that could happen here. We had a full assessment done a few years ago, but I wasn't directly involved at the time and didn't get all the details. I've looked at the original electrical report, and I'm not sure how to interpret it—I'm hoping you can help. I made copies of the relevant parts, if you'd like to take a look." I handed him a slim sheaf of photocopies.

"Would y'all like coffee?" Eric asked from the doorway.

I glanced at Shelby and Barney, who shook their heads. "No, we're good, Eric. You can go on home now."

"You sure?" he asked. When I nodded, he went back to his desk to collect his things, and I turned my attention back to Barney. I let him read the documents I'd given him for a minute or two before I asked, "Can you tell me if any local codes or regulations have changed since that study was done?"

"Not much. And this looks pretty solid—I know the company, and they're honest. At least as far as the evaluation—I won't go so far as to swear their prices are fair."

"I looked over the report, but I'm not equipped to understand most of it. Can you give me a quick summary?"

"No problem. What you've got here is an old building—what, a hundred years old?"

"A bit over," I answered.

"Okay, a century old, and there've been several overhauls over the years, right? Brick and concrete construction, which makes it a pain in the patootie to run new wires. I think when you folks were thinking about renovating, they might have planned to do some serious demolition and then run new conduit in the new construction. That didn't happen, right?"

I shook my head. "It was a good idea, but we didn't have the money. Still don't. I guess what I'm asking now is, is there anything that is a potential hazard right now or that's likely to deteriorate and become one in the near future?"

Barney sat back in his chair. "That's hard to say. Electrical demands have changed in the last few years—lots more computers, better lighting. Nowadays they don't necessarily draw a lot of power, but it all adds up. And since you're not putting in new lines, the old ones get more and more loaded. If they're running where they shouldn't be, they could be subject to wear. And you can't discount the occasional mouse chewing on wires."

I shuddered. "I don't even want to think about that! We do have a current contract for pest control, at least. Unfortunately, mice like old paper and leather."

He looked at me levelly. "So what do you want me to tell you?"

I thought for a moment. "Well, you've already said that the last report looks solid, which I'm happy to hear. And we aren't in any danger of blowing fuses or breakers or whatever we have now?"

"Have you had a problem with power failures?"

"No, not that I can remember."

"Then you're probably doing all right, as long as you don't add much. Not that I wouldn't recommend a thorough overhaul. You could probably save money in the long run if this place was wired more efficiently and you put in low-energy lighting fixtures."

"That's a good point. Shelby, you listening?"

She nodded. "I am. It might be nice to work up some numbers showing how the cost savings would offset the installation costs. Barney, can you help us out there?"

"I could." He looked at Shelby, then at me. "I told Shelby I'd be happy to take a look at this stuff for you, but she may have mentioned I wanted something in return."

"Yes, she said that," I replied cautiously.

Barney smiled. "What do you know about Philadelphia baseball history?"

I hadn't expected that question. "Not much. I don't really follow sports."

Barney looked disgusted. "You've at least heard of the Phillies?"

Was he being sarcastic? "Yes, of course." I'd have to be blind and deaf not to know our city's own baseball team. Even the William Penn statue atop City Hall occasionally sported a Phillies cap. Hard to miss.

"They weren't always the Phillies, you know." Barney got a faraway look in his eye and seemed to be settling in for a long story. "They're the oldest continuous, one-name, one-city franchise in all of professional American sports. They were founded in 1883, but in the very beginning they were called the Quakers. That name was used on and off, as well as the Phillies, up until 1890, when they made the Phillies name official. They even had a permanent home by 1887—the Baker Bowl. Over twelve thousand seats it had. First one burned down in 1894, and they built a bigger, better one on the same spot, with more than eighteen thousand seats. Won their first pennant there, in 1915, and they kept on using it until 1938. Betcha don't know where it was?"

I shook my head. I could find the current stadia only because they were obvious if you drove past Philadelphia on I-95. I'd never been to an event at any of them.

"Little over three miles from here, up Broad Street. Nothing left now—coupla gas stations, some factories. What was still standing was torn down in 1950. Ah, but it had a great history. Babe Ruth—you've heard of him?" He was looking at me with a twinkle in his eye, clearly enjoying educating me. "He played his last major league game there. Woodrow Wilson was the first president to ever attend a World Series game—right there in the Baker Bowl."

Clearly I was in the presence of a rabid sports historian. I could sympathize with his enthusiasm. "I never knew! So tell me, what is it you want in return for sharing your electrical expertise?" I was pretty sure I could guess.

"I want to know what kinda stuff you got in your collections, about the team and the Baker Bowl."

"Surely there are better sources than the Society for information on the team?"

"I've looked." He ticked them off on his fingers. "The Atwater Kent—they had a good show there about local baseball a couple of years ago. The Philadelphia Sports Hall of Fame. The Philadelphia Athletics Historical Society, out in Hatboro. Even Comcast, and the architects for the new park."

"So what can we add for you?"

"My great-great-grandpa played for the original Quakers, the first couple of years. My great-grandpa went to a lot of games in that park, starting out as a toddler—he remembered seeing Ruth play there. I want to know more about the team and the players, maybe find a few photos. I bet you might have some records here that nobody knows about. You've got great stuff about the city, going way back. And Shelby here tells me a lot gets misfiled somewhere. So, say I was to look in one of those boxes that just says *Philadelphia photographs*, who knows what I might find? Especially if I know what I'm looking for?" He regarded me expectantly.

This was going to be a pleasure. "Barney, I would be delighted to provide you with an honorary membership to the Society and assure that you will have free access to our sports archives, in exchange for your advice on our electrical systems. I'm sure we can even find another enthusiast among our library staff who would be delighted to help you. How's that sound?"

"Sounds terrific." He beamed.

But I wasn't done. "Okay, Barney, we've got a deal. But I've got a condition, too."

"Yeah?"

"I want you to explain to me how that poor man came to die at the Let's Play Museum."

As I watched his face fall, I felt sad to have burst his happy bubble. "Awful thing," he said somberly. "Shouldn't have happened."

"So why did it?" I asked. "Or would it be easier to start with the *how*?" I checked my watch. "You want to take this someplace else, or do you have to be somewhere?"

"I got time if you do."

"Shelby? You want to join us?"

"I wouldn't miss it. How about the alehouse on Cedar Street?"

Perfect. An easy walk, and a pleasant place where we could talk without anyone listening in, and I figured Barney would be comfortable there. "Let me grab my coat and close up."

We all stood, and Shelby and Barney headed toward the elevator while I took one last look around, turned off my computer and the lights, and followed.

Outside it was cool and damp—probably rain coming. Luckily we didn't have far to go. Walking into the pub was like jumping into a warm bath of sound and color and smells, all good. We had no trouble finding a shabby booth in a corner that offered some privacy. We ordered a round of drinks (one of the plusses of taking the train in was that I could indulge—just a little—after work without worrying about driving home) and settled ourselves comfortably. The drinks arrived promptly, and we put in an order for a batch of bar munchies, which at least would be decently handled here, then we got down to business.

"All right, just how much do you know about electricity?" Barney began.

"I can plug something into a socket, and I know where my breaker box is at home. Assume that's it."

He sighed, a bit dramatically, I thought. "How about the difference between AC and DC?"

"We use AC in this country, right? And most of Europe uses DC?"

He looked disgusted. "Okay, I'll take it in baby steps. You do know what an electron is?" I nodded. "Current is the flow of electrons through a conductor—that's most often a metal wire—and it's measured in amperes. AC is most popular because you can increase or decrease it through a transformer. Like the wires to your house—lots of amps in the overhead power line, but it's stepped down to household level through a pole-mounted transformer."

"Got it. So outside power lines have more juice than lines in the house, right?"

"Yeah, more or less. Now, by code these days, the plugs you use have to be grounded. That's the third wire, if you take your line apart. You can see it in any box behind a plug or switch plate in your house. In the most basic terms, you've got three wires: the hot wire, the one that isn't hot, and the ground. The ground is what keeps you from getting fried when you get between the hot and the neutral wires, because a ground wire has a lot less resistance than a human body, and current likes to take the easy way. Doesn't mean it won't hurt, though. Look, most of your household stuff is twenty amps, okay? A milliamp is a thousandth of an amp. You grab something with sixteen milliamps and an average guy can hold on and let it go. Twenty milliamps and you stop breathing; a hundred milliamps and your heart short-circuits."

"That doesn't sound like very much. Why aren't there more fatal accidents?"

"OSHA—that's the Occupational Safety and Health Administration—says there are maybe two hundred a year, and a bunch of those are electrical workers messing with high-voltage lines. Not many household accidents, because the circuit breaker usually blows before anybody gets seriously hurt."

While I appreciated the general information, it wasn't what I was looking for. "So what are you telling me? That the accident at Let's Play required something out of the ordinary? Was it just a couple of crossed wires, or somebody forgot to attach something right, or would somebody have had to make a deliberate effort to increase the current and booby-trap it?"

Barney didn't answer right away. He'd finished his first drink and signaled the waitress for a second, glancing at Shelby and me to see if we wanted another. We were both still working on our first, and barely half-finished. Luckily the food appeared at the same time as Barney's fresh drink—I didn't want him to get sloshed before I had the information I was looking for. Shelby and I exchanged a glance, and she shrugged.

When Barney finally spoke, he didn't look at either of us, but stared into the depths of his drink. "I knew Joe Murphy. We're—we were—in the same union local."

"I met him before . . ." I left that thought unfinished. "He was working on the wiring at Let's Play, right?"

"Yeah, but that was pretty much finished. He liked to

help out—I guess Ms. Heffernan sweet-talked him into doing some extra last-minute stuff. We worked together on a couple of jobs. He was a real union guy—I'm a paid-up member, but I don't get involved in stuff with the local. Joe liked all the political stuff with the union. And he was a good bit younger than me. But he was a buddy—if he knew of a job that needed some extra hands, I could count on him to put in a word for me. I keep working pretty steady that way."

That made it a bit harder for me to ask my next question. "Look, Barney, I don't want to get you or anybody else into trouble, and if you're uncomfortable talking about this, I'll understand. Do you think Joe might have messed up with the wiring?"

"I don't think so. And there were other guys working on it, and the city inspectors checked it all out. Far as I know, it passed, no problem. No reason why anyone should have gotten hurt."

"Would somebody have wanted to hurt Joe?"

Barney shrugged. "I didn't know a whole lot about his personal life. He did okay with jobs. Better'n me. And he wasn't married, didn't have any kids to support. The union chipped in to help pay for his funeral, you know. He was just in the wrong place at the wrong time."

I didn't think Barney was going to say anything more about Joe. "That means that somebody else had to have rigged the wiring. Right?"

Barney nodded. He still looked uncomfortable—was he reluctant to point a finger at any of his colleagues?

I pressed on. "What I'd like to know is, how easy would it be to rig up something to shock someone on purpose? How much would they have to know?"

"I need another drink," Barney said. He waved at the

waitress and pointed to his glass, then turned back to me. "You think somebody screwed it up deliberately?"

I nodded. "Twice. Arabella swears she had it checked out by two different people after the first incident." When Barney stared at me blankly, I added, "There was an earlier incident where someone was shocked, but he's all right."

"Damn. You talked to the cops about this? I mean, both of these problems?"

"Well, yes, I told them what I saw the first time it happened—they contacted me after the second incident. Look, Barney, I'm just asking for information, for my own sake. If there's a way it could have been an accident—some rookie mistake or something came loose—then that will be the end of it. But if somebody set this up . . . Hey, it's going to give whichever electrician did the work a black eye, won't it? You have friends there?" I didn't want or expect him to betray any of his buddies.

"Yeah," Barney said reluctantly.

"So just tell me how this could have been set up without anybody noticing."

"You seen this exhibit thing?"

"I have. A bunch of different animals with interactive features, scattered around so the little kids can walk through them. The kids poke or pull something on one of the animals, and something else moves or flashes or makes noise. The outer shells are some kind of plastic, I think—and there aren't a lot of places where kids could stick a finger. So whoever tampered with one of them would have to have deliberately gotten inside one of them to get at the wiring. Or maybe the problem was somewhere else?"

Barney sat back when the waitress put his new drink in front of him. "Okay, sounds like typical residential-type voltage. You push the doohickey and it completes the circuit and the whatsis lights up or tweets or whatever. That too technical for you?"

"I'm with you so far. Simple circuit, with a switch of some sort."

"And I'd put money on it that there's a subpanel for the exhibit, running off the main feed. It wouldn't have been worth the effort to run new lines. You see anything like that?"

"Yes, there was something in the same room as the exhibit, I think, and Arabella said the exhibit had its own circuit. But shouldn't the breaker have tripped when Joe got shocked? It did the first time, with Jason."

"Should have, if there was an overload, but obviously, it didn't."

I nodded again. I appreciated his information, but I wasn't getting the answers I needed. What had gone wrong?

"There any water around the exhibit? A fountain? Or somebody spilled something?" Barney asked.

"I don't think so."

"Speaking of water, I've got to visit the head." He stood up and made his way through the sparse crowd toward the restrooms.

Shelby looked at me. "Lady, what are you doing?"

"Trying to understand what happened. Trying to help Arabella. Heck, I don't know. You know, if I hadn't been there when Jason got zapped, I would have seen the article in the paper and thought, oh dear, how sad, and then forgotten about it. But I was there, so I know there were two separate events, and if somebody has a grudge against the museum or Arabella, it bothers me."

"And so it should. But what are you going to do, even if you figure out how this could have happened? Don't you think the police are doing the same thing?"

"I certainly hope so! This is just for my own peace of mind. Plus I'll rest easier if I know that the Society is safe."

"You think Barney thinks you're crazy?"

I had to smile at that. "Maybe."

Barney returned and sat down again. "Okay. So, no standing water. The critter wasn't made of metal, so it's not a conductor. That leaves the switch. If the switch wasn't grounded right, *and* if there was some other metal conductor that the guy was in contact with . . . Was there?"

I tried to reconstruct what I'd seen. "I think—and this is only a guess—that Willy—" When Barney looked blank, I added, "That's a weasel who's sort of a friend of the hedgehog who's the star of the show. The weasel is the one who zapped Jason. As I recall, Willy is standing behind a gate to greet visitors, and I'd guess the gate is metal, and is probably bolted to something below the floor. I remember wondering if it was meant to keep the smaller children from climbing on the animals, and this was their solution. They can reach Willy's hand and his nose, I gather, but that's about it."

"Huh. I don't suppose you know much about the building's construction?"

I shook my head. "Nope. Old factory, brick exterior. But it's easy enough to see—when they refitted it for a museum, they left a lot of the structure exposed, and you can see the old ductwork and girders from the first floor."

"Ah," Barney responded. "So let's say the switch was the problem, and our guy was leaning over the railing to do whatever he was doing, and the railing was bolted to a metal girder for stability . . . that might just do it."

"So if someone knew that the gate was metal and it was secured to a metal girder, then all they would have to do is mess around with the switch on Willy?"

"That's about it."

It sounded far too easy.

"What's he do, this Willy guy? I mean, what's the interactive part?" Barney asked.

"I think he shakes hands, or maybe hands out something. When I was there, Arabella wanted to show me Harriet first, and after that we were kind of distracted, so I never actually saw it working."

Shelby spoke up. "I could make a good guess—I've given the books to plenty of my friends' kids. Willy's kind of a jerk, right?"

"So I gather, although apparently he has some redeeming qualities. He's just misunderstood."

Barney looked confused, but Shelby nodded. "Exactly," she said. "So he's going to be kind of smarmy, right? He wants people to like him, but he goes about it all wrong. Does he talk?"

"I don't know—not that I heard."

"Ladies, that stuff doesn't matter," Barney said. "As long as there's a button to push, to make the model do whatever the heck it does, it completes the circuit."

Obviously he was right. "So what does it take to change the switch and make it dangerous?"

"A screwdriver and a basic understanding of wiring. You could do it in a coupla minutes."

That didn't help at all. I checked my watch—it was getting late. "Thanks, Barney. I guess that answers my question. Given the way things were set up, sounds like almost anyone with some basic knowledge plus access to the exhibit could have rigged Willy to shock someone."

Barney shrugged. "Like I said, it's a simple switch, so any electrician would know how to do it quick."

I wasn't sure if I'd made any progress, but I had all the

information I could handle at the moment. "I appreciate your help, Barney. Let me know when you want to stop by and do some research into our baseball records and I'll set it up for you. And if I have any more questions about the Society's wiring, may I contact you?"

"Yeah, sure—as long as you keep me in mind when you get the money together to do something about it."

"I'll do that, I promise." I doubted we'd find funding before Barney retired, but I owed him that much. I stood up. "I've got to catch my train. Shelby, are you leaving, too?"

"I am. Barney, good to see you again."

Barney stood out of courtesy but said, "I think I'll hang around for a while. Nice to meet you, Nell—and I'll be coming around soon to check out your records!"

CHAPTER 16

The next morning I was editing the agenda for the Executive Committee meeting when I looked up to see Marty Terwilliger slouched against the door frame.

"You busy?" she asked.

"I'm always busy these days, but I can make time for you. Do you need something?"

Marty came in and sat down with a thunk that had me worrying about the chair. "We need to talk about the Executive Committee meeting."

That was something I'd been putting off. Since I'd only held this job for a couple of months, I wasn't exactly settled into a routine yet. The Society's full board met quarterly, and the last one had been a doozy; most board members had gone away stunned and baffled. The Executive Committee was a subset of the board, made up of the core members who actually got things done, including Marty, and I had scheduled a committee meeting for tonight. Marty was right: we needed to talk about progress or lack thereof; I hadn't even finished my reports. It was going to be another busy day.

I sighed. "In general, or you have some particular issues?"

"Both." Marty laughed at the look on my face. "Relax. You're doing as well as anybody could have expected, under the circumstances. But the board needs reassurance, and there are some specific issues we need to review. Assuming, of course, that you don't waste a lot of time on the Let's Play problem?"

"Why would I? Although Hadley Eastman dropped in on me, with steam coming out of her ears."

"Why?"

"Why was Hadley here, or why was she steaming? She thinks I told Arabella that I thought *she* might have been the target of the incident, which I didn't. Well, not exactly."

Marty snorted. "Hadley Eastman apparently thinks everything is about her and her damned hedgehog. From what I've heard, she's a real drama queen. She's gone through three publicists in the last couple of years."

"And you know this how?" I was always amazed at what and who Marty knew. She was definitely plugged into a lot of social networks—the kind that predated electronics.

"One of my nieces worked for her for a short while. She quit. Said Hadley treated her like a slave and never even said thank you."

"Based on my very short acquaintance, that doesn't surprise me. That's how she treated Chloe, the assistant who was with her when she came to my office. But she *is* successful."

"Maybe."

I cocked my head at Marty. "Maybe? Have you heard something?"

Marty shrugged. "A friend of mine said that her books

aren't selling as well as they used to. Publishing is fickle— one day you're hot, the next day you're not. Maybe this whole mess is a boost for her sagging career."

"Marty! Are you saying she electrocuted someone just to sell books?"

"Gets her name in the papers, doesn't it? Look, I'm only guessing. But from what I've heard, I wouldn't put it past her. Of course, she wouldn't get her own hands dirty, but I'm sure she could find someone to do it for her."

"Well, I assume the police will look into that. She said they'd paid her a call."

"Good for them. That Hrivnak woman isn't stupid, even if she lacks tact. Uh, there's one other thing . . ." Marty glanced over her shoulder, then got up and closed the door. "It's about Arabella."

Now I was really curious. There was something to know about Arabella that required closed doors? "Is this something I need to know?"

"Maybe. I just thought I'd fill you in on some of the background, in case it comes up in this investigation. I think I told you already that she's divorced, and the split was messy?"

"Yes. And I've met her daughter."

"The divorce happened, oh, about twenty years ago, I guess."

I laughed. "Marty, I was in high school then. Even if I had been here, I wouldn't have paid any attention to Philadelphia gossip."

"Oh, right—I forget you're just a baby. Anyway, it wasn't pretty. Arabella was married to a blue-collar guy, and she was working in some low-level position at Let's Play. Like front desk, or maybe it was the gift shop. Her daughter was pretty young. The guy left her, and she was stuck with the kid and the mortgage. She really struggled for a while."

"So how did she end up running Let's Play?"

"I'll give her credit—she hauled herself out of the pits, without any help. I can't imagine how she managed, but she kept the job and worked her way up. She took night classes in business administration, to fill out her résumé. She worked damned hard—and made friends with all the board, which didn't hurt. I've got to say I admire her. She may seem sweet, but she's got some real grit."

I tried to read between the lines of what Marty was saying. "Are you telling me she's a phony?"

Marty shook her head vehemently. "No, not at all. From everything I've ever heard, she really is a nice person. But you see the sweetness up front—there's some steel behind it."

"You think she had something to do with what's happened?"

"No, I'm not saying that. She's worked too hard to make the place what it is, and no way would she jeopardize it. It just doesn't fit. Just keep in mind, she's a lot tougher than she looks."

"Has she made enemies along the way?"

"Maybe. There's always somebody whose nose is out of joint about what's being done, or what's not. Look, Nell, you're in a position to know something about all this. You've worked at several different places, and you know people at others. Isn't there always some malcontent on the staff, someone who thinks he or she got passed over or isn't getting enough attention? That kind of thing can fester. Maybe that's what happened."

I nodded. "I can see that, I guess. It just seems so incongruous, when you apply it to a children's museum. Everything there is supposed to be cheery and happy."

"That's the way they want it to look, and believe me, they work hard to keep up that public image. But it's a business, like any other. Have the police decided whether the death was accidental or deliberate?"

"If they have, they haven't shared it with me. But the very fact that Detective Hrivnak is looking into it says something. She is a homicide detective, after all. By the way, I talked to an electrician—I'll fill you in on what he said about the Society's wiring—and he told me how the accident could have happened. I say *could* because he'd have to have more details to be sure. But how do we know if the person who set it up was thinking about murder? Maybe he just wanted a nasty accident, but not a death. Assuming, of course, that it wasn't just sloppy work. Still, I could see one mistake, but two separate events? That has to be deliberate, doesn't it?"

"Maybe. Anyway, that's not something we should worry about. So—the meeting. What've you got on the agenda?" And we turned to the business of the Society. I was happy to tell her that we had no new problems since I'd taken the helm, but unfortunately most of the old ones were still with us. Marty outlined what she thought were the most pressing issues at the moment, most of which I'd already included on my agenda—they didn't change much from one meeting to the next. Then we went over the one-page agenda I'd prepared, and Marty agreed with my priorities.

When we were wrapping up, I added, "We need a new registrar."

"I know. I haven't forgotten. You're looking?"

"I've talked to Latoya and Melanie, our human resources coordinator, and Melanie says she's posted the listing, but there's a snag."

"Money," Marty said bluntly.

I nodded. "Yes. We were lucky with Alfred—we got away with underpaying him for years. We're going to have to offer more if we want to attract qualified applicants. And that will probably throw the entire senior staff scale out of whack. You have any suggestions?"

Marty sat back in her chair. "Welcome to senior management. You know as well as anyone that salaries here are low, but we haven't had the budget to meet even cost-of-living adjustments. That's why the turnover's been so high, particularly among the junior staff—they stay a year or two to get the experience, and then they move on to someplace that pays better. There are no easy solutions, you know, unless you find an angel."

"You mean a major donor? This is the kind of funding we can't make up through grants, even if anyone were making them these days."

"Have you thought about recruiting new board members? A couple of our current ones are making noises about retiring, especially after the last few months. Not what they signed up for. They thought they were joining a sleepy historical institution, and instead they've gotten nasty headlines and drama."

"Marty, I've only been in this job for two months. I haven't had time. Of course I know what our budget problems are. I just haven't come up with any brilliant ideas—yet."

"I know, it's early days. And I know you're doing your best, Nell. I'll see what I can do about Alfred's position. I seem to recall promising you I'd guilt-trip the family into creating an endowment in his honor—maybe that could make up the difference? You should have reminded me."

I grinned at her. "That's what I just did—didn't you notice?"

She nodded her approval. "Smooth. You're learning fast." She stood up. "Well, I've got something to follow up on in the stacks."

I rose as well. "Let me walk you out—I want to talk to Felicity anyway."

Marty and I chatted as I escorted her to the elevator. She went up; I took the stairs down, to seek out librarian Felicity Soames, who knew where everything in the collections was. I found her at her post at the high desk in the reading room.

"Hi, Felicity," I whispered. "Do you have a moment?"

Felicity looked around the room: it was moderately busy for a weekday. She nodded to her assistant, who was circulating with a rolling cart, collecting documents for reshelving, and she parked it and headed for the desk. "Where do you want to go? Is this hush-hush?"

I suppressed a laugh. "No, I just wanted to ask a favor. Can we just step into the lobby?"

I could swear she looked disappointed. "All right." She led the way to the lobby, and we found two chairs near the monumental grand staircase. "What's this about?"

"I've been doing a little horse-trading. After what happened at Let's Play, I wanted to make sure our wiring was in good shape, but I didn't want to have to pay for a full review. So I found an electrician who was willing to look over the last report and tell us if things were up to par, but he had a price."

"And how does that involve me?"

"He's really into Phillies history, and he wants some help looking through our archives." I stopped, since Felicity's face had assumed a strange and wonderful expression. "What?"

"The Quakers?" she said.

"Yes, I think he mentioned those. Why, do you know about them?"

Felicity produced as close to a grin as I'd ever seen on her. "It's my secret vice. I *love* sports history, but nobody else here seems to share that. I'd be happy to help him."

"Great! I said I'd give him a complimentary membership, so he can come in when he has time. I'll send him straight to you."

"Thank you! Do you know if he's done a lot of research?"

"He said he's checked out some of the other local collections, but he's looking for something more specific, and he thinks we might have it."

"Wonderful." Felicity sighed. "I love a challenge. Was that all?"

"For now. Thanks for helping out, Felicity."

"My pleasure. Really. Well, back to work."

She headed back to the reading room, and I went to the elevator. One more stop and I could settle my debt to Barney. I dropped in at Shelby's office on the way to my own.

"Hey, lady," Shelby greeted me. "What's up?"

"If you recall, I promised Barney a free membership, so he could work on that Phillies stuff. Can you process that?"

"Sure will. Definitely a good trade."

"I thought so. And I just talked to Felicity, who is apparently a secret sports fan, so she'll be happy to help him out. I'll write a cover letter for you, so you can send him his membership card."

"Felicity's the head librarian, right? I love it when a plan comes together. Don't you? And that Felicity has hidden depths."

"I do, and she does. Thanks for bringing Barney in."

"My pleasure. And I'll get right on that membership."

I went back to my office with a feeling of accomplishment. As I walked toward my door, Eric waved a message slip at me.

"Agent Morrison, that FBI guy? He wants you to call him. You want me to place the call?"

I snagged the slip from him. "Thanks, Eric. I'll do it myself."

CHAPTER 17

Back at my desk, I looked at James's message. It was his work number, rather than his cell phone, which surprised me—trouble? Or good news? I dialed, then waded through a couple of layers of receptionists until I reached him.

"Hello, Nell," he said when he picked up, all business.

"James," I replied in the same neutral tone. "You called?"

"Yes. Thanks for getting back to me. I need to talk to you about something."

"Business?" I acknowledged a small feeling of disappointment, then squashed it.

"Yes. Can you meet me after work?"

If he could be businesslike, so could I. "Sorry, I can't—committee meeting tonight. Lunch?"

He hesitated a moment before answering. "No time. Coffee?"

"Okay. Where?"

"How about the Doubletree again? Half an hour?"

Not his office, not my office, but the very public hotel down the street. Interesting. "Fine."

"See you then." He hung up before I could add anything more.

I sat back in my chair, mildly baffled. If this was about the Society, he could have met me here, but his tone suggested it was not about the two of us, whatever *we* were. Something about the missing collection items? But again, he wouldn't be coy about that. Ergo, it had to be something about the Let's Play problem. Had something changed since the last time we had met? At that point I ran out of deductions and resolved to wait until we got together to think about it further. I turned my attention back to the agenda for the Executive Committee meeting.

Collections: acquisitions were on indefinite hold, both because of a shortage of funds and because we didn't have a registrar to catalog anything right now. Membership: holding steady for the moment, but would members renew when the time came? Fundraising: on hold. Shelby seemed competent, but she wasn't yet up to speed on the inner workings of our organization, and that would take time. Right now I felt like a nurse, trying to soothe everyone and keep them calm. Not to mention, keep our name out of the press, at least in any negative way.

So I did what I knew I could do—ran numbers, assembled information, talked briefly to staff members, and tried to cobble together reports that were accurate, short, and as optimistic as I could make them. I'd only roughed out a few before I had to leave to meet James—luckily he'd picked a spot just down the street.

James was waiting at a table and stood when he spotted me. I tried to gauge his expression: I was reading *cau-*

tiously welcoming. "Thank you for coming on such short notice," he said.

"Thank you for picking a convenient location." He held out my chair and I sat. "So, what's this about? And why so formal?"

A waiter appeared. James ordered coffee, and I followed suit. When the server had left, James began, "I know I told you that there was no way I could involve myself or the agency in what happened at Let's Play." He sighed. "Turns out, there may be a reason for the FBI to take an interest after all."

"Oh really?" I racked my brain for a list of the FBI's responsibilities and couldn't find *children's museums with electric hedgehogs* there.

"What do you know about Arabella's husband?"

Only what Marty had told me, but I wasn't going to mention that. "Next to nothing. I know that she was married a long time ago and had one child—in fact, I've met her daughter, Caitlin. She's head of exhibits at Let's Play. The husband's been out of the picture for years, I gather. All that was long before my time. Why do you ask?"

James stared pensively over my head. "Arabella's husband, Nolan Treacy, was Irish-born. He was active in raising funds in Boston for the IRA, back in the eighties. And he was a member of the local electrician's union."

I sat back, somewhat stunned. It took me a few moments to line up the pieces: IRA meant terrorism, which is why James finally had reason to be sitting in front of me talking about it. I decided to start with the simple stuff. "I thought the IRA was dead, or at least dormant."

"Yes and no. The leadership in Ireland has backed off the violence, but there are still some Irish-Americans who have had a hard time letting go. Things were very heated in the eighties, when Nolan was living here. Problem is, we don't know where he stands now. It could be that he's one of the ones who don't want to give up the fight."

"Isn't it kind of a stretch, to connect Irish extremists with an accident at a small Philadelphia museum?"

He shrugged. "Maybe. In fact, probably. But the connection is there—a straight line from Arabella to a subversive group with Philadelphia ties. We have to at least consider it. That's our job."

"So you're on the case?" This time I smiled.

"Looks like it." He smiled back.

This was encouraging, except for one troubling fact. "Why are you telling me this?"

"For one thing, I'm telling you that I'm involved, so you don't trip over me."

"But I'm not involved!"

"But you know Arabella."

"Are you going to talk to her?"

"Of course. In fact, we already have. She says she hasn't heard from her ex in years, and that's fine with her. I gather their parting was less than amicable."

"He walked away and left her to pick up the pieces, including financially." I spoke before I had time to think.

James was quick to react. "And how do you know this?"

"Marty."

He sighed again. "Of course my cousin would stick her nose in. Why am I not surprised?"

"Hey, all she knew about was Arabella's side. She didn't say anything about Irish radicals."

"I suppose not. If it's not a Philadelphia family, she's not interested."

"Do you doubt what Arabella told you? About a clean break?"

"I have no reason to doubt it," James said carefully. "But her profile at the place might have planted an idea in our boy Nolan's head."

"Why? He wants to heat things up again for the IRA? Why here, why now? Or he's got a long-standing grudge against Arabella? Marty said he dumped her, rather than the other way around. He envies her success? It all seems kind of far-fetched. Wait—are there hedgehogs in Ireland? Maybe he can't stand to see them exploited."

James did his best to suppress a smile but finally gave up the effort. "I hadn't considered the hedgehog angle, but I'll take it under advisement."

"You do that. Or, wait—maybe he had an affair with Hadley, years ago, and gave her the whole hedgehog idea, and she wouldn't give him credit and now he's taking revenge."

James shook his head. "Nell, I know stranger things have happened, and we have to look at all sides of this, but remember that someone died at Let's Play."

My laughter drained away quickly. "I know, and I don't take that lightly. But the whole thing seems so odd. Why go after a beloved and harmless institution?"

James sat back in his chair. "From a political perspective it makes sense. People expect attacks on major institutions, like government or the military. But hit them where they don't expect it, go after the safe, ordinary places, and it really rattles them. It's effective and simple."

"I hadn't looked at it like that, but you're right. What a sad commentary. And if it had been a child who was injured or killed, it would have been so much worse."

"Exactly." We both fell silent for a few moments.

"Was there anything else?" I'm not sure what answer I hoped for.

"Not right now. Nell," he began, fumbling for words, "I'd like to get together with you again, but can we get through this thing first?"

"The electric hedgehog case? All right. I've got a lot on my plate right now, too—there's an Executive Committee meeting tonight, the first since I took over, and I'm still looking for a registrar so we can get back to reviewing our collections."

"I see you've filled a couple of positions."

"How do you know that?"

"For one thing, a young male voice keeps answering your phone. And I assume, since you're a competent fundraiser, that you made it a priority to fill your empty position ASAP?"

"Right on both counts, although it was the other way around. Shelby Carver is the new me—she came through a human resources ad. And she found Eric Marston—he's the voice on the phone. So far, so good, although it's only been a week or so. I'm more worried about filling the registrar's position. That requires a different level of skills, and I'm not sure how far news of our recent troubles have spread."

"I wouldn't worry about it, in this job market."

"Marty said she'd help. I hope it's not another relative, but I guess I can't complain if she comes up with a good candidate. And I know she cares about the Society."

"It'll all work out." James stood up. "I've got to get back to the office."

"So do I. Let me know if you learn anything else."

"If I can."

CHAPTER 18

Back at my desk, I dug into those reports again. Luckily most of the Executive Committee members were busy people, and they appreciated brevity. I hoped it would be a short meeting, and at least I had no catastrophes to report, no crises to resolve. Just business as usual, as we slid into the new calendar year.

I had just gotten my head back into report mode when Eric called out, "Ms. Heffernan is on the phone for you."

"Thanks, Eric. I'll pick up." I lifted my handset. "Hi, Arabella. Is everything all right?"

"No new disasters, if that's what you mean. Can you come out and play for a little while?"

For a moment I wondered if I'd heard her correctly. "What are you suggesting?"

"I'm just so tired of dust and paint smells and noise, and I need to get out of my office because the pesky phone keeps ringing. How does lunch at the Reading Terminal Market sound?"

My mouth started watering immediately. I was torn, but I knew that the reports would still be sitting here after lunch. "Wonderful. Can I meet you there?"

"Noonish? I thought I'd walk over—I can really use the exercise. How about we meet at the corner by the tunnel?"

"Sounds good to me. See you then!" I'd walk over, too, which would let me feel less guilty about indulging in lunch. And maybe I could pick up some good stuff to take home with me. Even though it was only a few blocks away, I seldom went to the Market, and I missed it. I welcomed Arabella's impromptu suggestion.

The Reading Terminal Market is one of Philadelphia's most enduring institutions. When the Reading Railroad became the largest railway in the country in 1892, the Market opened next to the imposing bulk of the arched train shed. The above-ground trains are long gone, and the train shed is part of the Pennsylvania Convention Center now, but the Market continues to thrive, providing a magnificent array of vegetables, meats, fish, prepared food, and a whole lot more. There are quite a few Amish vendors, mixed in with Asian ones now, and a smattering of names that have been in place for decades. The place is almost always crowded, as both urban and suburban shoppers pass through on their way to and from home and work. Why did I always forget how much I loved the place?

Arabella was waiting on the corner when I crossed Market Street and scurried down the block. Despite the pale sunshine and brisk breeze, she looked warm and happy, her cheeks glowing like apples. "Hi, Nell!" she called out gaily as I approached. "I'm so glad you could make it! I know you must be busy."

"I am, but I needed to get out and clear my head as much as you do. Where shall we eat?"

"Ooh, I love the Down Home Diner."

One of my favorites, too. "Sounds good to me. Let's get inside before my ears freeze off."

We made our way quickly to the nearest door in the tunnel and ducked inside. A young waiter held up two fingers; we nodded and followed him to a booth, where we sat and shrugged off our winter coats. After we'd given our orders—chunky sandwiches and some of their outstanding fries, along with coffee—I sat back and sighed with anticipation.

"I'm so glad you thought of this. How are things going? Will you be able to open the exhibit on time?" I hated to cast a damper on Arabella's mood, but the problems at Let's Play had to be weighing on her mind.

Arabella didn't appear too upset at my question. "I think so. We were just putting on the finishing touches when the . . . incident occurred, so I think the schedule is holding."

"That's good news. Do you think people will be reluctant to visit, given . . . what's happened?" I noticed that we were both talking in euphemisms.

"I doubt it. You don't have children, do you?" When I shook my head, she went on. "Many of our visitors are too young to have any grasp of what's happened."

Not so their parents, I thought, but kept silent. Arabella seemed very matter-of-fact about a death in her building, but she did have a business to run. "Hadley Eastman stopped by the other day," I said.

Arabella made a face. "That woman! I'm sorry I ever agreed to work with her. What did she want from you?"

"Somehow she got the idea that I'd pointed a finger at her for this accident."

Arabella sighed. "I'm sorry—that's probably my fault.

She came in and started yelling at me, and I just said whatever I could to make her stop. I might have mentioned that you thought Hadley could have been the target."

Having faced the wrath of Hadley, I wasn't surprised. "I forgive you. So she's not easy to work with?"

Arabella gave a ladylike snort. "I won't say what I'd like to, but to put it politely, she's demanding, arbitrary, and self-centered. I could go on, but I won't. It's funny, in a way—she's the complete opposite of a hedgehog, shy little creatures that they are. And Harriet is so sweet!"

"But Hadley *is* prickly."

That brought a laugh from Arabella. "That she is."

Our sandwiches arrived, and we dove in with enthusiasm—particularly for the accompanying fries, which were best eaten hot. When I slowed down, I asked, "How did you two connect in the first place? Did you approach her with the idea of an exhibition?"

"I did not! Of course, you know how long exhibit planning takes. About two years ago her publisher approached us."

"Really?"

Arabella nodded. "We set up a meeting, and her editor and the publisher's publicist were there. They said they wanted Hadley to do more outreach to children, and they thought we'd be a good match, since she's from this area. I knew *of* her, of course—we even carried her books in the gift shop—but we'd never met. So I said, sure, let's do it. I thought it would be a good draw, and I loved the books. Harriet's such an appealing figure."

"And then you met Hadley?"

"Looking back, I think she was on her best behavior the first couple of times we met. She was pretty quiet and let her editor do most of the talking—at least until we signed the contracts. Then she showed her true colors. She wanted this, she wasn't happy with that, everything should be bigger—particularly her name."

"How did you manage to smooth things out?" I asked, honestly curious. If Arabella was the businesswoman Marty made her out to be, she must have applied her skills to this problem.

"We did a lot of haggling, but eventually we agreed on most things. I know our audience, I told her—better than she does, apparently. She may write charming books, but she has no idea how to translate them into an interactive display. I think she wanted the children to file through and admire her works silently, but that's not our style at Let's Play. We want the kids to handle things, play with things. Sure, it's hard on the exhibits sometimes. But children are wonderful—they don't see the chips in the paint, they see a character they love. Not that we haven't made provisions for freshening things now and then, over the life of the exhibit."

"Are you considering making it a permanent exhibit?" I asked.

"Not if I can help it!" Arabella replied vehemently. "I don't want to deal with that woman any longer than I have to. Besides, we've already made commitments for the space for the year after next."

I marveled at how fast things moved in the world of children's museums, compared to our staid institution. It usually took us the better part of a decade to change anything.

I looked at my plate to find that all my food had mysteriously disappeared, save for a lonely french fry lurking under a piece of lettuce. I promptly snared and ate it. There was a line of impatient lunch seekers waiting by the door, and the waiter had long since tossed our bill on the table. "Shall we settle up and walk around a bit? Maybe we can find something tasty for dessert along the way."

"Wonderful. There's so much to see here. I even enjoy people watching, especially children—too bad there are so few children here during the day, and I don't get over here much on weekends. Oh, and we have to go see the pig! It's a tradition of mine."

Even I knew about Eric Berg's sculpture of Philbert the pig, the Market's mascot. He was located roughly in the center of the Market, sitting on his cash box, mouth eagerly open. Philbert attracted a lot of donations, which went toward supporting healthy eating programs. "Sure," I said, sticking some cash in the bill folder and gathering up my coat.

We strolled through the crowded market aisles, pointing out the interesting and exotic goodies we passed. Arabella's enthusiasm was refreshing. She made no effort to act like a serious grown-up but instead responded like the children she so enjoyed, all but squealing with glee when she spied something absurd like a giant ear made out of chocolate. The Market offered plenty of inspiration.

We reached Philbert and stopped to pay him homage as people swirled around us, intent on their lunch-hour errands. Philbert sat next to one of the main seating and eating areas, although he turned his back to the throng. Arabella approached him to rub his snout, fishing with her other hand in her roomy bag for a contribution. She fed him with a pleased smile, then looked up—and froze, her pink cheeks turning parchment white in seconds.

I followed her gaze but saw nothing out of the ordinary. Most of the tables were filled, primarily with ones and twos. People were leaving and being replaced in a steady stream, their purchases clustered around their feet. At the far end was a table of four men, who had no purchases and only soft-drink bottles on their table; they appeared deep in conversation. But they did not look out of place in the rich ethnic mix of shoppers. I touched Arabella on the arm, and she jumped. "Arabella, are you all right?"

She turned to me quickly. "Oh, yes, I'm fine. Maybe I just overdid it a bit. I've been under a lot of stress lately, as you can guess. Perhaps I'll just catch a cab back to the museum. Please, you go on shopping. I'll be fine once I get off my feet."

"If you're sure . . ." I said dubiously.

Her color was already returning. "Don't worry about me. I'll talk to you soon. And thanks for coming out to lunch with me!"

She turned on her heel and headed straight for the side exit, where I knew cabs lined up waiting. I watched along the long aisle until she left the building, then turned back to the cluster of tables. The four men had dispersed without a trace.

After making a few purchases of vegetables, I walked slowly back toward the Society. What could have startled Arabella so? I had a sneaking suspicion that she had unexpectedly recognized someone among the lunch goers. One of the men at the table? On the sidewalk I stepped aside, pulled out my cell phone, and hit a number—James's private line. I didn't have time to go through all those receptionists.

"Nell?" James's voice at last. "What's up?"

"Do you have a picture of Nolan Treacy?" I said without preamble.

"Of course. Why?"

"Could you email me a copy to my office? I'm on my way back there now."

"What's going on?"

"I'll explain when I get to my office. Please?"

"Okay."

"Thanks." I hung up before he asked for more explanation.

Back at the Society I hurried to my desk, nodding briefly to Eric as I passed. I sat down at my computer, logged into my email, and found James's message, with an attachment. When I opened the attachment, it was a single image. I printed it out, then studied it. It clearly wasn't recent, and the quality was poor—it was badly pixilated.

Was this one of the men I had seen at the Market? I couldn't say for sure, but neither could I rule it out.

As I sat with the picture in my hands, the phone rang. Eric appeared at the door and whispered, "It's that FBI agent," not that James could possibly hear Eric if he was on hold. Or maybe he could: I had no idea how far the capabilities of the FBI stretched.

"Thanks, Eric. I'll take it. Oh, and could you close the door behind you?"

When he was gone, I picked up the phone. "What's this about, Nell?" James demanded.

I took a breath. "I just had lunch with Arabella Heffernan, at her invitation. We went to the Reading Terminal Market. After lunch we were strolling around and she stopped suddenly and looked like she'd seen a ghost."

"And?" James said impatiently.

"It occurred to me that she might have seen her ex-husband among a group of men sitting at a nearby table. That's why I asked you for the picture."

"Was it him?"

"Hard to tell. This is an old picture, right?"

"Yes, maybe fifteen, twenty years ago. Nobody's had

any official reason to photograph him since, not here in the U.S. at least—and he's a foreign national, so it's not like we have access to his driver's license or anything. What did you see?"

"A bunch of ordinary-looking guys having a soda in a busy place. Seriously. That's all I can tell you. But Arabella went white and hightailed it out of there as fast as she could. She took a cab back."

"Hmm. I'm going to have to talk with Ms. Heffernan."

"James, don't chew her head off, please. She looked honestly surprised, and none too happy. If that was what she was even looking at. She claimed not to feel well—it's possible it could have been the smoked eel or something else that turned her off."

"I'll bear that in mind. Talk with you later?"

"I've got that meeting tonight. Call me when I get home?"

"Will do."

And he was gone. I felt bad about siccing the FBI on Arabella. Of course, if she *had* seen Nolan Treacy, they needed to know. Maybe it was just a coincidence, but if so, it had to be verified that it was nothing more. Maybe Nolan had turned into a sober, upright citizen and renounced his activist ways, but the FBI needed to be sure. So why did I feel so bad?

With a sigh, I turned back to the reports on my desk.

CHAPTER 19

I approached my first Executive Committee meeting as president of the Society with a little trepidation. The Executive Committee—the subgroup that actually ran the place—met once a month, but the Christmas holidays had intervened in December, and I think the board members, still reeling from the events of the fall, had wanted to give me a little breathing room in my new position before meeting again. I'd kept the key players informed, at least. For the meeting now I'd prepared all the reports that I thought were needed, but I wasn't sure if they were going to be enough. I hated committing to paper our lack of progress in several significant areas. But I was doing the best I could. I hoped they would recognize that. Sure, I'd known the members of the board for years, but in an entirely different role. I still had no idea how they would treat me after my sudden elevation to leadership. I knew I had Marty as my champion, but it would take more than one person in my corner to make this work. Plus the board was still reeling from a slew of unwelcome revelations a couple of months earlier, and I had to address their concerns and look like I was handling things. I wasn't sure what I could tell them that would reassure them, but I had to try.

Most of the members smiled at me as they walked in, which I chose to interpret as a good sign. It felt really strange to be standing at the head of the table when the members congregated in the board room. I'd sent Eric home: the board secretary could handle the minutes from this meeting. Marty gave me a nod when she walked in and took her seat.

At five thirty I began. "Thank you for coming—I know how busy you all are. I'll try to keep my remarks brief, since it hasn't been long since our last meeting, but that one was a bit unusual." A couple of the board members chuckled. "I can report that we don't appear to have lost any ground since then, although the holiday season is historically slow. At least it gave us some breathing room. If you'll look at your information packets . . ." I led them through the reports that they should have read but probably hadn't: membership status, the final income numbers from our November gala (the last bright moment before the storm), and the status of acquisitions and major grant proposals (nil for both). The treasurer provided a simplified update on the state of our finances, which were, as usual, precarious.

When we'd run through the formal reports, I said, "I've had some success in filling some of our vacant positions. I've hired Shelby Carver to fill my former slot. I hope she'll introduce herself to you soon."

An emeritus member rumbled, "I hope you're being careful filling positions these days. Background checks and the like. We don't want to make the same mistake again."

I debated about how to respond. It was all too easy to fabricate résumés and even cover your tracks in this electronic age, and I'd been relying on Melanie's due diligence—and my gut reactions—with Shelby and then Eric. "Shelby is very well qualified, and she's already provided a lot of help. Of course, she's barely started, so I can't speak to her fundraising abilities, but give her a chance to settle in. In addition, I've hired a new assistant."

"He's a he, isn't he?" the secretary asked. Predictably it was John Rittenhouse, one of our older board members. "He sounds young, on the phone. Nell, you've got to remember that this person represents the Society and is often the first contact that our major donors have with us. He has to be right for the position."

"I understand your concern, and I haven't offered him the position on a full-time basis yet—he's on probation. But so far I've had no reason to complain. Eric has been careful, polite, discreet, and he can think on his feet. And in case you don't know it, I really need someone at that desk to keep me from being overwhelmed by the insignificant stuff. I assume you'd all prefer me to deal with more important issues?"

No one argued with me. I pressed on. "I've been moving slowly to fill the registrar's position. We need someone who is well qualified, but we're somewhat hampered by the salary we can offer. It's just not competitive in today's market."

"You've advertised the position?" Lewis Howard, one of our most long-standing board members, asked.

"We already have, but few people were looking for jobs around the holidays, even in this economy. I expect interest will pick up now. But of course we all recognize that our collections management is on hold as long as the position is vacant. We still have a lot of sorting out to do."

"All the more reason to make sure you find the right person."

Marty winked at me before jumping in to say, "You may remember that at the last board meeting I suggested that we start a fund in Alfred's memory, with the income going toward enhancing the salary for collections management positions. That, after all, is our core mission—to preserve and protect our collections, and to make them accessible to the public. We can't do that if we can't find them, and that means we need to hire a well-qualified registrar. I'd like to make a formal motion to create this endowed fund, and I'd like to make the first contribution of twenty-five thousand dollars. I hope you'll all contribute."

Hooray for Marty! She'd not only stepped up—presumably with money collected from her extended family—but she'd also challenged the others to join her. She knew how to play the game. Before anyone else spoke, I stepped in. "I can ask Shelby to look into grant funding to supplement the income further. And maybe we can suggest that the board will match all funds collected?"

Marty nodded. "Good idea, Nell. There's a motion on the table. Do I hear a second?"

The motion passed, and I gave an inward sigh of relief.

The meeting wound down after that, and I noticed that a couple of members were looking at their watches. I was ready to adjourn when John Rittenhouse spoke up once again. "Maybe this is none of our business, but I've been reading about that problem at Let's Play. I'm worried that it's going to open up what happened here all over again. I mean, it looks like there's a black cloud over Philadelphia museums, and some nosy newshound is bound to pick up on that."

"How do you propose we address that, John?" I asked. "For public purposes, the police are calling it a tragic accident. Beyond offering our sympathies, what can we do?" If he didn't know, I wasn't about to tell him that I was already involved.

"Are you saying it wasn't an accident? Do you know something more than what's been announced in the news?" He didn't voice the next logical thing—that I had contacts with local law enforcement who could tell me more.

"No, I don't. From what I know of Arabella Heffernan, she's a lovely person and a good administrator. I know full well the difficulties of the situation she faces, and I hope she—and Let's Play—can weather them. By the way, I think in light of what happened at Let's Play, we should revisit the state of our own electrical systems, so that we can reassure the public that our building is safe." I didn't mention that I'd already started that process.

"How much will that cost us?" someone grumbled, and we were off on a tangent once again—one that at least led away from Arabella and her problem.

After a few more minutes the meeting broke up and the members dispersed. Marty lingered behind. "You want to grab some dinner?" she asked.

I considered for about three seconds. "Sure, sounds good. I owe you for stepping up on the registrar position. Just let me get my stuff." Luckily I'd driven in today, anticipating the late meeting, so I didn't have to worry about catching a train.

We meandered over to the restaurant on the corner and found a quiet booth. Once we were settled and had ordered, I said, "I thought that went pretty well. Of course, we're all

still on good behavior, and there hasn't been time to ac-
complish much—or to screw things up."

Marty gave a slight nod. "I haven't heard any com-
plaints, but then, they know I'm on your side, so maybe
they wouldn't talk to me. Look, I'll cut to the chase: Jimmy
told me about Arabella's ex."

"The so-called IRA terrorist? Why would he tell you?"

Marty shrugged. "He asked me what I knew about him,
back in the day, not that I could tell him much. Plus I think
he's keeping an eye on you—and trying to keep you out of
trouble."

I should have figured that James would go to his cousin
Marty as the local expert on Philadelphia society. But I
didn't like the way the rest of that sounded. "Marty, I don't
need babysitting. I do think the whole terrorist connection
is kind of far-fetched, especially the idea that this guy
would come back now just to make trouble at Arabella's
museum. And if James is pursuing this just to keep an eye
on me, you can tell him to quit it. It's a waste of FBI
resources."

Marty smiled." Look, if there's a legitimate threat, he's
got to look into it. And if you want him to back off, *you* tell
him. But I think it's kind of cute that he wants to keep you
out of trouble."

Cute was not the word I would have chosen. *Annoying*
came closer. "Why would I get into trouble?"

"You've already gotten together with Arabella a couple
of times. And don't forget Hadley."

"Hey, Hadley came to me, not the other way around."

"Drama queen, that one. Why don't you tell Arabella to
take care of her own problems? Not to mention Hadley?"

Our food arrived while I turned over answers in my
mind. "A couple of reasons, at least where Arabella is con-

cerned. As for Hadley, I'm happy to tell *her* to take a hike. But I like Arabella and I don't think she had anything to do with this, and she doesn't deserve this kind of trouble. I certainly know what that's like. And I also feel a professional stake in this; like it or not, if the public believes there's a threat to our Philadelphia cultural institutions, all our attendance—and our revenues—will drop. You'll notice that the topic even came up at the board meeting, and they're usually pretty clueless about things like that. The sooner this is cleared up, the better off we'll all be. Do you want any more reasons?"

Marty laughed. "Okay, okay, I get it. But just watch your back, will you? If you want to hold on to this job, you have to keep the board happy. That's your first priority."

"I know." I savored my excellent lasagna, which gave me a chance to change the subject. "Marty, did you already know about Arabella's ex-husband's ties to the IRA? You hinted at something in her past."

"Like I told James, I didn't know the details about him specifically, I just knew there had been problems. And as I've said to you before, I admire what I know about Arabella. It sounds like she pulled herself up by her bootstraps under difficult conditions. But I have to say, it makes me wonder—could she really have been that naive back then, married to an IRA activist? If she's really as smart as she appears to be now, could she have really been in the dark about her husband's activities? Just think about it, that's all."

I didn't like what I was hearing. James was giving some credence to the terrorist angle, and now Marty was issuing vague warnings? Had Arabella really seen Nolan at the Market? Or was she seeing ghosts now? Her reactions had certainly seemed sincere enough. And if it really had been him, why was he here now?

Marty had résuméd talking, and I had to force myself to pay attention. "How's Shelby working out?" she asked.

"Good, I think. She may not be old Philadelphia, but when she turns on that southern charm, it works. You should have seen her handle Hadley, getting her out of my office fast, before I said something I'd regret. I'll have to see how she does with grant proposals. Speaking of which, thank you so much for that funding for the registrar's position. I'll do my best to see that we match it with grants and donations from this end."

"I'll make sure you do. I had to call in some favors to get my share, but I thought I owed Alfred that much. Uh, off the record, Jimmy chipped in, too."

"Why off the record? Is he worried that he'll look like he feels guilty about something? Obviously, if he didn't want me to know about it, he isn't using it to impress me. Or buy his way into my affections."

"Could he?" Marty asked.

"Could he what?"

"How do I put this . . . you interested? Because if you aren't, I can tell him to back off and save you the trouble."

"Marty! We've had like one and a half dates, if you want to call them that."

"Yeah, right. Okay, I'll shut up about it and let you two muddle along. How's your lasagna?" And the talk drifted to impersonal things.

It was late when I drove home, but at least the roads were empty and I made good time. I had to laugh at Marty playing matchmaker. I knew she was mistress of all the intricacies of local family connections, past and present, but I'd never thought about her trying to forge new ones, particularly within her extended Pennsylvania clan. Should I be flattered? More important, was I interested in James? Maybe, maybe. But right now I didn't have time to think about it.

CHAPTER 20

The next morning was our regular biweekly staff meeting, held before the doors opened to the public. I had two new employees to officially introduce, which was good. More important, I had to crack the whip and get everyone to focus on their jobs, now that the holidays were behind us and people weren't distracted by things going on in their lives outside the building. Some people actually *had* lives outside of the Society.

I'd warned Shelby and Eric to be there early, and they were already in their seats, looking eager, when I arrived. One of them had even thought to bring coffee and goodies, a surefire way to win friends among the staff. I smiled at the latecomers who straggled in, and called the meeting to order a few minutes after nine.

"Good morning! I know you're all busy, so I'll keep this short. First of all, I wanted to officially introduce the person who will be filling my former role as director of development, Shelby Carver. Since she's been here nearly two weeks already, she's probably introduced herself to all of you by now. Shelby, you want to say anything?"

Shelby beamed at the group. "No, ma'am. I think I've met all these nice people already. And if anybody has any ideas for a good grant project, just stop by my office and we can chat."

"Good idea. If there's anything I've learned working here, it's that you never know what's going to catch a funder's eye, and you staff members here know what the real needs are. We want to know what you'd like to see implemented. Of course, we still have a long way to go to beef up our security systems, and before you say it, I know you'd all like to see a small raise in your piddling salaries." A quiet laugh rippled through the group; they'd heard this before. Nobody here had had a raise in all the time I had been here, more than five years now. But I'd keep trying, because the staff members deserved it, and they couldn't be expected to work purely for the love of local history. Not forever, anyway.

"And there's one more new member here, Eric Marston. He's my new assistant, and that's a pretty big job, at least from my perspective. Please make him welcome. I suspect either he or Shelby is responsible for the tasty treats here?" Eric blushed and smiled. "Eric, you're learning fast! The best way to win over people here is to feed them. One other staffing issue—we're still looking for a replacement for Alfred Findley, so if any of you knows of someone who might be interested in the registrar job, please let me know. A computer wizard might be helpful, since Alfred was the only one who really knew how the cataloging database works. Okay, anything else we need to talk about?"

The meeting shifted to small administrative details and scheduling issues. Out of the corner of my eye I noticed

Front Desk Bob peer into the room—he was holding the fort out front while we met. I raised one eyebrow, but apparently he wasn't looking for me. He nodded toward Eric. Eric looked confused but excused himself and headed out the door.

After a few more minutes the staff scattered to their respective tasks, and Shelby and I shared the elevator up to the third floor. "I need to talk to you about looking for some funding for Alfred's position," I told her. "Marty Terwilliger announced at the board meeting last night that she's started the ball rolling with an endowment fund to help support collections management, and we want to use it to supplement the salary for the position. In fact, she's guilt-tripping the other board members to ante up, too. Can you check through the funder database and see what might fit?"

"Sure will," she replied. "You have a job description for the position?"

"Talk to Melanie—she does, and she's updated it recently. Alfred Findley was here for years, and I understand the computer side of things has changed just a bit. He understood it, but I don't know what kind of instructions he left behind. Or . . ." I stumbled over my words, distressed at my own oversight. "Or you should talk to Latoya, since she was his boss." Heck, *I* had to talk to Latoya to update her about Marty's offer. "And FYI, he was some kind of distant relative to Marty, which is why she's helping out financially."

"Marty seems to be related to just about everybody around here," Shelby remarked as we arrived at the development office.

"That she is. That's what makes her so useful on the board. Have you had a chance to talk to her?"

Shelby shook her head. "Not more than in passing."

"She's worth getting to know. Maybe we should all have lunch one of these days."

"You figure things'll be slow for a while?"

"Maybe. A lot of our members are retired and older, and they don't like to come out in winter. Just wait until summer—we actually get tour busses stopping by."

"Kind of like a magical history tour?"

"You've got it."

I was about to go back to my office when Eric appeared in the doorway, looking worried. "Sorry, Shelby, but can I borrow Nell for a minute?"

I met his concerned gaze. "We're all set anyway. What do you need, Eric?"

Eric didn't answer but urged me toward my office, bypassing his desk outside. Once in the office, he said, "Hadley Eastman's assistant, Chloe, is downstairs. That woman fired her with no notice, and she's real upset."

I wasn't surprised, given what Marty had told me and what I'd seen firsthand of how Hadley treated Chloe, but I wondered why she'd come here. "I didn't know you two were friends."

"We aren't—the only time I've ever seen her was when she was here with Hadley this week. But maybe I'm the only person who's been nice to her lately. Anyway, do you mind if I bring her up here? I figured you didn't want her to sit in the lobby weeping—it might scare off some of our patrons."

I was confused. Why was Chloe so upset? I would think that she'd rejoice that she was finally free of prima donna Hadley, but maybe she was in dire financial straits and couldn't afford to lose the job. And maybe . . . she could tell me something about Hadley. "Sure, bring her up."

"Thank you, ma'am. I'll try to find a quiet corner and see if I can calm her down." Eric headed back toward the elevator, and I took my seat behind my desk and tried to figure out what else I was supposed to be doing at the moment. At least I could check off the Executive Committee meeting, which I thought had gone as well as I could have hoped, and the staff meeting, too. What next?

I'd managed to put in a constructive half hour clearing necessary paperwork when Eric rapped on my door, with a teary-eyed Chloe hovering reluctantly behind him. "Nell, sorry to bother you again, but I thought you really ought to talk to Chloe. About Hadley."

I wondered if I'd ever work my way through the pile of papers on my desk, but I did want to hear what Chloe had to say, especially if Eric thought it was important. "Sure. Chloe, come in and sit down."

Chloe came in and sat timidly. "Look, I'm really sorry to be a pest. Eric told you Hadley fired me?"

I nodded. "I'm sorry to hear that, although I understand that happens a lot with her."

Chloe nodded. "Yeah, I knew that, but I thought I could handle her. And I thought at least I could learn something about publishing and stuff. Maybe it would have been okay if it hadn't been for what happened at Let's Play."

Eric was still hovering in the doorway. "Eric, come in and shut the door, and sit down," I said. "You're the one Chloe asked for, right? Why was that, Chloe?"

Chloe sniffed. "Eric was nice to me the other day when Hadley was throwing one of her hissy fits. Which she does maybe every ten minutes. It's like, Chloe, carry this; Chloe, get me that. No matter what I do, it's not enough. I would have quit weeks ago, but I'm flat broke. And she owes me money. Not just my salary, but she's always asking me to get her a latte or pick up her dry cleaning, and she never remembers to reimburse me for it."

I was beginning to get impatient. Was I supposed to take care of all of the local orphans and strays? "Was there something different that set her off this time?"

"The police asked for her records. Her correspondence with her publisher, stuff like that. She went off the deep end, said that was private, and they should get a warrant."

"That's probably true, and she's within her rights." And then I realized that as her assistant, Chloe probably knew what was in those files, and I could ask her . . . It was slippery moral ground, but I wanted to help Arabella, and I really didn't like Hadley. I decided to approach this indirectly. "Chloe, did the police question you?"

Chloe nodded, new tears springing to her eyes. "I didn't know what to do. I mean, I had to tell the truth, didn't I? Even though I knew I'd lose my job. Which I did."

I chose my words carefully. "Did Hadley have something to hide?"

"Maybe. I'm not sure."

I took a deep breath. "Maybe you should tell me what you're worried about, and then I can help."

"Could you? But, I mean, it's not like I have anything real to tell anybody."

"Were you working for Hadley when the planning started for the exhibit?"

"No. That was about three assistants back, but at least they left pretty good records."

"Was Hadley pleased with the way things were going at the museum?"

Chloe snorted. "Ha! Is Hadley ever pleased about anything?" She leaned forward in her seat. "Look, here's what I know. Based on what I found in the files, and what I've overheard, Hadley's publisher told her that her sales numbers were dropping and maybe she should look at some new ways to expand her audience. The message was, either the numbers pick up or you're toast. So after she went into a royal snit, she started thinking about things she hadn't tried, and she brainstormed with the publicist and they came up with the idea to approach the museum. I mean, Hadley's local, so it was a logical tie-in. And the publicist promised to chip in some promotional bucks for the exhibit and getting the word out. This was maybe two years ago?"

That matched what Arabella had told me. "Did you get the impression that Hadley thought she was doing the museum a favor, or vice versa?" I asked.

"You've met Hadley—what do you think? But the memos that went back and forth made it sound like the museum was calling the shots. I mean, everybody benefitted, but the museum set the timetable and the scope of the display, not Hadley. Anyway, the announcements about it went out in all the museum's promotional stuff, so that was good exposure for Hadley. And to be fair, I think once she realized what was on the line, she did pitch in and try to help. But it might have been too little, too late. That silly hedgehog is a nice character and all, but she's kind of out of step with the times, isn't she? Kids these day, even the really young ones, want something more than cute talking animals."

"Did anyone tell Hadley that?"

Chloe shrugged. "I don't know—maybe. Not me, that's for sure. I think her agent kept trying to let her down gently—there was a little bump up in sales when the exhibit was announced, but not as much as the publisher wanted to see. So this exhibit opening was really, really important to Hadley."

I mulled over what Chloe had told me. Hadley needed a success, or her career might be on the line. Or at least, she needed to get some attention. But would that have included rigging the exhibit display to do harm? Would that include a deadly weasel? Maybe that was Hadley's idea of taking her work in a new, edgier direction. Or she hoped to milk the event for a lot of tearstained network interviews, defending the beloved hedgehog and pals? Based on what little I'd seen of Hadley, I wouldn't put it past her. But if she had somehow been behind the incidents, why had she stormed into my office and ranted at me? How could that benefit her? Unless she wanted to make this an even bigger story by piggybacking off the Society's recent unpleasant events . . .

I realized Eric and Chloe were looking at me expectantly. "Chloe, what did you tell the police?"

"All of this. I mean, I couldn't give them the documents, but I could tell them what I knew, right?"

"And how did they respond? Wait—was there a detective named Hrivnak there?"

"A kind of chunky woman? Yeah, she was there. I don't think she got the whole hedgehog and publishing thing, but she was paying attention to what I told her."

I had trouble envisioning Meredith Hrivnak in a children's museum—she wasn't exactly the maternal type. But would the detective see a motive for Hadley to sabotage the exhibit, or the opposite? Hadley wasn't a warm and fuzzy person, either, and she had her eye fixed on the bottom line, selling books. Did disaster sell?

But there was still one big sticking point: how could Hadley have done it? "Chloe, how much time did Hadley spend at the museum while the exhibit was being installed?"

"Lately, lots. She really wanted to make sure they got it

right. I mean, she even bitched—oh, excuse me— complained that they hadn't made Harriet look happy enough, and that Willy looked too snarky. I think they had to change Willy's head a couple of times before she was satisfied. It was kind of creepy—she kept the heads sitting around at her house so she could decide which one she liked best."

Now that was interesting. If Hadley had had the heads at home for a while, she could have had someone else rig the wiring for her, or figured it out for herself. From what Barney had told me, the whole setup wasn't particularly complicated. Even if there had been multiple tests of the equipment, Hadley had been in and out of Let's Play often enough that it was possible she could have tweaked Willy after the testing was done. But it was hard for me to make the leap from diva behavior to rigging Willy's wiring. "Is Hadley good with her hands? I mean, does she make things, do any craft work?"

Chloe shook her head. "Nope. She can barely keyboard. Didn't you notice her manicure? No way she'd risk those nails, much less actually do some real work."

I couldn't say that I had—I just wasn't tuned into that kind of thing. "When did she decide which head she liked best?"

"Early last week, I think—I'd have to check her calendar. Arabella or Caitlin would know. I know the installation crew was getting really fed up, and I think Arabella had to put her foot down: no more changes."

"And when was she there last?"

"The Wednesday that the guy died, when she and Arabella got into a fight over the heads. After that, last week, maybe? Monday or Tuesday, I think."

Opportunity *and* motive. I wondered how hard the police were looking at Hadley. But I was still troubled by the mechanics of rigging the head. I'd read that short brochure on wiring, and I was nowhere near ready to deliberately cross wires to achieve what had happened. I didn't think Hadley was any better qualified than I was, so she must have had help. "Chloe, is Hadley seeing anyone?"

"In the time I've worked with her, she's dated at least three guys that I know of, and I'd bet there are some that I didn't. She goes for the young blue-collar type—hunky but not too intellectual. That way they're too intimidated to argue with her, and they think she's brilliant because she writes books, even if they're only children's books. And she doesn't keep them around long."

That was promising. The right construction worker could certainly know the rudiments of electrical wiring. I wondered if the police had already gone down this road.

Chloe seemed much calmer now. "Listen, I know this is real pushy, but do you have any job openings here?"

Smart girl, to seize the opportunity. And she had given me some useful information. "I can't promise anything, but I can certainly ask. It's likely to be something low level, like shelving books, if that's okay."

"After working with Hadley, that'd be great—books don't yell at you. Thank you, Nell. I mean it."

I glanced at Eric. "Why don't you show Chloe the library, and I'll call Melanie?"

Eric grinned. "I'd love to. Chloe, follow me."

I watched them leave, and then I picked up the phone. Luck was on Chloe's side: it turned out we had a short-term slot with grant funding, doing some reorganization of one of our collections. It might not last long, but it would let her get back on her feet. Chloe had helped me, and I was happy to be able to repay the favor.

CHAPTER 21

I headed downstairs in search of Eric and Chloe, to give Chloe the good news, but instead I found Barney waiting in the lobby.

"You got your membership card already?" I asked.

"Yes, ma'am, I did. Shelby hand-delivered it, and I thank you. I had some time between jobs, so I thought I'd check this place out. I'm just waiting for your guy here"—he nodded toward Front Desk Bob—"to track down that librarian you said could help me."

"Felicity Soames. Bob, I'll take Barney to the reading room. He's signed in, right?"

Bob nodded, and I led Barney through the catalog room into the large reading room beyond. Barney studied the soaring ceiling and the tiers of books around the perimeter and on the balcony above, and gave a low whistle. "Wow. Nice place. I wouldn't know where to start."

"You haven't looked at our collections before? You said you'd been doing research for a while."

"On and off. I don't get much free time, and it's just kind of a hobby, really."

Felicity was seated behind her high desk, surveying her domain. The reading room had a few people in it, and one of our shelvers was delivering requested materials to the patrons. I led Barney over to the desk. "Felicity, this is Barney Hogan, the person I told you about who's interested in what we have on baseball history."

Felicity's eyes lit up. "The Quakers, right?"

Barney grinned. "Yup. My great-great-grandfather played for them, and I'm hoping you have some team pictures."

Felicity looked at him critically. "He must have been a baby when he played for them."

It took Barney a moment to find the compliment buried in her statement, and then he grinned. "Yep, he was all of eighteen."

Felicity picked up her phone. "Let me find someone to cover the desk for me, and I'll show you what we've got." She spoke into the phone, then stood up. "When Nell told me about what you wanted, I started to do some digging, and I've already set aside some files about the team in back. Ah, Janie, there you are. If you can hold down the fort for a while, I'll get Barney started."

I was clearly superfluous, but since I knew next to nothing about local sports history, I wasn't insulted. "I leave you in good hands, Barney. Happy hunting!"

I'm not sure he even heard me, as Felicity led him toward the elevator and her office upstairs. It looked as though I'd made at least two people happy today.

As I was trying to figure out what came next on my to-do list, I realized I still needed to tell Latoya about Marty's offer at the Executive Committee meeting to fund part of the registrar's position. I was pretty sure that Marty hadn't discussed the issue with Latoya first; they didn't get along well. So Marty had told me—and the core board members—first and left me to deal with the fallout. But that was my job now. I squared my shoulders and headed for Latoya's office on the third floor.

She looked up when I reached her door. "Hi, Nell. Sorry I didn't make the staff meeting this morning, but I had a problem with my car, and I had to leave it with the mechanic. Did I miss anything?"

I took a seat across from her. "Kind of. At the Executive Committee meeting last night, Marty announced that she's setting up an endowed fund to supplement the salary for Alfred's replacement. I gather she still feels kind of responsible for what happened with him. I wasn't about to turn her down, and she's going to lean on the rest of the board to contribute. We haven't had a lot of interest in the registrar position so far, so I think we have time to sort out Marty's contribution. Do you have someone in mind?"

Emotions flit across Latoya's expressive features. Annoyance came first, but she smoothed that over quickly. "I have put some feelers out among my colleagues, but being able to offer a better salary should spark some interest."

So far she was playing nice. "I've also asked Shelby to look into any matching grants Do you have a job description for the position handy?"

The always well-organized Latoya reached into the bottom drawer of her desk and pulled out a piece of paper, then handed it to me. "Of course. This is what I gave Melanie."

"Thank you. I'll give this copy to Shelby. Anything else we need to discuss? Do you have the documentation for the cataloging software?"

"I'll have a complete package together for interviews. I

should tell you that I've been working with the FBI to refine the list of what's gone missing. I think we're making progress, but we shouldn't expect too much. Sadly, I think some items are gone forever."

As was Alfred. "I know, but I hope we've done all we can."

"Was there anything else, Nell?" Latoya looked at me expectantly.

I stood up. "No, that's all. I just wanted you to know about the funding change."

"Thank you," she said gravely—and waited for me to leave.

I left. Maybe I was her boss now, at least on paper, but she'd never had much time for me before, and some of that attitude still lingered. We'd have to work on that.

I dropped the registrar job description on Shelby's desk and went back to my own. The next time I looked up it was three o'clock, and I hadn't even remembered to eat lunch—again. I was interrupted by a phone call from Felicity.

"Nell, Barney's about to leave, but he wanted to thank you first. You have a minute?"

"Sure, I'll be right down." I could use the exercise—maybe the blood would return to my brain if I actually left my chair. It seemed to work, because I had a thought as I walked to the stairs, or maybe a series of thoughts. Barney was probably in his sixties and apparently had been an electrician and union member most of his adult life. Could he have known Nolan Treacy? Would he know, or could he find out, if Nolan was actually in Philadelphia at the moment? It was worth asking.

I found Barney and Felicity in the catalog room, still deep in conversation. Barney was clutching a thick sheaf of photocopies, and he looked dazed but happy. Felicity was doing much of the talking, and Barney nodded now and then. They didn't notice me until I was a few feet away from them.

"You look like you've had a successful day," I said.

Barney nodded vigorously. "Yeah, really. Felicity here was great—she really knows her stuff."

"Well, of course I do—that's why I'm head librarian," she said, softening her statement with a smile. "But I love all that early baseball history. I'm so glad I could help! I'll keep looking, if you've got the time to come back again?"

"Sure, I'd love to."

As I watched the two of them smiling at each other, I wondered if I had started something more than research here. I knew exactly nothing about Felicity's personal life, and even less about Barney's, but I'd never seen either look so animated. Interesting.

"Barney, if you've got one more moment, I'd like to ask you something," I said.

He tore himself away from Felicity's gaze. "Oh, sure, no problem. What?"

"Maybe we should take this someplace more private?" It wasn't the kind of question I wanted to ask in the middle of a busy—well, sort of busy—public room. "Thanks, Felicity," I said, then led Barney to the old boardroom under the stairs.

He looked confused. "What's this about? You still thinking about electrical problems?"

"Kind of." There was no simple way to lead into this, so I just jumped right in. "Barney, have you ever known an electrician named Nolan Treacy?"

"Nolan? Yeah, sure. We were both in the union back in the eighties, and then he left town. I hadn't thought of him in years until recently."

My radar went into overdrive. "Why recently?"

"He's in town, visiting, and came by the union hall, a week or two ago, looking for his old mates. We all went out and had a few drinks. Why're you asking about him?"

So Nolan could have been in town in time for the Let's Play accident. "Did you know he was once married to Arabella Heffernan, the woman who runs Let's Play?"

Barney sat back in his chair, clearly surprised. "That I didn't! Back in the day, we weren't exactly buddies, and we never talked about families, just about work. But he was really into the whole Sinn Fein thing back then. Kept asking us all to contribute to the cause, that kind of thing."

"Before he left Philadelphia?"

"Yeah, and then he just fell off the map. Somebody said he went back to Ireland. I know I didn't hear from him again until the other week, like I said."

I wondered if I'd end up in hot water with James if I kept asking questions. I should just tell Barney to talk to the FBI, but I didn't know how he'd react to that suggestion. "What's he doing back here in Philadelphia?"

Barney shrugged. "Said he was just visiting."

"How did he seem to you?"

"What're you getting at? He used to be a real jumpy kind of guy, with a gift of gab. But we're both twenty-some years older now, and he's more laid-back—like we all are, I guess. I know he's got kids back in Ireland, too—he showed us pictures."

So Nolan had remarried, after he left Arabella. His visit sounded completely innocent—or was he hoping to set up something more? I was so not prepared to deal with this kind of thing. "Did he say whether he'd seen his ex-wife?"

"Didn't come up. Why all the questions, Nell?"

I had to decide which way to go, and I opted for the simple truth. "The FBI is looking at him for the electrical accident at Let's Play, since he was connected to Arabella, and he may have terrorist ties."

Barney stared at me for a moment, then laughed out loud. "You've gotta be kidding. Hey, we were all young then, and most of us had Irish relatives, so some of us were into that whole scene. But that's a long way from doing anything violent, apart from handing over some cash now and then. Are you saying Nolan went back to Ireland and got into it there?"

"I don't know. But the FBI apparently has reason to check it out. Do you know where he's staying?"

"He didn't say. We talked about getting together again, but we didn't set a time. But I think you're barking up the wrong tree here. The idea of Nolan being a terrorist . . . You might as well suspect me. It's a sad turn of events when old pals can't get together for a drink without being suspected of plotting the overthrow of something or other. And him, a man with kids? I can't see him going after a kiddy museum."

"Was he angry with Arabella?"

"How the hell would I know?"

Great, now I was making him angry. "Barney, I'm sorry if I've upset or insulted you in any way. I'll admit I find it far-fetched, too, that a guy who hasn't been in Philadelphia for decades would show up now and stir up trouble. But he is an electrician, and he did have some sort of terrorist ties, once upon a time. Wouldn't you rather the FBI checked it out, before someone else gets hurt?"

Barney didn't look convinced. "I guess. You want me to ask around, see if anyone knows where to find him? That way he can clear things up."

"I don't want to make trouble for anyone, including Nolan, but maybe he should know that the FBI would like a word with him. Again, I'm sorry if I've caused any hard feelings between us, and I appreciate the information you've given me. Are we okay?"

"Sure, no problem. You've done me a great service here, getting Felicity to help me out, and it's the least I can do to thank you. I'm sure it'll all be nothing, in the end."

"Good. I'll see you out. And I hope you'll come back again."

"Already planning to—Felicity said she had some ideas where to look next. You've got a whole lot of stuff here."

"Don't I know it!"

I escorted Barney to the front door and then headed back to my office, wrestling with an internal debate: should I call James and tell him what Barney had said about Nolan? Maybe I was worried about nothing. Maybe James had already confirmed that Nolan was in town. Maybe it really was Nolan whom Arabella and I had seen at the Market.

I decided to say nothing for the moment. I didn't want James to know I was meddling in his business. Upstairs, half the offices were dark already—people tended to leave on the dot of five on Fridays, especially at this time of year when it was cold and dark out. Eric had left a neat stack of phone slips on my desk. The top one was from Arabella. Did I want to talk to her now? I checked my watch: nearly six. I didn't have her home number, so I would call her office and leave a message, and clear my conscience.

I was surprised when she answered her phone. "Oh, Nell, thank you so much for calling me back. I really need to talk to you."

"Now?"

"No, I can't tonight. Is there any way you could come by my house tomorrow morning?"

On a Saturday? I considered turning her down but realized with embarrassment that I had no weekend plans. She sweetened the pot by promising breakfast, but she didn't say anything more about why she needed to see me so urgently. Still, she wasn't the hysterical type—although I could imagine that dealing with Hadley had pushed her over the edge—so I assumed she had a good reason for asking. Besides, driving into the city would take me no more than forty minutes, so what excuse did I have to say no? "Tell me how to get there."

CHAPTER 22

As arranged, Saturday morning found me driving to the city. Arabella lived in a quiet neighborhood east of the Philadelphia Art Museum. She had probably bought it years ago when she first married, when the neighborhood had been a bit seedier—and more affordable—than it was now. The house itself, when I located it, proved to be small and charming, its trim newly painted, its brass knocker gleaming. I parked on the street, then approached the door and knocked. I heard the tap-tap of shoes on what must be bare wooden floors, and then Arabella opened the door.

"Oh, good, you found it. Nell, I'm so sorry to interrupt your weekend, but I thought this was important. Come on in. Can I get you some coffee?"

She led me down the narrow hall with a steep staircase along one side, to the living room at the back. I stopped on the threshold, because there was someone else there I thought I recognized: "You're Nolan Treacy."

The man had risen when I appeared, and now stepped

forward to offer his hand. "I am. I hear my name's been getting tossed about lately."

"It's come up," I said cautiously.

Nolan raised both hands in protest. "I'm a respectable man with nothing to hide."

Arabella interrupted. "The FBI got in touch with me the other day to ask if I knew where Nolan was. I hadn't seen him since we split up, decades ago, but it turns out he's been in town for the past few weeks. The FBI talked to some of his old friends, and they passed the word to him, and he got in touch with me late yesterday. I wanted you to hear what he had to say, Nell, since you've been so helpful to me. Unfortunately it doesn't seem to get us any closer to figuring out who messed with the exhibit, but I guess we can eliminate a few possibilities. Let me set the food out so we can eat. I'll just be a minute." Arabella bustled toward what had to be the kitchen. I stood in the doorway, unsure of what to do next. Nolan looked equally ill at ease.

"So," I finally began, "you and Arabella were married?"

"We were, years ago. Nineteen eighty, it was. Caitlin was born in 1985, but we were already having problems by then. I returned to Ireland shortly after we split in 1990."

I felt uncomfortable talking about such personal matters with a man I didn't know. Heck, I barely knew Arabella. "What brought you back now? Have you been back to this country since you two split?"

"I haven't. I had a lot of things to sort out, back home, and I guess my life kind of went on. Arabella divorced me after I left. I've remarried, and I'm a father again now."

"Come help yourselves," Arabella called out.

I got up and made my way to the dining room, relieved to be able to put off this conversation. Arabella had laid out a pretty spread of breakfast goodies, nicely arrayed on fine china. Was she showing off for Nolan? Given the way she was keeping as far away from him as possible, I guessed that there was no lingering affection on her part. I wondered about the whole story behind their split, but no way was I going to ask. I took a plate and filled it, and when we were all ready, we returned to the living room.

"I don't mean to spoil this lovely food, Arabella, but can you tell me, why was it so urgent for you to speak with me in person?" I asked.

She sighed, and set her plate down on a delicate side table. "I thought you'd want to hear the story. The FBI asked me if I knew where Nolan might be staying. At the time I told them the truth, which was that I hadn't seen him, or at least I wasn't sure—and then yesterday he called me out of the blue." She sent an angry look Nolan's way. "I didn't want to meet him alone, and that's why I asked you to join us. But I don't know what to do about the FBI. Should I call them? I don't want to get myself in any trouble about this by not telling them. I thought perhaps you had more experience dealing with the FBI?"

I wondered why she hadn't just asked me for a contact name at the FBI, but I could see that she might hesitate at just turning her ex-husband over to them, whatever her past or current feelings were. I tried to work out the best way to explain my odd connection to the FBI, and settled for the simplest. "When we had our problems at the Society, I got to know the local agent in charge, James Morrison. Normally he wouldn't be involved in the investigation of the incident at Let's Play, but when they found the connection between you and Nolan, he was called in." Both looked blank, so I added, "The IRA terrorist angle."

It took Nolan a moment to figure out what I'd said, and then he burst out laughing. "That old business! So that's what this is about? That was mostly blather back in the day—it was a different time, and tempers ran a bit high. But beyond sending a few punts back to the boys at home, I was never *really* involved with the IRA or anything like it. I'm almost flattered that they'd see me in that light, but it's got nothing to do with this now."

Arabella was watching him coldly. "You certainly talked a good line, Nolan. That was one of the things that split us up—you were always going off to some bar to recruit people or collect more money."

Nolan looked at her. "That's what I told you, love, but mostly I wanted to get out of the house. I'll admit it now—I wasn't ready for marriage then, especially after Caitlin came along. I was too young and too full of myself. It wasn't fair to you, and I figured the best thing I could do for you was to walk away."

Arabella's color darkened. "Well, thank you so much for running back to Ireland and leaving me with a baby and a mortgage and no way to support myself! You never sent a penny. You never even asked how we were."

Nolan held up his hands in surrender. "I was wrong, Bella. I signed the divorce papers, didn't I? I figured you were better off without me. I did think you'd remarry, though."

Arabella was not placated. "And when did I have time to find a new husband? I was holding down a job and taking classes at night and trying to be a mother to Caitlin. And after the way you'd treated me, I wasn't exactly eager to find a replacement."

"I'm sorry—I know it can't have been easy. You've done well for yourself, though."

If I'd been uncomfortable before, it was ten times worse being in the middle of a couple rehashing old grievances.

"Listen, you two—you can argue all you want about what's past, but what's it got to do with the mess at Let's Play?"

Arabella took a moment to steady herself before she answered. "I apologize, Nell. You're right—you don't need to hear about our dirty laundry. But this FBI inquiry really threw me, because I didn't expect it, and until this morning I hadn't seen Nolan for years."

"You saw him two days ago at the Market, right?"

Arabella nodded. "I thought I was seeing a ghost. I couldn't be sure, and he looks so much older."

"Ah, you cut me to the quick, darlin'," Nolan said lightly.

Arabella turned back to face him. "Don't you make a joke of it, Nolan. You left me in the lurch. Now you're back, and so far all you've done is make more trouble for me. Don't you realize this is serious? You've got the FBI looking for you now, and the police."

"I'm sorry. You're right, of course. But it's just a case of bad timing. You can't think I had anything to do with that problem at your museum, can you?"

"I don't know what to think, and it really doesn't matter. What counts is what the FBI and the police think. You're an electrician, or at least you used to be, and you've had ties with organizations on their watch list. That makes you suspicious to them. You certainly could have set up that death trap at Let's Play, and if you're wondering about motive, they might guess that for some insane reason you had decided to get back at me by attacking what I've made of myself, what I love. Can you even see that? Or are you still completely clueless?"

I'd had enough. "All right, that's it. The quickest way to move forward is to talk to the FBI. I'm going to call my friend. Nolan, if you really want to clear up old issues—

and if you have nothing to hide—you should talk to him." Before he could respond, I turned on my heel, stalked to the hallway, and called James on my cell phone. Without thinking, I hit the speed dial for his office first and was startled when he answered. "What are you doing in your office? It's Saturday."

"So I've been told. Hunting for terrorists, among other things. Why did you call my office if you didn't think I'd be here?"

"Force of habit. In any case, if you're looking for Nolan Treacy, I've got him."

"What? Where are you?" James sputtered.

"I'm at Arabella Heffernan's house. Want to come over?"

"Nolan's there?"

"Yes, unless he's sneaked out the back door in the last three minutes. You coming?"

"Yes." He hung up without formality.

I went back to the living room, relieved to see that Nolan hadn't vanished, though Arabella still looked none too happy to have him there. "Arabella, you might want to get out another coffee cup. Agent James Morrison is on his way over. Nolan, James is one of the good guys. If you play it straight with him, he'll do right by you."

Arabella finally smiled. "See? That's why I called you, Nell. You know how to make things happen."

I tried not to choke on my coffee.

James arrived precisely seven minutes later. Arabella answered the door and escorted him in, making twittering noises about coffee and pastries. He bore it with patience, but when he walked into the living room, his eyes fixed on Nolan Treacy and didn't move. Nolan stood, and the two men sized each other up. Arabella hovered between them, eager to keep the peace—it was, after all, her home. Me, I stayed out of the way.

"Mr. Treacy," James began, "were you aware that the FBI and the police wanted to speak with you?"

"Not until I spoke with my former wife yesterday. And it's Nolan, if you will."

"Won't you all please sit down?" Arabella pleaded. "Would you like coffee?"

Everyone turned down coffee, but at least James and Nolan took seats, which reduced the tension in the room. "What brings you to Philadelphia at this particular time?" James asked.

"Making amends for my sinful ways. Sorry, that sounded a bit flip. Let's put it this way: I've finally grown up, or so I hope, and I thought I owed it to Arabella to apologize to her face for the trouble I caused her, back when I left."

"How long have you been in the country?"

"A couple of weeks. All nice and legal—want to see my passport?"

"Yet you waited this long to contact your former wife. Why was that?"

"Cold feet? I was trying to get my bearings again, after so long. The city has changed a lot in twenty-odd years. People have changed. And then I heard about the trouble at the museum, and I thought maybe I shouldn't make her life any more complicated than it already was."

"Have you seen your daughter, Caitlin, yet?"

Nolan's eyes darted to Arabella. "I wasn't sure how she'd take me showing up out of the blue. She was no more than six when I walked out of her life. I thought I should test the waters with Arabella first."

I noticed that Nolan hadn't quite answered the question.

James launched his next question. "Were you planning to stay around long?"

"What're you asking? Do I have a home, a family, a job to go back to? The answer would be yes to all three. My wife understands why I need to do this. My children back home are in their teens, and I hope they have happier memories of me than those I gave Caitlin. I've been running my own business for years. But this . . . It's *closure* you say over here, isn't it?"

"Why now?"

Nolan looked away. "My health—I've got prostate cancer. I've probably got a good few years left to me, but it's an uncertain world. I thought I should get my traveling out of the way while I could still manage it."

James studied him silently. I held my breath. Everything that Nolan had said seemed reasonable, and I had little reason to doubt him, but the timing was troublesome. Nolan had come back to this country for the first time after twenty years, and a few days later there had been an electrical accident at the institution run by the wife he'd abandoned years earlier. Coincidence?

I didn't like coincidences. Neither, apparently, did James. "At the time you left this country, you were a member of the electrician's union. Are you still an electrician?"

"I am. I have my own business in Bagenalstown."

"Are you aware of the circumstances of the accident at Let's Play?"

Nolan didn't answer immediately, and when he spoke I thought I understood why—still covering for his union pals. "I might have heard mention of it, here and there."

"Could you rig up something like that?"

"I don't know the details, but I'd wager I could—sounds simple enough. But why on earth would I want to?"

James ignored the question. "Did you know the dead man?"

Nolan cocked his head. "And who would that be? I haven't been reading the papers, you know."

"Joe Murphy."

"No, may the poor soul rest in peace." Nolan shut his eyes for a moment.

"Were you aware that your daughter's boyfriend was injured before Joe was killed?"

Nolan snapped to attention at that. "No, sir, I was not! I know nothing about any boyfriend, but if he's my daughter's choice, why would I do him harm? This whole thing's a joke! Why would I come back to this country after twenty years and try to destroy Arabella's business and my daughter's happiness? You'd have to think me mad, man!" He sat back and glared at James.

I had to admit he had a point. Twenty years was a long time to hold a grudge, and if there were a grudge to be held, that honor went to Arabella rather than Nolan. I turned to James to see how he would react. His slumped shoulders told the story. He sighed. "Mr. Treacy, I have no reason to suspect you of anything. Your former connections with Irish malcontents put you on our local watch list, and I was asked to follow through on that. I'll choose to believe you when you tell me that you didn't know we wanted to speak with you. I've spoken with you now, and I don't doubt your story, although I would be remiss if I didn't verify it."

"Of course," Nolan said, gracious in his triumph. "I'll be happy to give you anything else you need."

"I'll ask that you keep me apprised of your whereabouts, at least until we've cleared this up. How long did you intend to stay in Philadelphia?"

"I'd planned to go home in a couple of weeks. I've booked my flight, if you want to see that."

"That shouldn't be a problem. Mrs. Heffernan, could I trouble you for some of that coffee now?"

We maintained a strained civility for as long as it took to consume a cup of coffee, and then I stood up. The men politely followed suit. "If you don't need me for anything else, I've got a desk full of paperwork waiting for me," I said, to no one in particular.

James looked surprised. "You're going to the office today?"

"I am. If you recall, I'm still the new kid at the Society, and I've got a lot of catching up to do."

"I'll walk you out," he said. He turned back to Nolan and Arabella. "You can stop by my office and leave me a list of names to verify your whereabouts, Mr. Treacy. I'll let the police know I've talked to you."

Arabella was fluttering. "Nell, thank you so much for coming by. And Mr. Morrison, I hope it wasn't too much trouble for you . . ."

"Not at all, Mrs. Heffernan. At least I've accounted for your ex-husband. Nell, let's go."

CHAPTER 23

On the sidewalk, after Arabella had closed the door behind us, James turned to me. "Can I buy you a cup of coffee?"

"Business?" I asked.

"In part." He smiled.

I smiled back. "I guess. I drove—my car's parked over there." I pointed across the street. "You want to meet somewhere?"

He named a sandwich place on Locust Street, and we split up to retrieve our cars. As I drove down Market Street toward City Hall, admiring the view, I was glad for some time alone to sort out what I had just witnessed. Nolan Treacy had surfaced in Philadelphia twenty-some years after he'd left. He told an appealing story, but was it true? If he was in fact an Irish terrorist, albeit low-grade, he would be good at making up stories, wouldn't he?

I parked in the lot across the street from the Society and checked my watch: there was no point in going to my office first. Instead, I got out and walked up Locust Street toward the restaurant. It was still early for lunch, and the chill in the air tended to discourage tourists, so most of the people on the street were moving quickly to get to their destinations. As did I. But James was already waiting at the restaurant when I arrived.

He held out my chair for me, and I shrugged out of my coat. A waiter appeared and handed us menus.

"Didn't I just eat at Arabella's?" I asked. I sighed and asked for coffee. James did, too, and ordered a sandwich to go with it. "So, what do you think?" I asked, once we were settled.

James smiled. "I'm not supposed to tell you, you know. But I have no reason to believe that Nolan is anything other than what he says he is. We did a basic check: he's a small-town Irish electrician, with the wife and kids he described. In fact, he's got a son working for him as an apprentice of sorts. His company did pretty well during the Irish boom years, but now he's got a bit more free time on his hands, which may be why he decided this was a good time to make this trip."

"Did you check his medical records, too?" I asked.

"No, we did not. Look, this isn't hush-hush spy stuff—we made a couple of phone calls to our counterparts over there. Nolan has no record with the Irish police, and it looks like his life is an open book. It's true that he flirted with Sinn Fein years ago, but so did a lot of people, and we have no reason to think that he's had anything more to do with them since."

My coffee arrived. I added sugar and sipped. "So he's a dead end."

"No, he's a loose end that I've just tied up. I get to write up a report and copy it to the police department. Not that they ever thought Nolan was a serious suspect, as far as I can tell."

I sighed. "Do they have any other suspects?"

He shrugged, which didn't tell me much.

"Is that a *no* or an *I don't know*?"

"Nell, do you really want to be in the middle of this?"

"No! But Arabella keeps calling me. And I did put you together with Nolan, didn't I?"

"Yes, you did. You've done your civic duty. But I'd guess Arabella would have shoved him in our direction anyway."

"You picked up on that, too? No love lost between them. I have to say, he did abandon her, and she has a right to be angry."

"Even twenty years later? After she's done so well for herself?"

"Well, apparently this is the first time she's been face-to-face with him since he left. She'll probably get it out of her system quickly." But for a moment my heart ached for Arabella, who was being buffeted from all sides: first the death at the museum, now the wandering ex. I hoped she was resilient.

"Let the police handle the incident, Nell. You can be a friend to Arabella, but that's all."

"You're telling me to stay out of it," I completed the thought for him. "I'd be delighted to. Is this the end of the business part of lunch?"

"It is. Unless there's something new at the Society."

"We're still waiting for you to find our collections. And still hunting for a registrar. I assume Marty mentioned what she wanted to do about that?" He didn't know that I knew that he had volunteered to help boost the funding for the position, and I wondered how he would respond.

I could swear he blushed. "She might have mentioned something. We're still working on the collections angle. Don't worry, we haven't forgotten. Don't give up hope."

"At least I've made a couple of people happy. I talked to this other electrician who's really into local baseball history, and I think Felicity is sweet on him."

James's eyebrow went up. "*Sweet on him?* What, are you a matchmaker now?"

"Anything to keep my staff happy."

James's lunch arrived, and we bantered over it, and over another cup of coffee after. It was fun. Three months earlier I would never have guessed I'd be having lunch with an FBI agent, much less flirting with him. Flirting? I thought I'd forgotten how. Anyway, it was a weird mix of business and pleasure.

Finally he said, "This is nice, but that blasted report should go out today."

"So you're going back to the office? I should, too. I can get a lot done when the administrative staff isn't around on the weekend—no interruptions."

"Would you consider scheduling something else on a weekend?"

"You mean, with you? I could probably fit that into my calendar."

"I'll call you. And I'll take care of lunch. You finish your coffee." He rose and headed toward the cashier. I stayed where I was and admired the cut of his topcoat. Nice shoulders under that grey tweed.

I felt good. The feeling lasted until I got back to the Society. I came in the front door and took a quick scan of the reading room. It looked fairly well filled for a Saturday, especially considering the season and the rather cold and gloomy weather. Of course, I knew well that a truly committed researcher wouldn't let anything deter him or her from the pursuit of a tiny but critical detail. Still, it warmed my heart that there were people here today, doing what we were here for.

Felicity beckoned me over and said in an excited whisper, "I think I found a picture for Barney!"

I replied in the same hushed tone. "That's great. Are you going to call him and tell him?"

I could swear she blushed. "I couldn't do that. Does he have email, do you think?"

"I can check the membership list when I go upstairs. Good work, Felicity. I know he'll be happy."

"I hope so."

She turned back to help a patron, and I headed for the elevator. I didn't make it, because Rich Girard waylaid me before I got there. "Can I talk to you about something, Nell?"

Rich had been hired to catalog the massive Terwilliger Collection of documents, and had been making steady progress, with Marty egging him on. Had Marty been pushing him too hard? "Sure, Rich. Is this about the Terwilliger Collection?"

He looked around. "Uh, no. Can we go to your office?"

"Sure." Mystified, I led the way to the elevator and then to my third-floor office, turning on lights as I went. As I had anticipated, none of the administrative staff was in today. Inside my office, I hung up my coat and pointed Rich toward a chair, then sat down behind my desk. "So, what's up?"

"It's about Eric Marston," he began, looking uncomfortable.

"Eric?" I hadn't expected to hear that.

"Yeah, your new assistant, right? Uh, how much do you know about him?"

Where was he going with this? "Not a lot. Shelby Carver found him for me, and so far he's been doing a great job. Do you have a problem with him?"

Rich wouldn't meet my eyes. "You know he's gay?"

I sat back in my chair and looked at him. Rich was the last person I would have suspected of homophobia. "I haven't asked about his personal life. Nor should you be interested in it."

He had the grace to look embarrassed. "Oh, no—hey, I don't care what he does on his own time. But, well . . . this is complicated. When you showed him around, I thought he looked kind of familiar, but I didn't think anything more of it. But last night, I was out with Carrie, you know? And we hit some clubs. And that's when I remembered where I'd seen him before." Rich stopped, apparently reluctant to go on.

"At a club?" I really didn't know the local club scene.

"No, outside a place, when I was walking by. With some cops. It looked like he was getting arrested."

Something inside me went cold. Eric hadn't mentioned anything about any criminal record, but then, I hadn't asked, had I? Nor had I requested that kind of background check on him. I had trusted my instincts, because I liked Eric and he had looked like he needed a break. Shelby had vouched for him, but I barely knew her, either. Had I been wrong? "When was this?" I asked, my voice tight.

"A while ago. Six months, maybe? I remember it was warm, so it had to be summer. Look, I really didn't want to bring this up, because he seems like a nice guy. But I know a lot of people are looking at the Society under a microscope these days, and I wanted to be sure that you checked it out."

He was right, much as I hated to admit it. "Thank you, Rich. You were right to bring it to my attention. Was there anything else?"

Relieved, he bounded out of his chair. "Nope. Cataloging's going great, and thanks for sending Chloe our way. That'll make things go faster, once I show her the ropes."

"I'm glad I could help." I watched his retreating back, then slumped in my chair. Damn! I fix one thing, and another one pops up. How could I discreetly find out if Eric had a history with the police? Well, duh—I could ask him. But he wouldn't be around until Monday, which gave me two whole days to stew. What was our liability if we hired people with criminal records? I had no idea, and I really didn't want to ask anyone and send up red flags.

Why was nothing ever easy? With a sigh, I turned to the waiting pile of paperwork. At least that I could do.

CHAPTER 24

I spent the rest of the weekend wondering what I would say to Eric on Monday—and wondering what my seat-of-the-pants decision to hire him said about my management skills. I hadn't had any training or preparation for stepping into the role of president, and I had certainly never coveted the position. I had been happy doing my former job, drumming up funding for worthy projects and making sure that our members were happy enough to keep renewing their membership, and to keep giving. Every dollar counted when you were as perpetually strapped for cash as the Society was.

Administration at the highest levels required a lot of skills, and I wasn't sure I had them all. There were definitely some things I could manage. I could put together a budget. I could prioritize projects and delegate tasks. I could stand up in front of a crowd and make an impassioned case for supporting the Society. All good. Where I was afraid I was inadequate was in managing people as a leader. I wasn't comfortable telling other people what to do, and frankly, I didn't like trying to manipulate them to do my bidding. I relied on goodwill and friendly persuasion and instinct. Had my instinct let me down with Eric? I hadn't asked him any hard questions, and had offered him the opportunity to prove himself on the job. So far as that was concerned, he was doing quite well. His lifestyle choices were his own business, unless he acted wildly inappropriately in-house, and in my time I'd seen enough extracurricular activities in the stacks to know that our policy was flexible, to say the least. As long as the work got done, administration didn't care what you did with whom, and I supported that policy.

But a criminal record was another matter. We were an institution that served the public, and our reputation was a very real asset. Undermine that and we were in trouble: donors had plenty of choices for where to spend their philanthropic allowances, and we were already on shaky ground after our recent scandal, with donors questioning our integrity. Employing known criminals after all that was definitely pushing the limits. If it was true. But I'd been working with Rich for the better part of a year, and I didn't think he would have brought this to my attention unless he was convinced that he had in fact seen Eric in a compromising situation.

And, I had to remind myself, I hadn't looked any more closely at Shelby, taking her at face value, too. Melanie had told me she was checking out Shelby's résumé, but had she? I made a note to myself: talk to Melanie on Monday and find out what her vetting process was, and what she'd found out about Shelby. Or Eric.

Stewing was getting me nowhere. I resolved to shove all Society-related matters into a closet in my head and shut the door until Monday. Everybody ran into a few glitches during transitions. Didn't they?

———

Monday I took the train in early. I liked arriving before everyone else. The old building was still and dim, taking its time to wake up in the morning. I'd always felt as though I owned it when it was empty, even before I had risen to the top job. Now it *was* kind of mine . . . along with all its responsibilities.

I was both relieved and dismayed to find Eric already at his desk, looking all shiny bright and eager. On the plus side, I could get this discussion over with quickly; on the minus side, it might ruin his day, or week, or life.

"Hi, Eric, you're in early. Can I talk to you for a minute, in my office?"

"Sure. Coffee first?"

"No, let's wait on that. Come on in, and shut the door."

He did, looking mystified and apprehensive. I hung up my coat and sat behind my desk, facing him. "Eric, I won't beat around the bush. Someone I trust said that not long ago you were seen outside a club, apparently involved with the police. Is there something you need to tell me?"

Eric's face fell, and his eyes filled with tears. "I'm sorry," he whispered. He waited a moment, then cleared his throat. "A few months ago I was arrested. The charges were dropped. It was the first and only time it happened."

Could I believe him? I knew I wanted to. "Eric, I'm counting on you to be honest with me. Can you tell me a bit more about what happened?"

"I'm not proud of it. Look, I didn't tell you that part of why I moved to Philadelphia was because my folks didn't want to have anything to do with me when they found out I was gay. I figured I might as well move somewhere new, and after college I ended up in Philadelphia over a year ago. I tried really hard to find steady work when I got here, but I didn't know the place, and the economy sucks, so I ended up temping. Which meant I didn't stay in one place long enough to make friends, and I was pretty lonely. When I had some money to spare, I'd do a little clubbing, but I wasn't into the party scene in college, and I wasn't looking to get into anything here. I was just trying to get out of my crappy apartment, you know?" He looked at me like a puppy, hoping for approval.

"Go on. How did you end up being arrested?"

"I guess I just read the signals wrong one night. I mean, I wasn't doing anything illegal, as far as I know. I thought I'd connected with this guy, and he said, why not come to my place? We'd both been drinking, so I said, sure, why not? And after that I'm not sure who said what. I swear to God, I never asked for money or anything like that. Heck, I even paid for our drinks. But when we got outside on the pavement, he told me he was an undercover cop and I was under arrest for solicitation."

I'd heard about such sweeps in the city, although I would have thought the local police had enough to keep themselves busy dealing with real crime without hassling harmless hookups between consenting adults. "Why did they drop the charges?"

"Apparently the arresting officer had a history of jumping the gun. He's a real homophobe, plus he'd been drinking—lots of people saw him. I was turned loose after a couple of miserable hours, and I don't think I've been out after dark since."

"So no criminal record?" I asked.

"No, ma'am." He swallowed. "Look, Nell, if this is a

problem for you, you can let me go, no hard feelings. I don't hide what I am, and I know that makes some people uncomfortable . . ."

I stopped him there. "And I'm not one of them. Eric, you've done a good job for me so far, and I don't care what you do in your personal life. But I do need you, and anyone else I hire, to be honest with me, because I'm responsible for this whole place. If you say this was just a misunderstanding, and there's nothing else like it lurking in your past, then we're good. Does that work for you?"

Eric broke out in a big grin. "It sure does. I like it here, and I enjoy working for you. You ready for coffee now?"

"I am." I watched his retreating back and sighed with relief. I did like Eric, and I didn't want to start hunting for another assistant. But this little tempest in a teapot had definitely put me on notice: check everything and everyone, twice. Like it or not, I was accountable for all things great and small at the Society.

I settled down at my desk to get something accomplished. Mondays were usually so peaceful, since we weren't open to the public—not that the patrons of the reading room downstairs were exactly a rowdy bunch. But there was something soothing about the silence of the place.

Until Eric came back with coffee—and with Shelby. She looked worried. My heart sank into my stomach. What now?

Before they could speak, I said, "Do I want to hear this?" I took the coffee that Eric handed me. He looked at Shelby.

"Probably not, but you should," Shelby said.

I took a sip of coffee, sighed, and said, "What?"

"Eric just told me what you just talked about. About his arrest and all."

"Did you know?" I wasn't sure what answer I wanted from her.

Shelby shrugged. "Not in so many words, but I knew there'd been some trouble. That's why I wanted to help him if I could, and I figured this job would be a great solution for everyone."

So far I didn't see any issues. "Then what's the problem?"

Shelby looked away. "I figured this was as good a time as any to come clean. You know that résumé of mine? It's kind of a fairy tale."

Great. Another imposter. "You told me you didn't have a criminal record. I remember distinctly asking you that."

"I don't! I'm as pure as the driven snow—at least as far as the police are concerned."

"But Melanie checked out your references, right?"

"She did. But . . . I kind of, uh, enhanced some of my experience, and then I told my friends back in Virginia to back me up. Melanie did her job, so don't blame her."

This day just kept getting better. I slumped back in my chair. "Tell me."

"Well, the general outlines are true. I didn't even lie about my age! I've lived here for two years, and I'm married to John and I have a daughter, Melissa. But a year ago John got laid off, and we spent a whole lot on Melissa's education, and now she wants this no-holds-barred wedding, so I'm really, really hard up for money. So when I saw this job listing, it sounded perfect."

"Do I dare ask what real experience you have?"

"Back in Virginia, I was a society wife—lots of parties and good works. I helped raise money for a lot of things, and I did a good job of it. Except I didn't get paid for it."

"So you're saying you have no professional experience in development?"

She shook her head. "Sorry, Nell. I *was* a member of my local historical society but never in any official capacity—not that they did much anyway. But I do love history," she ended lamely.

Great. I'd made a total of two new hires, and both had turned out to be keeping secrets. What was I supposed to do now? One part of me said I should boot them both out because they hadn't been completely honest with me. Another part said that I didn't have time at the moment to dump them and try to find two replacements. Still another part of me told me that I didn't want to fire them because I liked them both, and my gut said they were decent people who'd happened to get themselves into difficult situations and were just doing the best they could. Which sounded rather familiar.

Shelby and Eric were watching me like two cats keeping their eye on a large dog. I didn't want to be a dog; I wanted to be on the side of the cats. But I'd given up that option when I'd said yes to the board last month.

I laid both hands flat on the surface of my desk. "Okay, here's what we're going to do. I'm angry at both of you for misrepresenting yourselves to me, even though I understand the circumstances. I appreciate your coming forward, even though you might have been forced into it. To be honest, I need you both. Let's just leave things the way they are for now, okay? And if either one of you has forgotten to mention some other big black hole in your past, or if I catch you taking any shortcuts now, or lying to me or to anyone else, you'll be out of here so fast you won't know what hit you. With no severance and no recommendations. Got it?"

Eric nodded.

"Thank you, Nell," Shelby said softly. "I'm sorry."

"That's all we need to say. Now go get some work done, will you?" I said, trying to sound both benevolent and authoritative at the same time. It wasn't easy.

They left, contrite. I looked at my watch: it was barely nine o'clock. What else was this day going to bring?

CHAPTER 25

I decided to work through the lunch hour, and sent Eric out to find a sandwich and bring me something back whenever he was done. He was still acting like a whipped puppy, and he was thrilled to be able to do something for me. He'd been gone for half an hour or so when Front Desk Bob called up to say that Caitlin Treacy was in the lobby. What did she want this time? "I'll be right there, Bob."

When I entered the lobby I found Caitlin standing there, dwarfed by a large basket of not only cookies and flowers but also what appeared to be a stuffed animal lurking amidst the greenery. "Hi, Nell," she said. "Mother wanted to thank you for helping sort things out over the weekend." She held out the basket. I took it—and nearly dropped it. Arabella must have been *really* grateful.

"So she told you about it?"

"You mean about my father? Yes. Anyway, I've got to get back to Let's Play. And I've been using the advice you gave me the other day. It's been a big help. Bye." She turned to go, leaving me with a hefty basket and a lot of unanswered questions. Not much of a response for a woman who hadn't seen her father in twenty years.

Eric pulled open the door from outside and stopped to hold it for Caitlin. He continued to hold it, staring after her, until I called out to him. "Eric? Is that my lunch?"

He started, then turned to me. "Oh, sorry, yes. Who was that who was leaving?"

"That was Caitlin Treacy, Arabella's daughter. She works at Let's Play—she's the person who's handling the *Harriet* exhibit."

"Huh," Eric said, still looking puzzled. "I thought she looked familiar, but I've never been to Let's Play. Anyway, I assume you want to eat your lunch?"

"Definitely."

Upstairs I took my lunch to the staff room at the rear of the building, both to keep my desk clean and to hide out from anyone who might come looking for me. Since it was past the lunch hour, there was no one around, and I managed to enjoy a few minutes of peace and a good sandwich. I was just folding up the wrapper to throw it away when Eric appeared, looking triumphant.

"I knew I'd seen her somewhere!" he announced.

"Who? Caitlin?"

He dropped into a chair across from me. "Yes, only when I knew her she was Kathleen Treacy. I didn't put it together with Caitlin, or with Heffernan, her mother's last name."

"I thought you grew up in Virginia. How did you know Caitlin?"

Eric looked around, then leaned toward me. "It's kind of complicated. Maybe we should take this to your office. And ask Shelby to join us. I think she knows Kathleen, or Caitlin, or whoever she thinks she is, too."

"Okay," I said, mystified. I gathered up my trash, threw it out, and followed Eric back down the hall. As we walked, I asked, "What's with the confusion of names?"

"Something about honoring her Irish roots, I think. That's what I heard."

As soon as we reached his desk, Eric dialed Shelby, who appeared a few moments later. I led them both into my office and shut the door, and we distributed ourselves between the damask-covered visitors' settee and the matching armchair. "What's going on? Why so hush-hush?"

"Let me back up a minute," Eric began. "Shelby, you can fill in as I go. You're right, Nell—I grew up in Virginia. I knew pretty early that I was gay, but my folks thought that maybe a good private school could straighten me out—uh, pun intended—so for high school they sent me to Bishop's Gate School. It's a boarding school, and I think they were glad to have me out of the house. It was a good school academically, but it also had a reputation for helping out kids with issues, which I guess is what they thought I had. I did well enough there to get into a good college, even though it didn't change the fact that I liked boys. I met Shelby's daughter, Melissa, at Bishop's Gate, although she was a year behind me—and Caitlin or Kathleen or whatever she wants to call herself was a year ahead. But it was a small school, so everybody knew everybody else."

"Okay," I said cautiously. "So Kathleen Treacy from Philadelphia was at your boarding school in Virginia?" Something seemed odd there. "What's the problem?"

"Kathleen—can I stick to that for now? Because that's how I knew her." When I nodded, he continued. "Kathleen didn't want to be there any more than I did. She was one of the 'difficult' kids"—Eric made air quotes—"that the school took on. She didn't hide that."

I still didn't see where this story was going. "Look, you two, this is all very nice, but what's it got to do with anything?"

"Because Kathleen hated her mother, and she was always talking about it to anybody who would listen."

It must have been a small school. "Lots of teenagers claim to hate their parents, or so I'm told—obviously I can't speak from experience."

Shelby spoke for the first time. "Kathleen was there for four years, and I never once saw Arabella at any school event, and I was at most of them. Melissa wasn't a boarder, and she always brought home the kids with nowhere to go for Thanksgiving. And Kathleen was always among them, not that she was exactly sociable. But I really couldn't understand Arabella. Kathleen's an only child, right? Doesn't that seem rather harsh, to send her off and not even visit? The school wasn't all that far from Philadelphia."

I was beginning to understand their concern. "You're saying that Arabella, who runs a children's museum, didn't spend any time with her own child?"

Shelby nodded. "That's about the size of it. Of course, Kathleen said she didn't care. She didn't want to see her mother anyway. But that's what a lot of the so-called orphan kids said. I even took her out to dinner once, along with Melissa, but she wasn't exactly easy to talk to."

"It was more than teenage sulking?"

"I think so. I asked Melissa about it after we got through that endless dinner, and she said Kathleen was like that most of the time. Melissa said she had real trouble making friends, and she was always blurting out the most inappropriate things. You know, *I'm going to say what I think and I don't care who it hurts*."

"Interesting. She graduated, right?"

Eric answered. "Yes, she did, and she went off to college. She had good grades, and she worked hard—maybe because she didn't have many friends. I certainly wasn't one of them."

"So let me get this straight. We've got a young woman who had a few difficult years in her teens, and who said things that sound like what a lot of moody, resentful teenagers say. Her mother sent her away to school and didn't visit her much. But Arabella was a single mother after her husband left, and I heard she took a lot of night classes while she was working full-time. And she must have found a way to pay Caitlin's tuition. Sure, maybe Caitlin resented it, but now she's here working for the mother she claimed to hate back then. You don't think she just grew up and got past whatever her earlier problems were?"

Eric and Shelby exchanged a glance. "Maybe," Shelby said. "Look, I'm no expert, but I *am* a mother, and I think Kathleen might have needed more help than the school gave her, at least early on. Maybe you're right, and she grew past her problems and patched things up with her mother, and everything's peachy. And I'll admit it's been a few years since I saw her, but she's the last person I would have expected to move back and work for her mother. I would have imagined she'd head for someplace like California, to get as far away as she could."

I looked at each of them in turn. "Okay, let me say what you're not saying. You think Arabella's daughter could be behind the incidents at Let's Play?"

Shelby said carefully, "I wouldn't rule it out, based on what I know of her."

"But her boyfriend Jason was the first victim! And she's got to have been working at Let's Play for at least a couple of years. Why now?"

"That's true. But maybe the incident with Jason was a mistake or a warm-up for the real thing. Or maybe it's because Daddy's back in town and that's reopened a lot of old wounds."

We all fell silent, briefly. Nolan had implied he hadn't been in touch with his daughter since he'd arrived. Maybe he had ducked the question because he didn't want to upset Arabella further. "What is it you think I—or we—should do, then? Talk to Arabella? Ask Caitlin directly if she's killed anyone lately?"

"I don't know," Shelby said. "But it's better to have the whole picture, don't you think?"

"I guess." I didn't want to know this. I didn't want to have to go to Arabella and ask her whether her daughter was a potential murderer, and I wasn't about to complicate things by taking a vague suspicion to the police. So I made an executive decision: I would sleep on it. Maybe in the cold light of morning the situation would look clearer, or at least different. "I'd like a little time to think it over before I go to Arabella. She's got enough to worry about right now as it is. Are you comfortable with that?"

Shelby stood up. "I think that's fair, Nell. Maybe I'll call Melissa tonight and see if she knows anything more."

"Eric, are you good with this?"

"Sure. Let's hope it's just one of those weird coincidences."

I hated that word.

CHAPTER 26

At home that night I kept vacillating. I was not a mother, and I had little insight into the complexities of a mother-daughter relationship. But I had, of course, been a teenager once, and I knew it was a time of extremes, often hormone inspired, that led teens to say and do things that were overdramatic and sometimes irrational. Most of us survived the teen years and became normal, reasonable adults. Since Caitlin was working daily with her mother at the museum, I had to assume that they'd patched things up. I also had to believe that Caitlin was professionally competent; the exhibit planning and installation had gone smoothly . . . up until the point where someone had died, of course. And she'd managed to handle Hadley, which was definitely a plus in my opinion. Running a small museum was challenging under the best of circumstances—it seemed that the less money, the more internal clashes, as each department fought to defend its turf and compete for the small pot of available funds.

The next morning I woke up late. One look out the window and I decided that I couldn't face walking to the station and waiting in the spitting icy rain and gusty wind, so I decided to drive into the city. I went to work and threw myself into the day, and by the time I looked up it was lunchtime. How did that keep happening? At least if I kept skipping meals like this, I might lose a few pounds, which wouldn't be a bad thing. Of course, if I kept sitting at my desk digging through piles of papers that needed my signature or my sage comments, my derriere was going to spread far and wide—one reason why I tried to walk as often as I could around the city.

The phone rang. Eric answered it and then called out, "It's Mrs. Heffernan."

"I'll pick up." I matched my actions to my words. "Hello, Arabella. Thank you for sending the lovely gift basket. What's up?"

The tone of Arabella's voice immediately set alarm bells ringing. "Oh, Nell! Caitlin's missing."

"What do you mean, missing?" Had Caitlin suddenly decided that this whole museum mess was too much to handle? Had she and Jason fled to a happy island in the sun?

"Jason tells me that he saw her at breakfast and she seemed all right. Maybe a little stressed out, but we all are at the moment, aren't we?" Arabella laughed ruefully. "But she never arrived at work, and she's not answering her cell phone."

Was Arabella overreacting? Caitlin couldn't have been out of touch for more than a couple of hours. Maybe she had gone somewhere to clear her head. I stalled. "Is that unusual?"

"No, she's usually very conscientious. And she told Jason she was on her way to work when she left. Oh, Nell, I'm afraid something's happened to her!"

Since we still hadn't figured out who or what the attacks

at Let's Play were directed at, it was all too possible that there was something sinister about Caitlin's disappearance. Should Arabella talk to the police?

She had already thought of that. "I called that awful detective, and she said that Caitlin was an adult and we weren't even sure she was missing, so there was nothing she could do. Then she hung up on me."

That sounded like Detective Hrivnak, but I had to agree that from her perspective it was a reasonable response. So, we couldn't expect any police help right now. "What do you want me to do, Arabella?" I had to ask, even though I had no idea what I *could* do at this point. "Do you want me to come over?"

"Could you?"

"I'm on my way. See you in half an hour." I hung up and stared at my phone.

Eric appeared in the doorway. "Trouble?"

"Caitlin's gone missing. Maybe it's nothing, but Arabella's upset. It seems unlikely anything's happened, but on the other hand, if there really is something wrong and I didn't go over to help Arabella, I'd hate myself."

Eric nodded in agreement, then said tentatively, "Maybe this is out of line, but do you want me to come along? Maybe I can help?"

It wasn't a bad idea. He had known Caitlin during a difficult time in her life, and he might have some insights. "Okay, why not? After all, you know Caitlin, too."

It was after two when we finally left the building, bundled up against the harsh wind. The rain had stopped, but the sky was still densely grey. Even so, I decided it was too much trouble to try to extricate my car from where I'd parked, since it was unlikely I'd find parking easier near Let's Play, and all the cabs were occupied. "I guess we're walking. Will you be warm enough?" Eric's thin leather jacket was obviously intended for Virginia winters, not Philadelphia city gales, and the cheerful wool scarf wrapped around his neck wasn't much help.

"Don't worry about me—just keep moving fast and I'll stay warm!"

We did. It took about twenty minutes to reach Let's Play, and the young woman at the front desk sent us up to Arabella's office. When we reached it, Arabella bounced out of her chair and came over to hug me before I'd even taken off my coat.

"Oh, Nell, thank you for coming! I know I seem silly, but I'm so worried. Oh, excuse me—who's this?" She'd finally noticed Eric, hovering behind me.

"I'm Eric Marston, Ms. Pratt's assistant. I was at Bishop's Gate with Kathleen—Caitlin."

Eric stepped forward and offered his hand, and Arabella shook it cautiously, studying him. A frown flashed across her face and disappeared quickly. "Did you know her well?"

"Not very, but I thought maybe I could help."

I dumped my coat on a chair and turned to face Arabella. "Sit down and tell me what you think is going on. Why are you so worried?"

Arabella sat behind her desk and glanced briefly at Eric before starting to talk. "Caitlin's very responsible, very organized. She always plans, and she always does what she says she will. She told Jason that she was leaving for work."

"How does she get to work? Drive? Train?" Arabella had said something about Camden, across the river, when we first met, but I wasn't sure what that commute would be like.

"Sometimes she takes the train. Sometimes she and Jason come in together, but not today. She drove her car today, and Jason took the train in later. He's still taking it easy, and he'd just gotten up when Caitlin left."

"You've talked to him?"

"Of course. Do you think we should include him now?"

Why not? The more the merrier. Although on some level I believed that Caitlin would walk in at any moment and ask what all the fuss was about. Maybe she was out somewhere picking up supplies for the exhibit opening—assuming, of course, that it was going to open on schedule. Arabella picked up the phone and called someone to track down Jason. "He's still working here?" I asked.

Arabella nodded. "Just finishing up the last details. Thank goodness he wasn't seriously hurt. Caitlin would have been devastated."

"How long have they been seeing each other?"

"A year now?" Arabella said, clearly distracted. "Caitlin moved out of the house in June, I think, and they've been sharing a place ever since."

"Does she enjoy working here?" I wondered if Arabella would be truthful.

"Until this recent mess, I would have said yes. You must think it odd, that she's here. Fears of nepotism and all that. Eric—have I got it right?—I know you must have heard what she thought of me a few years ago, but we've worked hard to get past that. When I offered her the job at Let's Play, she was clearly the best qualified candidate for the position. She majored in business administration in college, but she took a minor in early childhood education. I was so happy when she joined us! And she's done a great job! She handled Hadley so much better than I could have—I simply have no patience with that woman. Oh, Jason, there you are."

Jason was slouching in the doorway. "Hi, Arabella. What do you need?"

"Jason, you probably don't remember Nell Pratt, given the circumstances under which you met—she was here when you were hurt. And this is Eric . . . ?"

"Eric Marston. I'm Nell's administrative assistant. And I knew Caitlin years ago, at school in Virginia."

"Jason, you haven't heard from Caitlin, have you?" Arabella asked anxiously.

He shook his head. "Nope, and my cell's been on."

"She seemed fine, as far as I could tell, when she came by yesterday," I volunteered. "Did anything happen after that, that might have upset her?"

Jason shrugged. "She got home a little late, but she seemed up. She mentioned seeing you, Nell, and she said you'd given her some good ideas. Caitlin's worked really hard on this exhibit. She felt guilty about my accident, too, since she's the one who brought me in to help—she knew I needed the work."

"You're a graduate student?" I asked.

"Yeah, at Penn. Money's kind of tight, so when Caitlin said she needed some temporary help finishing up the exhibit, I jumped at the chance."

"No aftereffects from your shock?"

"Nah. I had a headache for a day, but that's about it. Caitlin takes this whole exhibit very seriously—it's the first one she's handled by herself, and I think she wants to prove herself. And she's very detail oriented, which is why she was so bothered by the electrical shorts. That's something that shouldn't have happened, period."

"Jason," Arabella appealed to him, "do you have any idea where she might have gone? She didn't say anything about an errand? Something she had to pick up? Did she talk to anyone after she got home last night?"

"I don't . . . wait, there was a phone call, around nine. She picked up but didn't talk long."

"Did she say who it was?" I asked.

"I think she said it was her father."

"What?" Arabella exclaimed.

I was equally, if more quietly, surprised. I tried to remember exactly what Nolan had said about contacting Caitlin, and remembered again how he'd kind of ducked the question. "This wasn't the first time she'd heard from him, was it?"

Jason looked between Arabella and me. "No, I don't think so. She's been writing to him for months. Sorry, Arabella, she didn't want you to know."

I turned to Arabella. "She never told you?"

"No!" she snapped. "She knows how I feel about him. He abandoned us and never looked back. I've had nothing to do with him for years, decades even. How did they ever find each other? I wouldn't have known where to look for him."

"He's never contacted her? He *is* her father," I said, trying to defuse the situation.

"He never tried," Arabella said. "Not that I would've let him when Caitlin was younger. I can't say what went on when she was in college, but she never mentioned him to me."

"I think she started it," Jason said. "It's not hard to find people with the Internet nowadays, and Ireland's not that big."

"Do you think that's why he really came back—to see Caitlin?" I asked.

Jason shrugged. "I don't know. She told me he'd been in touch, but she was kind of secretive about him. She didn't want to bring him to our place, and I'm not sure she wanted him to meet me. It was like she wanted him all to herself, at least for now. Why, do you think maybe she's with him?"

"She used to talk about him at school," Eric said, speaking for the first time. I'd forgotten he'd even come along. We all turned to look at him, and he shrank back in his chair. "I got the impression that he was a sort of heroic figure to her. He was some kind of noble revolutionary who'd been forced to flee the country because he was being pursued by the authorities for his political activities—and because her mom pushed him away. The fact that he never got in touch with her meant she could idolize him without pesky reality getting in the way."

Arabella looked devastated. I stepped in. "Do you know how to get in touch with him?" I asked her. "I think he needs to be part of this conversation. Either Caitlin's with him, or he might know something."

Arabella shook her head, her jaw tight. "I don't know. I didn't ask, when I saw him."

"Jason, do you have any idea?"

"If I was home, I could look at the phone and see the listings for recent calls. Sorry—can't do it from here."

I thought for a moment. James no doubt had an address for him, but I didn't want to drag the FBI into this situation—yet. Barney Hogan had said he knew Nolan slightly, had seen him around town recently. Maybe he knew where Nolan was hanging out these days. Shelby would have Barney's number. I stood up. "Excuse me—I'm going to make a call."

I stalked out into the hall outside Arabella's office and called Shelby on my cell phone. When she answered, I said without preamble, "I don't have time to talk right now, but can you give me Barney's phone number? Does he have a cell?"

"Yes, ma'am—that's how I reach him." She read me off the number, which I copied on a scrap of paper.

"Thanks. I'll fill you in when I have time." I disconnected, then immediately called Barney, waiting impatiently through five rings. Thank God he finally answered. "Barney, it's Nell Pratt. I can't explain right now, but do you know where I can find Nolan Treacy at the moment?"

Barney, bless him, didn't waste time asking stupid questions. "He's made himself at home at O'Reilly's, on Chestnut. You want me to roust him from there? I'm only a couple of blocks away."

"Would you? And if you don't find him there, could you let me know, and spread the word that his ex needs to talk with him? It's about his daughter."

"I'll do that." He rang off. A no-nonsense man, exactly what we needed at the moment.

I went back to Arabella's office, where three sets of eyes swiveled toward me. "I've got someone looking for him. It may be a while. Does anyone have any more ideas? Jason, any friends Caitlin might contact? Arabella, is she close to anyone here at the museum?"

They both hesitated, just as the phone on Arabella's desk rang. She looked at it as though it were a snake, then reached out a hand and snatched it up. "Hello?"

I watched as her face fell. Not Caitlin, then. But not bad news, either.

"Nolan, you get yourself over here now! If Caitlin's not with you, she's missing, and you've got to tell me what you know." Arabella listened for a moment, then hung up. "He's on his way."

CHAPTER 27

Arabella had calmed down a bit by the time the front desk called to say that Nolan had arrived. We'd spent the intervening time going over the same sparse information. Caitlin hadn't called, and she still wasn't answering her phone. I had no constructive ideas, so I devoted some of my time to watching the rain dribble down the windows of Arabella's office. If the temperature dropped much, it would turn to sleet.

Nolan appeared in the doorway to the office, a cliché tweed cap dangling from his hand. Arabella didn't rise to greet him. She was sending a clear signal: this was her domain, and she was in charge here. The rest of us nodded at him.

"What's going on?" he demanded. "Something about Caitlin?"

"She's missing," Arabella said flatly. "Would you know anything about that? I understand you've been in contact with her for some time. A fact you neglected to mention to me."

It was interesting watching Nolan trying to decide what tack to take with his clearly angry ex-wife, as expressions chased across his face. Resentment? Contrition? In the end he said, "She tracked me down, said she wanted to know me better. I *am* her father."

Arabella pointed to a chair, and Nolan sat. "Yes, and a lousy one," she said. "Funny, you never had much time for her before."

Nolan held up both hands in a gesture of surrender. "I've admitted that, and I've apologized—to you and to her. I was wrong. I was young and stupid. But what's that do for us now? Tell me, why is it you think she's gone missing?"

"Jason, here . . ." Arabella began and then stopped herself. "Oh, right, you two haven't met. Nolan, this is Jason Miller, Caitlin's fiancé. They live together, in case she hasn't mentioned that. Jason said you and Caitlin talked on the phone last night. She left for work this morning, or at least that's where she told Jason she was headed, but nobody's seen or heard from her since. Do you know anything about that?"

"We talked, yes. We were going to try to meet up after she got off work today. She said she's been busy with this exhibit, but she really wanted to see me. That's all."

"You hadn't seen her before this?"

"I did, a time or two. Bella, what's all the fuss about? She's an adult."

"And she's under a lot of stress. There's the exhibit, and you might recall that there was a fatal accident here two weeks ago. She really doesn't need you in the mix, not right now."

Nolan shook his head. "She said she wanted to see me again. She didn't mention a thing about troubles at work. And as for the death, I'd only just arrived when that happened. Yes, before you ask, I saw Caitlin the same day as I landed. She'd been pushing for us to get together for a long time."

"Which she never told me," Arabella said bitterly. "What did you talk about?"

"This and that. We had quite a lot to catch up on, you know."

"Tell me, how long has this been going on?"

"A few years now. She was in college at the time. Like I said, she found me, not the other way around."

"Did she ask you for money?"

"She did not! Bella, that was always your fight, and I know I did wrong by you. But that wasn't what she wanted from me. She was curious, is all. Why shouldn't she be? From what she's told me, you tried to erase me from the face of the earth, to pretend I never existed. Was that fair to the child?"

"I was angry, Nolan," Arabella said. "You'd walked out on me, and even before that, you weren't around much."

Nolan's face was flushed now. "And I've bloody well apologized for that! What more do you want? You want me to pay for twenty years of back child support? Because I don't have it, you know. I can't make up for all those years, but I'd like to be able to talk to my daughter now without you blowing up in my face. She's her own woman now."

I was getting tired of watching this battle; it was time to step in and get things back on track. "Hey, you two, you can settle old scores later. What we need to do now is find Caitlin. I saw her yesterday, Nolan talked to her last night, Jason saw her this morning, and we all agree she seemed fine. Sometime after eight this morning she vanished, which is out of character for her. The police can't or won't do anything because it's been only a few hours. So either we can do nothing and wait for her to show up, or we can put our heads together and try to figure out where she is." I turned to Jason. "Did you talk about anything this morning before she left?"

Jason shrugged. "I was only half-awake. I got a cup of coffee, and I said something about how I kept having Willy the Weasel flashbacks, you know? The last thing I saw before the lights went out? And how Hadley had spent so much time messing around with the head that it was a wonder that we managed to get it installed at all. And then Caitlin said she had to go and went out the door. That was it."

"Does she usually keep her cell phone charged and on?" I asked.

He nodded. "Absolutely. It's part of her routine. She comes home and plugs it in as soon as she walks in the door. In the morning she grabs it on her way out. Always."

"Arabella, nobody saw her come in today? Could she be somewhere in the building?"

"I already looked everywhere I thought she might be."

"Do you have security cameras?"

Arabella laughed without humor. "No, of course not. No money, and no real need. What's to steal?"

I was running out of ideas. "Does she have any medical problems? Fainting spells? Blackouts? A drinking problem? Anybody?" I looked around our small group. "Jason? Does she take any medications?"

"Vitamins. Allergy pills. And she sometimes has a glass or two of wine in the evening when she gets home, but I've never seen her get drunk." He was looking at Arabella rather than me as he spoke.

"Excuse me," Eric broke in. I think we had all forgotten he was there again. "Was she on any medication when she was at school? Because I seem to remember something . . ."

Arabella shut her eyes for a moment. "She's going to hate me for this," she said, almost to herself. Then she looked around at all of us. "Caitlin has Asperger's syndrome, a mild form. She doesn't like to talk about it—but you know, right, Jason?"

He nodded, looking miserable. "Yes."

"What's that?" Nolan asked.

"It's a fairly mild form of autism," Arabella said, "and it affects mainly a person's social interactions. It's like they simply don't understand what other people are thinking and feeling. So they have trouble making friends. Sometimes they focus on something to the point of obsession. They can be very invested in routines. I probably should have seen it, but I was so busy, and I suppose I didn't want to see it. I could fool myself that she was shy or awkward. I should have wondered why she never had any friends, didn't want to bring anyone home or go to sleepovers. I probably didn't do her any favors by sending her the message that it was just the two of us against the world. Once we had a diagnosis, her problems made a lot more sense."

"She seems to function very well, Arabella," I said. "Those years at school must have done her some good. It looks as though you made a good decision, even if it was hard on you both."

"Thank you, Nell. It *was* hard. She needed more help than any of the local schools could offer. That's when I decided to send her to Bishop's Gate. I did a lot of research, and Bishop's Gate has been very successful in helping children like Caitlin function well in society. Of course, she hated me at the time, and we had some incredible fights. I'm sure Eric can fill you in on her behavior there—

apparently she was a real hellion for the first six months or so. Thank goodness the school could cope with her. I know I couldn't have." Arabella took a breath and then went on. "We didn't get a real diagnosis until right before she went to Bishop's Gate. I just thought she was hard to handle, and I blamed myself. Caitlin was always a difficult child. Even as a baby, she was colicky, and she cried a lot."

"I remember that," Nolan volunteered. "That was one of the reasons I couldn't stand to hang around the house—she was always whining or screaming, early on."

"She outgrew that, you know," Arabella said, a touch of anger in her voice. "But she was always a handful. She challenged me, all the time. It's like the terrible twos went on for years. Her standard response to everything was *no!* first, then *why?* She resisted everything I said. I was always the bad guy, the disciplinarian. She adored Nolan—she was always a daddy's girl. Looking back, I guess I'd have to say he was one of her fixations. And then he left. Maybe you thought you were only leaving me, Nolan, but Caitlin took it a whole lot harder than I did. And it took me far too long to see that there was something really wrong, not just acting out. Nolan left, and I had no money. I had to find a way to support myself and my child, and that meant I had to work long hours, take classes to improve my credentials. The city schools weren't good, so I sent her to a local private school, the best I could afford. She was a scholarship kid, but even so, money was tight. Which meant I had to keep saying no to her, because there were too many things we simply couldn't afford. I was lucky to hang on to the house through it all."

"I'm sorry, luv," Nolan said quietly. "I didn't know. Not that I could have helped you much—I was pretty strapped myself."

"Well, as you can see, we managed," Arabella said bitterly. "But Caitlin was harder and harder to handle, and puberty only made it worse. Then her school stepped in and insisted that I get her psychological testing, and that's when we found out about the Asperger's."

"She's really all right now, Arabella," Jason volunteered. "I mean, even with all the stress she's been under—moving in with me last summer, working full-time, putting together this exhibit—she's kept it together. Even when I was shocked, she was there with me all the way."

"Maybe that was the final straw?" Arabella said sadly. The phone on her desk rang, and she snatched it up. "Caitlin? Is that you?" She nodded at us all to indicate that it was her daughter, listened intently for a moment before saying, "Okay, I will," and then replaced the receiver. She looked up, different emotions fighting in her expression.

"Caitlin's at Hadley Eastman's, of all places. She says I have to come out there, right now—she wouldn't explain."

"Did she say anything else?" I asked.

Arabella shook her head, bewildered. "No, she just said to get there as soon as possible."

"How did she sound?" I asked.

"Really worked up—all her words were rushing together. So, now what?"

"Go to Hadley's. Do you know where she lives?"

Arabella started rummaging through the stacks of papers on her desk. "I know I've got it here somewhere—she insists on sending me letters, all the time . . . Ah, here it is. Someplace in Gladwyne. That's your territory, Nell. Will you drive? Please? I'm too upset to handle driving in this weather right now."

I knew *of* Gladwyne—it wasn't far from my own town of Bryn Mawr. However, it was in another category altogether when it came to status; I couldn't afford a doghouse in that neighborhood. Hadley must have done well for herself with the *Harriet the Hedgehog* books. "Okay, I suppose. Luckily I drove to work today," I said.

"I'm coming, too," Nolan announced.

"We don't need you there," Arabella began, but Nolan cut her off.

"You've complained that I haven't been part of her life. Well, that can change, beginning now. Tell me, Bella—do you think everything's all right with our daughter?"

They exchanged a long silent look before Arabella finally answered. "I . . . don't know. I think . . . maybe something's wrong. And I have no idea why she'd have gone to Hadley's, now of all times. Nell, maybe we should have a man along?"

To do what, beat up Hadley? But I wasn't going to argue. "Fine. Nolan, you can come. Jason, how about you?"

"Of course I'm coming. I love Caitlin, and I'm as worried about her as anyone here."

"All right, it's the four of us." I stood up, relieved to have something concrete to do. "I'm going to go get my car, and I'll come by and pick you up. Half an hour, maybe. Arabella, you look up the directions to Hadley's house. Eric, let's go." I turned and left before anyone could argue with me, with Eric trailing behind.

Back on the street we walked at a fast clip. "Okay, Eric—what the hell was going on in there?"

"Nell, the more I think about it, the more I recall there having always been something a little off about Caitlin. Maybe the Asperger's explains it—nobody ever mentioned that. I don't know. But you can find out what's going on."

"That's my plan. It's probably all totally innocent— maybe Caitlin had some last-minute brilliant idea for the exhibit, and she wanted to clear it with Hadley. Or vice versa. She's an adult, and she doesn't have to check in with her mom every time she blows her nose. I have to assume that she thought whatever it was, was important, to go haring off to the suburbs like this. The best way to find out what Caitlin's up to is to ask her."

We reached the Society in a record fifteen minutes. "Eric, you can hold the fort while I go take care of this. I probably won't make it back to the office today."

"Will do. But let me know what happens, if you can."

"Just as soon as I figure it out myself," I promised.

CHAPTER 28

I really wasn't happy making this trip. I still wasn't convinced that there was any real problem here; that Caitlin hadn't just gotten caught up in some new excitement about the exhibit and not bothered to tell anyone where she was. Why she wanted Arabella to meet her at Hadley's was an open question, but chances were still good that it was legitimately work related.

But even Arabella thought there was something odd about the situation, and I didn't like what I was hearing. Caitlin had been a troubled girl, although to all appearances she had moved past that. But maybe the stresses of her recent responsibilities for the exhibit, coupled with the unfortunate accident, had triggered something?

The weather had definitely taken a turn for the worse. It was already dark, even though it was barely five, and the temperature was dropping. I had to scrape a thin layer of ice off my windshield. The same ice coated the streets, although the early rush hour traffic wore it away quickly. I was pretty sure that the ice would be worse outside of the city. I hated driving in winter.

I arrived at Let's Play without mishap. When I pulled up at the front door, Arabella, Nolan, and Jason were waiting just inside and hurried out quickly. Nolan opened the front door for Arabella, then climbed into my rather messy backseat. I pointed us toward Gladwyne. Unfortunately the most direct route required taking the Schuylkill Expressway, known affectionately as the Surekill. Predictably, some idiot, or maybe several idiots, had tried to drive as though there wasn't any ice, and managed to slam into each other, blocking all but one lane. The flashing lights of the police cruisers and the multiple tow trucks reflected off the wet surfaces—further distracting and slowing the other impatient drivers. Worse, the wind had picked up, blowing the icy rain sideways, and straight into my windshield. I should have had the brains to check the weather report this morning before I'd decided to drive into the city, but it was too late now.

There was no alternate route. We just had to wait it out, a slow and slippery mile at a time. "Why don't you try Caitlin again, Arabella?"

"I have been, every five minutes. The phone goes straight to voice mail."

"Have you or Caitlin ever been to Hadley's house before?" I tried to picture the three of them socializing and failed, but I held out some hope that Arabella might be able to navigate the lanes of Gladwyne.

No such luck. "No, Hadley's always come into the city. We aren't exactly friends, you know. Just between us, that lady is a royal pain in the ass," Arabella said. Nolan snorted from the backseat.

Traffic inched forward again. Particles of sleet slid down my windshield, driven by the wind.

Arabella started talking softly. "I was so happy when Caitlin told me she wanted to work for me—there was a job opening at Let's Play, and I truly believed she could handle it. She'd been doing so well, at Bishop's Gate, and then at college. She could have found a job somewhere else—she has the skills—but I was so pleased when she came to me, I guess I didn't ask too many questions. I thought maybe we could move past the early problems and maybe even be friends, if that's possible for a mother and daughter."

"And it's been, what—two years now?"

"Going on three," Arabella said proudly. "It may sound horrible of me, but her Asperger's is actually an asset. She doesn't usually have to work with people, but she's very good with organizing things and following through. She's terrific at keeping track of details. I had no qualms about letting her manage the exhibit process. I'm proud of her. Of course I kept an eye on her, but I didn't interfere, and everything has gone smoothly."

"I know she's been really happy there," Jason volunteered from the backseat, "especially since she's been working on this exhibit."

Arabella turned in her seat to look at him. "Thank you, Jason. I'm glad to hear that."

"What about handling Hadley?" I asked.

Arabella gave a grim laugh. "After I'd met Hadley, I realized that *nobody* could manage her—people skills were irrelevant. Hadley is so absorbed in Hadley that she wouldn't notice anyway. So, to the best of my knowledge, Caitlin had no problem dealing with her. At least, Hadley never complained, and I'm sure she would have if she could have found a reason."

We all fell silent; the others were lost in their thoughts, and I was using all my attention to focus on the increasingly slippery road. After inching along at a snail's pace for half an hour, the Gladwyne exit was finally approaching. I turned with a sigh of relief—and promptly slid down the ramp, managing to stop at the stop sign at the bottom of the slope only by pumping my brakes carefully for half its length. Luckily there were few other cars taking this exit, and few on the street in front of us. "Which way now?"

"Oh, that's right—I have the instructions." Arabella fished in her purse and pulled out a sheet of paper, squinting to read it. "Left, I think. Yes, left."

I turned left, fishtailing only slightly. The two-lane road was poorly lit and slippery. "How far?" I asked, wrestling with the wheel and moving no faster than twenty miles an hour.

"It looks like two miles, and then you'll turn right."

It was definitely white-knuckle driving. We passed a road sign that showed a horse and rider, another clue that this was an upscale community. Probably a horse would be moving faster than I was at the moment. Still, I was in no hurry, and I saw no need to risk life and limb in order to find out what beef Hadley and Caitlin were hashing out.

The turn loomed on the right, and I slid into it, past a "Dead End" sign. If anything, the new road we were on was narrower and darker than the one we'd left, flanked by looming old-growth trees tossing in the wind. "How much farther?"

"About a half mile. The house should be on the right, if these instructions are accurate. The number's 78."

We crept along, peering through the bleared windows, looking at mailboxes and, in some cases, massive pillars flanking a drive. The houses were set back from the street, and based on the number of windows I could make out through the gloom, substantial in size. Nice neighborhood, or it would be if I could see it, but I was too busy trying to avoid hitting a tree.

"There!" Arabella pointed toward a mailbox. I pulled into the winding driveway—slick as glass—and crept along it until we reached what seemed to be the front of the house. From the look of it, every light in the place was on. There were two cars parked along the driveway. "That's Caitlin's," Arabella said, pointing.

I parked behind it, turned off the motor, and sighed in relief. We'd made it this far. How we'd get back again, I refused to contemplate. Maybe Hadley would put us all up for the night. I had to suppress a hysterical giggle at that thought; I was pretty sure that Hadley would not be a willing hostess.

I carefully turned off the lights and removed the key. "Well, let's go see what's going on."

We formed a rather shaky procession toward the door. No one had sanded the front steps—handsome slabs of stone, now coated with a thin, glistening sheet of ice. At least the front light was on, so we could see where to put our feet. Arabella and I inched up, each of us clinging to a rail on either side of the steps. Nolan and Jason brought up the rear. When we reached the top, Arabella pushed the doorbell, and somewhere inside the house we could hear a pompous bong-bong-bong echoing.

Arabella and I exchanged glances, and then she pounded on the door. "Hadley? Caitlin? Anybody home?"

"It's open," Caitlin answered from somewhere deep in the house. "We're in the living room."

I let Arabella go first. After all, this was her daughter and her problem; I was just the chauffeur. Nolan and Jason followed. We had to guess which way the living room lay—the house was long but shallow, presenting an impressive front to the driveway, but with little going on behind. Ersatz Tudor, probably early 1920s, I thought, as we navigated through a surfeit of exposed dark beams and rough-textured plaster, punctuated by heavy but dim wrought-iron light fixtures. The living room proved to be at the far end on the right side. We were guided in part by a holiday tree still set up against one wall, blazing with hundreds of small white lights, shining like a beacon down the dark hallway. As we came closer, I saw what I assumed were little animal ornaments dangling from the tree. When we came even closer, I realized that they were all tiny figures from the *Harriet* series. Maybe it was a permanent installation. I suppressed a shiver; it was supposed to be cute, but the figures actually made it look as though the tree was infested by vermin. Dead vermin, all hanging by their little necks.

When we reached the arched doorway to the room, I bumped into Arabella, who had stopped suddenly. I looked beyond to see Hadley and Caitlin, standing maybe five feet apart. But what was most noteworthy was that Caitlin was holding what I guessed was a Taser, not that I'd ever seen one up close before, and it was pointed at Hadley.

Then there was a loud crack, followed several seconds later by a thud that I could feel through the soles of my feet, and all the lights went out.

CHAPTER 29

We all froze. The brief glimpse of Caitlin and Hadley facing off in the living room was burned on my brain, but I wasn't sure what we were supposed to do next. It was nearly pitch dark—which meant the power failure went beyond Hadley's house. The neighborhood? The county? It didn't matter. Here we were, stuck in the dark.

Arabella spoke first, her voice surprisingly calm. "Caitlin, what is going on here? What are you doing? Was that a Taser? Put it down, please!"

"Hello, Mother," Caitlin replied in a surprisingly cheerful voice. "You didn't have to bring everyone—I just wanted you to come. Dad, what are you doing here? And Jason? And . . . Nell?"

"I drove," I said shortly. "We were all worried about you. Hadley, where are you standing?" I really wasn't sure if the situation was dangerous or simply ridiculous, but there was no point in all of us bumbling around in the dark until we knew what was going on, and I didn't want to risk running into a Taser.

"I'm over here," Hadley responded. At least she hadn't moved since we'd first seen her. "Will you tell this little bitch to put that thing down?"

Caitlin spoke up. "Sure I will, now that you're all here. And it's not even charged. I wasn't sure she would stay put until you got here without it. But now that I've got witnesses, I don't think Hadley's going anywhere."

"Caitlin, I was worried about you. Are you sure you're all right?" Jason said anxiously.

"I'm fine, Jase. Really. Now you can all hear Hadley's story," Caitlin told him, in an incongruously cheerful voice.

"Darlin', where the hell did you get that infernal device?" Nolan demanded.

There was a small clunk as Caitlin set something down on some invisible piece of furniture, on the side of the room away from Hadley. "It's perfectly legal, you know. I got it when Jason and I moved to Camden—our neighborhood's not the greatest. Jason, you didn't need to come. I've got this under control."

"She attacked me!" Hadley shrieked. "She came into my home and said she had to talk to me, and then she pulls out that . . . thing. She's crazy! Do something! Call the police!"

"First things first," I said firmly. "Hadley, do you have any flashlights?"

"Uh . . . there's one in the kitchen, maybe, although I'm not sure when I changed the batteries. And another one upstairs next to my bed. I think."

"Candles, maybe?"

"Oh, yes, I have candles—over there in the sideboard."

In the darkness there was no way to see where she was

pointing. "Can you find them for us, please?" I asked, gritting my teeth—and hoping she wouldn't take the opportunity to bolt. At least there were several people between her and the door. I heard the sound of movement, then a thud and a muffled "sh . . . oot." Then a drawer opening and the rasp of a match, and Hadley emerged from the gloom clutching a candle. "There are more," she said.

"Then light them, will you?"

I could see well enough to notice the glare she sent my way, but she complied without comment, and shortly we had five stubby candles burning, arrayed on a low table in the center of the room—enough light to see by. I checked the room to find the Taser, sitting like a black beetle on a table several feet away from Hadley and Caitlin.

With light, we were ready to get down to business. Arabella began, "Caitlin, will you tell us why you thought it was necessary to come all the way out here and hold Hadley at . . . Taser point?"

"It got you here, didn't it?" Caitlin said, and then turned contrite. "I'm sorry, I know it was wrong. But I was getting desperate. I mean, she's the great Hadley Eastman, and I'm a little nobody at the museum. Everybody believes her, and nobody listens to me. And the exhibit was about to open—or not open, if this mess isn't cleared up. I couldn't handle the idea of all my—our hard work going to waste, just because Hadley didn't want to take any responsibility for what happened."

In a way it made sense to me. Caitlin had done a great job under difficult circumstances, and I couldn't blame her for overreacting when it looked like it all might come to nothing. Maybe the Taser was a bit over the top, but as Caitlin had said, it had worked, and here we were.

Arabella looked from Caitlin to Hadley and back again.

Then she straightened up and said gently, "All right, Caitlin, we're listening now. What is going on?"

"She"—Caitlin pointed at Hadley—"she's the one who sabotaged the exhibit. She's the one who's responsible for Joe Murphy's death. The one who nearly killed Jason."

"That's ridiculous!" Hadley said. "Arabella, I hate to tell you, but I strongly suspect that your daughter is mentally unstable. Can't you control her? If you don't remove her from my house, I *am* going to call the police."

"Hadley," I said, "I'm not sure you want to do that—it would make all our lives a lot more complicated. I for one am willing to hear what Caitlin has to say. Besides, I don't think they'd get here very fast, and I don't think any of us will be leaving for a bit. If that crash was any indication, I think there's a pretty big tree down out there."

Caitlin gave me a long look, then nodded once. "Thank you, Nell. I don't trust Hadley. I'm sure she could tell you a great tale and convince you of her side of things. After all, she's a storyteller, or she used to be. I'm not as good with words. All that I ask is that you hear what I have to say. She"—Caitlin jerked her head toward Hadley—"can have her turn when I'm done."

I looked critically at Caitlin. She seemed to be under control, and she knew she had our attention. Hadley, on the other hand, looked ready to foam at the mouth. "Then let's all sit down," I said.

Hadley rallied enough to bristle. "Excuse me, this is *my* house. Who are you to give orders?"

I spat back at her, "The sooner you sit down, Hadley, the sooner we'll sort this all out."

Arabella and Hadley both sat, as did I. Nolan and Jason stationed themselves against the wall on either side of the arched doorway. Nolan's eyes were wary, but Jason focused only on Caitlin. Caitlin began to pace back and forth. I hated to admit it, but I did feel better having a couple of men watching my back, at least where Hadley was concerned. Nolan could probably be counted on to side with his daughter in any argument—I just hoped she had something worth hearing.

I cleared my throat. "Caitlin, you've accused Hadley of being a party to Joe's death. What's the story?"

Caitlin continued pacing back and forth, keeping a safe distance from Hadley. "Hadley and I have been working on this exhibit, what, two years now? She's a bitch to work with."

When Hadley started to protest, I gave her a look that shut her up. She could wait her turn.

"I know I'm not really good with people—I never have been," Caitlin went on. "But Hadley was something else. I mean, she did *everything* she could to slow things down, mess things up—and then she tried to blame it on me. I had misunderstood her instructions, she said. I had forgotten to order something, or tell the workmen to do something. After a while I started making detailed notes after each meeting with her, just so I'd know it really wasn't me. It wasn't."

"Caitlin, darling, why didn't you tell me about any of this?" Arabella asked.

Caitlin looked at her mother briefly. "You'd given me this project to manage. I wanted to prove I could handle it. I mean, even I know that difficult people are part of the business, and I wasn't going to run to Mommy every time I had a problem."

"She's making this up," Hadley spat. "I made reasonable requests, suggestions, and she ignored them all. She was going to do things *her* way, no matter what. But Harriet is *mine*—of course I fought to maintain my vision."

So far I thought both women's accounts sounded equally plausible. So how did any of this bickering lead to a death? "Hadley, this is Caitlin's turn—let her finish."

Caitlin smiled briefly. "Thank you, Nell. So, like I said, I started keeping notes. I can tell you about every conversation we had, and we had plenty. You know, Hadley, I was beginning to wonder just why you spent so much time onsite, 'supervising.'" Caitlin made air quotes. "I mean, I know you didn't particularly trust me, but there was a lot of day-to-day construction stuff that you didn't need to approve, not personally. And then there was the whole business with the weasel heads."

Arabella and Nolan looked confused, so Caitlin explained. "Hadley pitched a fit the first time she saw the model for Willy the Weasel. Dad, you probably don't know, but he's the bad guy in the stories, only he's not completely villainous, so we didn't want him to look too smarmy. Anyway, Hadley thought we got his expression wrong the first time around. Okay, I could understand that. After all, she created him, and I agreed that it was important to get it right. So I asked our fabricators to make another one—at our expense. They did—and Hadley hated that one, too."

"He looked mean," Hadley said, pouting.

"Maybe he did," Caitlin replied, "but I thought it was interesting that you didn't complain about any of the other figures, including Harriet, who's the centerpiece of the show. But I went along with you, and we had a third head made. So we had *three* heads, and I showed number three to Hadley, and she *still* wasn't happy. Then she decided to take all of three them home and study them for a bit, get to know them, and then decide which one she preferred. I said, fine, sure—just make sure you bring back the one you decide on by the beginning of the month, because we have to install it and make sure everything works the way it should before the exhibit opens for the public. I didn't want any screwups."

Like a fatal accident? Or a murder? "Then Hadley made a decision?" I prompted.

"Yeah, at the last possible minute. She sat on them for weeks, and then finally, after about seven reminders, she came waltzing in with head number two and told me that she thinks it's the one that best captured the spirit of Willy, even though it wasn't perfect. So I gave the head to the installers to, well, install. Which they did, that same morning. That was the day that Jason almost got killed."

"Wait a sec—we'd tried it out that morning and it worked just fine. And then I got zapped in the afternoon," Jason protested. "What happened in between?"

"Good question, Jason," Caitlin said to him. "Well, you might recall that Hadley here just happened to stop by at lunchtime that day, to be sure we had it right."

"Caitlin, love, would you mind telling me just what goes on with this Willy creature of yours?" Nolan said.

"Oh, right—you haven't seen it. It's what we call an interactive exhibit. The kids can touch the figures and make them do something. Since Willy's the villain of the piece— the one kids love to hate—the kids get to twist his nose. It's a switch—if you twist it hard enough, Willy says *Ow!* It's hard on the piece, so we had to make it sturdy, and we've got lots of spare parts on hand so we can replace them regularly."

"We want children to be able to play with our exhibits, Nolan," Arabella explained. "That's the philosophy of Let's Play. We don't want to keep telling them, *Be careful, don't touch.*"

"So you've got a simple switch rigged up in Willy's

nose," Nolan said, "and when the nose is twisted, the circuit is closed, it activates the voice recording that goes *Ow*?"

"Exactly," Caitlin said. "Willy's bending down to shake hands with the children, and the kids can grab his nose easily. It worked fine the first few times we tried it. Then Mom invited Nell to see it in action, and Jason was trying to demonstrate how it worked when he was knocked out. He grabbed the nose and zap!"

Nolan looked troubled. "Sounds like a simple connection—hard to go wrong with it. You've worked with your installers before?"

Caitlin nodded. "Plenty of times. Plus we've had the city inspectors in more than once, to make sure everything was up to code. I've got the paperwork. We didn't cut any corners."

"So you're saying that nothing could go wrong, but it did," Nolan said slowly. "And you think Hadley here had something to do with it?"

"I can't believe what I'm hearing!" Hadley jumped out of her chair, then retreated behind it when Caitlin glared at her. "I'm an author, for God's sake—not an electrician. I wouldn't know where to begin to tamper with it."

"I'm not so sure about that," I said. "What about one of your boyfriends?"

Hadley's stricken face was a treat to observe.

CHAPTER 30

"Who told you?" Hadley snarled. "That little twit Chloe?"

I wasn't about to rat out Chloe. "You know, if you were nicer to the people who worked for you, they might be a bit more loyal to you."

"They're all out to suck my blood. All of them. They think working for a successful author will jump-start their tiny careers in publishing. Ha! It takes years of trying, and swallowing a whole lot of rejection, to get where I am today."

"And where is that, Hadley?" I asked.

She glared at me. "I'm a *New York Times* bestseller! My *Harriet* books are in stores everywhere! A generation of children has grown up with her tales as bedtime stories. Harriet's been optioned for animated films, and there's some interest in a television series. Everybody knows me!"

Hadley's tone was becoming increasingly shrill, and I was beginning to wonder how much longer she could delude herself about her success. Sure, the world knew of Harriet the Hedgehog, and had for a generation. But that was part of the problem: the world had moved on, and Hadley couldn't or didn't want to accept that. She was yesterday's news now. As Chloe had pointed out, she needed this exhibit as much if not more than the museum did.

But if that was true, why would she try to destroy it? That didn't make any sense. "All right, what do *you* think happened at the exhibit, Hadley? Why did Jason get shocked, and why did Joe die?"

"Why do you think I know? She"—Hadley pointed at Caitlin—"*she* was the one in charge. Ask her!"

"Caitlin's already given us her side of the story, Hadley. What's yours?" Arabella said with surprising patience.

"I didn't want to do it," Hadley muttered, her shoulders slumping. "The exhibit, I mean. Sure, I've known about your tacky little museum for years. I didn't want Harriet to be cheapened by showing up there."

"We have tens of thousands of visitors each year, Hadley," Arabella replied tartly. "How many books have you sold in the past year?"

Hadley brushed aside Arabella's comment. "I don't pay attention to that kind of thing. But my publisher thought it was a good idea, and they hinted that they might be reluctant to publish the next book unless I agreed to promote a bit more aggressively, so I went along with it. And once I'd said yes, of course I spent a lot of time there, making sure your people got the details right. Obviously there were problems with that." She sniffed.

"Was Caitlin correct about the Willy heads?" I asked.

Hadley shrugged. "More or less. The first version was completely unacceptable—Willy looked positively evil, and I couldn't have that. So we tried again. And again."

"And did you in fact keep the heads here, in your house?"

"Yes."

"Do you still have the others, the two that didn't go into the exhibit?"

Hadley cocked her head. "Yes, they're in the basement. Do you want to see them?"

She stood up, and I held up a hand to stop her before she could go any farther. I didn't want to let her out of my sight until we had the whole story. She sat again. "Why don't you tell Nolan where to find them?"

"The basement. The door is off the kitchen, at the other end of the house." Hadley pointed vaguely back the way we had come in. "I'm sure you can find it. Don't touch anything else."

I wondered briefly if Hadley's remark had rankled; did she expect him to steal the silverware? I looked at Nolan, and he gave me an odd half smile before turning and heading toward the other end of the house. "Can I have a torch, darlin'?" he said. "Oh, that'd be a flashlight to you."

When Hadley didn't answer, I said, "Take a candle and check the kitchen." He complied and disappeared down the dark hallway.

I turned back to Hadley. "Go on, Hadley. You decided which head you wanted to use. Did you deliver it to the museum yourself?"

She nodded. "That Chloe person was still around then. I'm going to have to replace her, especially with this exhibit opening. It will go forward, won't it?" she asked, glancing at Arabella.

Arabella didn't reply immediately. "It all depends on whether we can determine how this death occurred." I noticed she didn't use the word *murder*. "If we can't convince the public that the exhibit and the museum are safe, then no one will come."

"I'll sue!" Hadley shrieked. "Look at the contract—I made sure I had a good lawyer, and I'm sure there's some sort of default clause in there."

"Hadley," Arabella said with something like pity, "do you really want to be associated with an exhibit where somebody died? What kind of a message does that send to your young readers—or their parents, who actually buy the books?"

As I watched them talk, I wondered if that had been Hadley's plan all along: scotch the exhibit, then collect whatever compensation she had wangled into the contract—and maybe enjoy a resurgence in sales as a result of the publicity. That would beat holding an exhibit that no one visited. I wondered just what else was in that contract, and how Arabella and the museum would fare, if this sad event weren't cleared up quickly. Would a failed exhibit and a cloud hovering over the museum be enough to force Let's Play to close its doors permanently? Arabella didn't deserve that. Nor did she deserve to have her daughter—and employee—accused of murder.

Did it all come down to money? And if so, who benefitted? Hadley would receive widespread local and possibly national exposure, which I had no doubt she would milk as far as possible, maybe resulting in increased book sales. Assuming, of course, she wasn't arrested for murder. The museum? If Hadley turned out to be the villain, then Arabella and her crew would benefit from the same publicity, if it was spun right, and a combination of curiosity and sympathy could attract droves of museum-goers, and therefore boost revenues. And what about Caitlin? No matter how things went, she had certainly gotten her parents' attention. Would she have gone as far as killing someone to achieve that? The only person I was willing to rule out at the moment as a suspect was Nolan. Maybe. After all, he had been in town at the right time. But for the life of me, I couldn't see any reason why he would bear a grudge toward Arabella.

And what was taking Nolan so long? The basement couldn't be all that big. I thought I could hear some banging around below my feet.

It was time to get to the point. "Hadley, let me see if I've got this right," I said. "You brought the head you chose back to the museum two weeks ago, and the installers attached it. Jason says they tried it out and everything was working fine."

"I don't remember what day it was. That's why I have an assistant, to keep track of things like that."

Caitlin, who I thought had shown remarkable restraint through Hadley's story, spoke for the first time in a while. "Tuesday, definitely. The installers attached the head in the morning, and we tested it. Then you came by at about one to check it out."

"If you say so," Hadley said. "I don't remember."

"Arabella, you invited me over on Tuesday afternoon," I said, picking up the thread. "That's when Jason was hurt. So if someone did something to the installation, it had to have happened between Tuesday morning and Tuesday afternoon.

"My memory's still kind of shaky," Jason said, "but I remember it worked fine the first time we tried it."

Jason's accident had looked convincing enough, and I'd seen it up close. Maybe it was possible he could have rigged it to limit the damage, and then used himself as a test dummy, but why on earth would he do such a thing? But who had the expertise to do it? Arabella had been married to an electrician; had she paid attention to the details of wiring? As for confirming Hadley's whereabouts, I had an idea.

"Hadley, do you keep a calendar?"

She sniffed. "My assistant does. I have no idea where."

"Would Chloe know what your schedule was that week?"

"Probably. But she's gone."

"I know where to find her." Hadley and I locked eyes, and I thought I saw fear in hers. "Did you provide her with a computer or some other device to keep track of things for you?"

"No. She had her own. She never asked for one."

Probably because she knew that Hadley wouldn't spring for one. "So you personally don't recall where you might have been Tuesday afternoon?"

"I told you, she was at the museum Tuesday after lunch," Caitlin said. "She wanted to make sure we hadn't screwed up attaching the new head."

"All right!" Hadley all but shouted. "I was at the museum. But so were Arabella and Caitlin and Jason and God knows how many other people. Any one of them could have tampered with the exhibit."

That was true enough, although I wasn't sure who else would have a motive. But there was one more piece: Joe had died on Wednesday. "Arabella, you had the wiring for the new head checked on Wednesday, the day after Jason was hurt. I assume you tested it again?"

"Of course we did. One accident was more than enough, and I wasn't going to take any chances. Caitlin and I were both there. It was working fine. I even called in an outside electrician to check things out—I paid for that out of my own pocket."

"Hadley, where were you on Wednesday?"

Hadley looked victorious. "I had a signing out in Chester County. I worked from home in the morning, then Chloe drove me to the bookstore there. We were there for a couple of hours—with plenty of witnesses."

"And after that?" I pressed.

"Chloe brought me home. I fixed supper and went to bed."

"Alone?"

"Yes, alone! Then some reporter called around eleven that evening to say that someone had been killed at my exhibit, and what did I have to say? That must be on record somewhere—I was quoted in the paper, you know."

Score one point for Hadley. If she had sneaked into the museum after hours to mess with the exhibit, she'd have had a rather narrow window of opportunity between the closing time for the museum and nine o'clock when Joe died. Which made things look worse for Caitlin. When had Jason come home from the hospital? Had they been together Wednesday night?

It wasn't easy to try to sort out any kind of time line while keeping up with the conversation going on in front of me. Joe had died on Wednesday, but Hadley hadn't fired Chloe immediately. Of course, it had taken the police some time to put together the pieces and arrive at Hadley's door, and from there to Chloe. After Chloe had talked to them and spilled some of Hadley's dirty little secrets, Hadley had dumped her fast, and Chloe had come running to Eric for sympathy. Last week. Why had Hadley bothered to fire her? Surely she should have known that Chloe had no choice but to talk to the police. Was it just Hadley acting out of pique, which was apparently her normal operating procedure, or did she think that Chloe had pointed the police toward Hadley, deliberately or unintentionally? Did Hadley's sliding book sales give her a real motive?

Apparently Hadley sensed my hesitation, because she launched into attack mode. "Excuse me, Nell, but who the hell appointed you investigator here? I've talked to the police about the events at Let's Play, told them everything I've told you, and they seem satisfied. My reputation is on the line as much as anyone's. And nobody has shown that I had a clue about what happened, or if I had even wanted to do something like that, how I could have. I have trouble programming my cell phone. Do you seriously think I could rig the wiring in the exhibit? And how was I supposed to set a death trap when I was miles away? Why aren't you looking at Caitlin—she's been part of this from the beginning. Maybe she thought she'd failed at her job and was trying to destroy the exhibit before it even opened. Maybe she has a lifelong beef with her mother. I don't know—but I do know that I've had enough of this discussion. I'd like you to leave now."

Nolan appeared in the doorway from the hall, holding a flashlight. He looked a bit absurd with a Willy head tucked under each arm, but his expression was far from amusing—or amused. "You've had some electrical work done recently, haven't you?"

Startled, Hadley turned to confront him. "Yes, I have. So what?"

"Because, lady, you have a serious problem."

CHAPTER 31

"What do you mean?" Hadley demanded.

"Whoever did your wiring—the most recent stuff—was an incompetent hack. You're lucky the place hasn't gone up in flames."

"Why?"

"Jaysus, aluminum wiring alongside knob-and-tube, junction boxes hacked to bits and shredding the wires. How long ago was this done?"

"Just a few weeks ago. What's wrong with it? "

"This place was built, what, in the twenties? That old knob-and-tube stuff—it's not bad, so long as you don't mess with it. In fact, looks like no one did until recently. Of course, you're seriously underpowered by current standards, but if it's just you and you don't run too many appliances at once, you'd get by. I take it you didn't fix it yourself?"

"The old wiring? Of course not!"

Nolan grinned. "Didn't think so. So you hired someone. Where'd you find this yahoo?"

"I . . . don't remember. Someone recommended him, I think."

I noticed that Hadley wasn't meeting anyone's eyes, and then I recalled Chloe's comments about Hadley's blue-collar boy toys. "Was this an electrician friend? A rather close friend?"

"What do you mean?"

I was getting increasingly tired of her evasions. "A boyfriend. Were you dating any electricians?"

Her expression changed then. "Yes," she whispered.

And then the penny dropped. "Was it Joe Murphy?"

Hadley nodded.

We all sat in stunned silence for a moment. My brain was in overdrive. Joe had dated Hadley. Joe had worked on Hadley's house while the Willy heads were in the basement. Joe was apparently a lousy electrician, if Nolan was right. And Joe had been electrocuted while working on the exhibit at Let's Play. But how to connect the dots?

"Okay, Hadley, can you walk us through this? When were you and Joe . . . together?"

"I don't want to talk about this," Hadley said in a tight voice.

Too bad. "Hadley, I'm afraid you have to. Did you mention to the police that you and the victim had had a relationship?"

Hadley shook her head like a sulky child. "I didn't see what difference it would make. It was over by then anyway."

Apparently Hadley was missing a few screws. She didn't realize that the police might like to know that she had been intimately involved with the dead man? But in Hadley World, Hadley's interests came first. "When did your relationship end?"

"Last month."

"How long were you together?"

"A few weeks, maybe?"

"And how many relationships have you had with, uh, other people, say over the last year?"

"A few. Five, maybe?" Hadley contemplated her mantelpiece, avoiding my gaze.

Chloe had been right. A rapid turnover of well-muscled and not-too-bright boyfriends was not what people wanted to hear about a children's book writer, so maybe it wasn't surprising that Hadley had kept it quiet. I tried another tack. "When did you bring the Willy heads home?"

Now she turned back to look at me. "You mean, were Joe and I seeing each other then? Yes. They were here while I was seeing Joe."

"But you two broke it off before you took the final head back to the museum."

"Yes, it was over by then."

"How did he take the breakup?"

"He was angry. I don't know why—I never promised him anything. He couldn't have thought we had any future together. I mean, look at me—look at who I am. He was just an electrician. It wasn't serious."

"So you used him for some quick sex and then dumped him," I said bluntly.

"You don't need to be crude, Nell," she replied. I noticed she didn't deny the allegation.

"Did he show you how the Willy heads worked?"

"No. I didn't really care, as long as they worked correctly. He was helping me with them. He would show me how fast Willy could speak, that kind of thing. He wanted to be sure they would stand up to heavy handling—kids can be kind of rough, you know. But I didn't want the final one to be too scary."

I turned to Nolan, who had set the two remaining heads down on the floor at his feet. "Nolan, can you take a look at those and tell me if they're wired correctly?"

"Piece of cake." He picked up the first one and peered inside. We all waited silently while Nolan poked and prodded inside the two heads. Finally he said, "They seem fine to me. It's a pretty simple circuit. I'm not up on all the fancy electronics like the recorded voice bit, but the connections inside look right. Can't speak as to how they went on the body."

That was good to know, especially since Hadley had sent Joe packing before she had delivered the head to Let's Play. "Did Joe know which head you had chosen, Hadley?" I asked.

"I don't think so. I really didn't make up my mind until the last minute. Arabella was being so pushy about it, so in the end I just grabbed one."

I could hear Caitlin laugh briefly.

"Hadley, you'd had months to make up your mind," Arabella said, clearly exasperated. Then she turned to me. "Nell, where are you going with this?"

"I'm trying to figure out who rigged the Willy model in the exhibit. And why. Hadley, was this all just a big publicity stunt to get your name in the papers?"

Hadley jumped out of her chair. "No! Look, I know you think I'm shallow and self-centered, and maybe I am, but I would never put anyone at risk."

"Are you sure? Maybe you didn't think anyone would die, just get a nasty shock. Which Jason did. And maybe you were disappointed when that didn't get any publicity and decided to up the ante the second time around. Maybe you'd already planned your tearful press conference."

"Nell!" Arabella burst out. "That's not fair."

I swung back to her. "Look, Arabella, if we don't get to the bottom of this, your museum is in deep trouble. You want me to be nice and polite under the circumstances? Hadley had motive and opportunity—and I gather she doesn't like you or Caitlin much. Why shouldn't she be a suspect? If she could pin this on you or Caitlin, she'd come out smelling like a rose."

Hadley was standing rigidly, her fists clenched, and the tears were spilling down her cheeks now. "I swear, I didn't do this. I may be a lousy person, but I wouldn't kill anyone. Believe me, Harriet isn't worth it. You think I don't know she's past her prime? Just like me? Sales are down, and so's my income, and that's all I've got. Sure, I've thought about how I could use this to my advantage for publicity, but when Joe died, I just couldn't."

Did I believe her? I decided I did. She was right—she was shallow. But I couldn't really see her as a cold-blooded killer. I looked around at our little group. "Then what happened?"

I was surprised when Nolan was the first to speak. "Have you thought that it might have been Joe's own doing?"

That was the last thing I expected to hear. "What, he killed himself in a very public way because Hadley rejected him?"

"Nah, nothing so fancy as that. But the lady had hurt his pride by dumping her, right? Maybe he figured messing with Hadley's exhibit was a good way of getting back at her. And maybe he screwed up the wiring himself and paid the price. After what I've seen downstairs, it wouldn't surprise me. The man took far too many shortcuts. Sloppy work."

"And of course he had access to the figures at Let's Play," Arabella added slowly, "since he was part of the installation crew."

"That's how I met him," Hadley said softly. Then, recovering her more imperious tone, she continued. "So let me get this straight. You're saying you think that he might have rigged Willy's head to get back at me?"

"I think so," I replied. "Jason received a jolt. That incident never went public, so it didn't get the result Joe wanted—he probably didn't want anyone to die, but he hoped that someone would get hurt badly enough that it would make the news. His first attempt went wrong, but then he had to wait all day Wednesday. He or one of his buddies repaired the wiring, and Arabella had it checked out, twice, and then he went back and changed it back again, only this time something went wrong. He didn't have much time, and he was probably working in the dark so no one could see him. Does that make sense?" I looked around at the group. "Nolan?"

"Could be," Nolan said. "I'd have to see the wiring in that head to be sure. I assume the cops have it?"

Arabella nodded. "They do."

"Then we should give them the other two, for comparison."

"Of course," Hadley said. "Just make sure they're back in time for the opening."

The gall of the statement rendered me speechless. Caitlin, who had been silent through this discussion, finally spoke. "So I was right—you *were* responsible, just not quite directly. But you were willing to let the police suspect me, and my mother, and Let's Play, rather than come forward and tell them the whole story, just because it made you look bad. What did we ever do to you?" I noticed that Jason had drifted closer to Caitlin, and he now had his arm around her.

"It wasn't personal."

"How lame is that?" Caitlin burst out. "You were thinking, *Sorry, but I'll take any likely candidate for killer, as long as it isn't me?*" She turned to Arabella. "Is it too late the pull the plug on that damned exhibit? Because right now it would feel really good to take a sledgehammer to the whole thing."

Arabella actually smiled. "Sweetie, I understand how you feel, believe me. But we're only a couple of weeks from opening, and we simply can't afford to have a huge hole in our scheduling right now. Nell, what do we do now?"

Nell Pratt, resident expert on law enforcement. I sighed. "We tell the Philadelphia Police what we know, and we give them the other two heads and tell them to compare them to the one they have. We tell them we believe that Joe may have been responsible for the faulty wiring, and he was stupid enough to electrocute himself. It's sad, but there's a weird sort of poetic justice to it."

"Will they believe that, Nell?" Arabella asked.

"I don't know. It makes as much sense as anything else, and I'm sure they'd be happy to close the case. If you're lucky, there'll be some evidence, if they know what to look for. And if you're *very* lucky, you, the museum, Caitlin, and Hadley will be exonerated, and the exhibit goes on as planned. Hadley, you're going to have to repeat what you've told us to the police, but I doubt that it will go public—unless you decide you really want that kind of publicity."

"I think not," Hadley said. "I'd like to come out of this with some shred of dignity. We'll just call it a tragic accident, due to an electrician's error, and he's already paid the price. Is that acceptable to you, Arabella?"

"I agree that would be best, Hadley."

"I don't suppose we can do this in time for tomorrow's paper?" Hadley said.

The woman was a piece of work. "Unlikely," I said. "Besides, we—or Arabella and you—need to talk to the police before you call the news folks."

"All right," a subdued Hadley replied.

I needed to clear my head. Had we really figured out what had happened—and come up with a noncrime? I took a candle and walked into the hall and pulled open the door a crack to check the weather. I had expected to see ice. What I hadn't expected to see was the massive tree trunk that spanned the road we had arrived by, and a few sparking wires that it had brought down with it.

"Uh, guys?" I called over my shoulder. "I don't think we're going anywhere tonight."

CHAPTER 32

Why was I not surprised that Hadley gave a small shriek from what sounded like pure frustration? But it was pitch black; the entire neighborhood was dark. I turned and made my way back to the living room. Luckily Nolan had held on to the flashlight he had been using.

"Tree down?" he asked.

"Big one, across the road. I guess we're stuck."

"I don't want to stay here," Hadley whined. "Can't we go to a hotel or something?"

Was I the only person who wanted to strangle the woman? "No, Hadley. Unless you have a helicopter handy, we can't get out."

"Does that fireplace work, Hadley?" Nolan asked.

"What?" Hadley looked around the room as if she was surprised she had a fireplace. "Oh, I guess so. I know I've used it, but not lately. Why?"

When she didn't say more, Nolan prompted, "You might like some heat tonight. Would you have any wood for it?"

"Oh. Maybe in the garage? It's at the other end of the house—there's a door leading from the kitchen."

"I'm on it. Do you have any more candles or such? Those are almost out"—he pointed to the still-flickering but quickly fading candles on the coffee table—"and I don't want to leave you all in the dark."

Finally Hadley roused herself to action. "Yes, I think there are some in the desk. I'll get them."

In short order she had retrieved more of the same short, squat candles and a lighter. I suppressed the image of Hadley and her man-of-the-moment enjoying an intimate candlelit interlude in front of the dying fire. At least we had light.

"Grand. I'll go check out the wood."

"I'll help," Jason volunteered, disentangling himself from Caitlin. Maybe he'd had enough drama for the moment. The two men disappeared down the hallway, Nolan's flashlight bobbing in front of them.

I waited a few moments for Hadley to take charge—it was, as she had pointed out, her house—but she seemed lethargic. Finally I said, "Hadley, we may be in for a long night. We'd better plan to sleep here, preferably in this room, if Nolan finds any wood. You have blankets, pillows?"

Hadley sniffed. "I guess. I don't have a lot of guests."

Why did that not surprise me? "Well," I said patiently, "why don't you go collect what you have? And what about food?"

"I don't know."

Maybe it would be faster to strangle her now. "Do you have a gas stove?"

"Yes. Why?"

"Because if it's gas, we can light it manually, so at least we could have something hot to eat and drink."

"Oh. All right. I'll go get the blankets and stuff." Hadley

picked up a candle and went down the hall, toward the other end of the house.

When she was out of earshot, I sighed. "Arabella, Caitlin, I do not know how you put up with this woman. She seems to switch between demanding and helpless at the drop of a hat."

"I will say it was always difficult to pry a decision out of her. Are we really stuck here, Nell?" Arabella asked.

"I'm afraid so. I don't know how long it will be before they send someone out to fix the wires, and even then they'll still have to get the tree out of the way. So, yes—it looks like we're having a slumber party."

"With s'mores?" Caitlin asked, and I thought I could detect a bit of a giggle in her voice. I think it was the first time I'd heard her say anything remotely funny in the time I'd known her.

I gave her a smile. "I doubt that Hadley's larder runs to marshmallows, but maybe we can scrounge up something to eat. Let's go see." I picked up another candle and led the way down the hall toward the kitchen.

There we met Nolan and Jason, emerging from the dark garage, each with an armload of wood. "This is most of it, but it'll do for now," Nolan said. "Where's herself?"

"She's looking for blankets. Can you get a fire started?"

"Not to worry. The first ten years of my life, we had nothing but turf to keep us warm. I'll see to it."

"All right, then—food."

Fifteen minutes later we were huddled in a tight half circle in front of the small fire that Nolan had built. Well, most of us were: Hadley maintained a distance, perched on a chair behind us. She had come up with a motley assortment of blankets, and we were noshing on the rather eclectic mix of items we had found in her refrigerator and cupboards—mostly crackers, olives, and cheese, plus a couple of shriveled apples. It would do for now, and since we had all missed dinner, we weren't complaining.

"This certainly is an unlikely turn of events, don't you think? All of us camped out here?" Arabella said.

"No," Hadley replied bitterly. "If anything can go wrong, it will, at least if I'm around. This whole mess was my fault. I knew it was a bad idea to keep flogging poor Harriet, but that's what my publisher wanted, and I couldn't argue. I am sick unto death of that little rodent."

"Hedgehogs aren't rodents," Caitlin commented. "Didn't you do any research?"

"Ha! Market research, more like it. My editor wanted something small and cute but that hadn't been done to death, and, presto, a hedgehog was what I got."

"But you've done so well with Harriet," Arabella said. "This house, renown, book tours."

"This house is mortgaged to the hilt, and my royalties are down to four figures a year. Unless Harriet becomes the first animated hedgehog vampire rock star, preferably with psychic powers, I'm broke." She stood up abruptly. "I'm tired, and I want to sleep in my own bed. Everybody's got enough blankets and pillows and all?"

"We'll be all right," Arabella said. "I guess we'll have to wait until morning to see what our options are for getting back to Philadelphia."

"Fine. Good night." Hadley picked up a candle and disappeared toward the other end of the house. The rest of us tried to make nests with the quilts and pillows we had. Since the floor was carpeted, it wasn't too uncomfortable, although I certainly wasn't used to sleeping on the ground—or with a crowd. Jason stayed close to Caitlin, while Arabella and Nolan staked out opposite sides of the room.

I was dozing off when Caitlin said quietly, "I'm sorry, Mother."

"For what?" her mother responded.

"For getting in touch with Dad, behind your back. I just wanted a chance to get to know him."

Arabella sighed. "I shouldn't have kept you apart for so long. Whatever our problems were, he's still your father." She paused for several beats. "Was your reunion what you expected?"

Caitlin laughed quietly. "No. Sorry, Dad—that's not your fault. I guess I'd built you up into some kind of hero. You know—revolutionary, misunderstood by my petty bourgeois mother. And, Mother, I thought you had driven him away."

"It wasn't like that, love," Nolan said. "I'll take my share of the blame. And I could have tried harder to see you."

"I know. It's just that I was angry for so long, and Mother was the most convenient target. Mother, I really felt like you were too busy to bother with me, so you shipped me off to boarding school."

"I know it sounds awful when you put it that way, Caitlin, but I had to make a living, to support us, since your father wouldn't. And I did think it was the right thing for you."

"I think it was. They're good at what they do there at Bishop's Gate, and they really helped me with the Asperger's."

I lay still, trying not to intrude on this belated family truth-telling. Caitlin was still speaking, in a near whisper. "In the beginning I hated you for it. I mean, there you were, playing Mommy to half the snot-nosed kids of Philadelphia, but you sent me away and then couldn't take the time to visit me. It took me a long time to get over that."

"I'm sorry. I can see how it must have looked to you." A pause. "Are you past it now?"

"I'm here, aren't I? I'm working with you, and for you, which I never would have imagined. And you were right—the school helped me deal with my problems. There were some good kids there, and I could make friends. I couldn't do what you do, but I'm doing an okay job at Let's Play, aren't I?"

"You're doing a fine job, darling. And I'd say that even if I weren't your mother. If we ever get past this nonsense, the exhibit should be a big hit. In spite of Hadley."

"You still awake, Dad?'

Nolan spoke from the opposite corner. "I am. I'm sorry I missed all those years, but I hope we can do better in the future. Maybe you'd like to plan a trip to Ireland, meet your half brother and sister?"

"I'd like that," Caitlin said. "Maybe in the spring—Let's Play is pretty busy in the summer. And not during spring breaks. But I'm sure I could work out something."

The voices faded. The low fire crackled and spit. Outside it was quiet, except for the occasional crack as a branch fell from the weight of the ice. I fell asleep.

I awoke to full daylight. Checking my watch, I saw that it was nearly nine o'clock. The fire was long dead, and three out of my four companions were still lumps under mounds of blankets—Nolan was snoring in an armchair, and Jason and Caitlin were snuggled together like puppies. The fourth, Arabella, I could hear down the hall, talking with Hadley. I disentangled myself from my own wrappings and, after a quick stop at the bathroom, I stumbled down the hall. Halfway there I encountered the smell of coffee and picked up my pace.

Hadley and Arabella were seated across from each other

at a small table. There was a window behind them, and through it I could see a glittering array of ice-coated trees and shrubs—and an alarming number of broken branches dangling. "Morning," I said. "Is there more of that?" I nodded toward their mugs.

"On the stove. Nolan showed me how to light the burner last night. I *can* manage to boil water," Hadley replied.

I helped myself and sat down. "Any word from the outside world?"

"The power's still out, but I think I saw a utility truck."

"I hope so!" Arabella said. "There's a lot to be done, and we have to talk to the police before we move forward."

The idea of meeting with the law didn't appear to bother Hadley now. She stirred her coffee idly and stared into space. I definitely preferred this resigned Hadley to the bitchy and demanding one, although I wondered if this mood would last.

"Hadley, do you have flour and eggs and sugar?" Arabella asked. "Maybe I can put together a meal."

"I don't know. Try that cupboard over there." Hadley gestured vaguely.

I fled the scene of unlikely domesticity and retreated down the hall, away from the living room, where there were sounds of stirring. I retrieved my cell phone from my bag and punched in the number to my office. Eric answered promptly. "President's office."

"Eric, it's me."

"Nell! I was worried about you—it sounds like a real mess out there in the burbs."

"You've got that right. I'm not even home—I'm still at Hadley's house. Long story, but we're all good. How's it look there?"

"Roads are clear, so it's business as usual. Do you think you'll make it in?"

"I hope so, but we've got to get a tree out of the way first." As we spoke, I could hear the welcome sound of chain saws in the lane in front of Hadley's house. I peered out the window in the front and could see that the morning sun was well on its way to dissolving the layer of ice on the windshield of my car. "I think it's happening as we speak, so I can probably make it by noon." Then I was struck by a sudden thought. "Eric, can you ask Shelby to get in touch with Barney Hogan and have him call me this afternoon?"

"Yes, ma'am, I can do that. Everything okay?"

"I think so, or at least it will be. Thanks, Eric—see you later." I hung up and thought a moment. There were five of us to transport back to the city, and three cars: mine, Hadley's, and Caitlin's. I wasn't sure if the police wanted me to have any part of the coming discussion, but it might be best to be available, just in case—which meant we should all head for the city.

"I think they're working on that tree now," I said to the others. "We can head for town as soon as the road is clear. Do you need a ride, Hadley?"

There was a flash of the old Hadley, and I could almost hear her saying, *As if I'd ride with any of you.* "I'll follow you in, in my car. Although we should speak to the authorities together, don't you think?" Hadley said to Arabella, who nodded.

"I agree," I said. "But I don't think you need me. I'll go in to work and be available if the police want to talk to me, but I think between all of you, you've got it covered. Oh, and don't forget to take the Willy heads with you."

CHAPTER 33

A tow truck had hauled the trunk of the fallen oak to the side of the road in under half an hour, and I managed to beat my estimated deadline and arrived at the office by eleven. I made a mental note to keep a change of clothes at the office in the future, not that I expected occasions like this to come around too often. At least, I hoped not. Caitlin had taken her parents and Jason in her car, and Hadley had promised to follow shortly, as soon as she checked her property for any storm damage. I wasn't sure I trusted Hadley to follow through with making a statement without some encouragement, but I couldn't exactly hog-tie her and throw her in my trunk, appealing though that idea was. Even by the light of day, I thought the scenario we had worked out the night before still made as much sense as anything else. I hoped the police would agree.

Eric was hovering anxiously at his desk, waiting for me. "Thank goodness! The news reports made it sound like a battle zone out there in the burbs."

"A lot of tree damage," I told him, "but once we reached a main road, things were fine. Did I miss anything here?"

"Nothing worth mentioning. So, tell me what went on last night?"

I checked my messages: nothing urgent. "Go get Shelby. She should hear it, too."

Eric was gone in a flash and returned in moments with Shelby in tow. I wondered if she'd been waiting for my arrival. "Sounds like you had an interesting evening, lady," she said, sitting in a chair opposite the desk. "So, spill it!"

"Shut the door and sit down, Eric. And I trust you won't mention this to anyone else yet. Arabella, Caitlin, and Hadley should be on their way to police headquarters as we speak."

"So who did it?" Shelby demanded.

"Apparently nobody," I said, and watched their expressions with amusement. "Seriously, it looks as though the whole thing was a stupid accident. This is how we worked it out last night. Hadley was more or less ordered to go along with this exhibit by her publisher, because her sales were way off, along with her income. She wasn't happy, and I gather she made life miserable for everyone, but she didn't have a choice." I paused before adding, "Hadley also has a taste for well-muscled young men, as Chloe informed us."

"Do tell," Sheryl said drily, and winked at Eric.

"Yes, and Hadley connected with one of the electricians who was working on the exhibit—the late Joe Murphy."

"No!" Eric said. "But she didn't kill him? Did he reject her?"

"She says she dumped him, but I wondered if she might have had a hand in his death. It seems unlikely, though— she doesn't have the skills, and she does have a pretty good alibi. Maybe being accused of murder would have been a great way to get some publicity, but definitely the wrong kind. In any case, I think she's used to discarding the, uh, objects of her attentions rather quickly, and nobody's ever cried foul, before now."

"Did Hadley volunteer all this delightful information?" Shelby asked.

"Not at first. But when Nolan went down to the basement to retrieve the Willy heads they didn't use in the exhibit, he saw the house's wiring and told us it was a mess—the worst combination of original old wiring combined with some recent shoddy patches and quick fixes. Apparently Hadley asked Joe to do a little work for her, and he did a lousy job. Which led us all to conclude that it was his sloppy work on the Willy the Weasel head that killed him."

"Wait, I don't understand," Eric said. "What did Hadley know about this?"

"That part she didn't want to share. My take is, Hadley had a fling with Joe and got bored with him—which she did with a lot of guys, according to Chloe—and told him it was over. Apparently he wasn't too thrilled about that. I'm guessing he tinkered with the exhibit to get back at Hadley."

"By killing someone?"

"I don't think that he meant to go that far—he was aiming for an accident. I think he wanted to discredit Hadley's exhibit. He probably thought that Hadley would be the one to suffer most if there were an accident with the exhibit— the museum might pull the plug on it. I don't know if he had anyone in mind, but it was Jason who got shocked and ended up in the hospital."

"That wasn't enough?" Eric asked.

"No, because there wasn't any publicity, and that's what he was looking for. After Arabella had everything inspected up one side and down the other, he tried again. He was probably in a hurry, and working in the dark, so the most likely scenario is that he screwed it up and it killed him."

"Wow," Shelby said. "So Hadley didn't know anything about all this?"

"So she says," I replied. "Once she'd sent Joe on his way, she didn't give him another thought—she had no idea how he felt. She is possibly the most self-centered woman I have ever met."

"And Arabella and Caitlin had nothing to do with any of it?" Eric asked.

"I think Caitlin figured out that Hadley was involved, once she put together the time line, with Jason's help, and that's why she went out to her house to confront her and asked her mother to join her. Hadley was eager to blame anybody else, and Caitlin was upset about that. But instead of just Arabella, we *all* showed up and then we got stuck there, so we had plenty of time to work it out." I decided to leave out the part about Caitlin's threatening Hadley with a Taser. "After all that, there was no murder involved, just stupidity."

"How's Let's Play going to come out of this? Aren't people going to wonder what else might not have been done right?" Shelby asked.

I sighed. "It's a problem, but there's not much that can be done about it. But I did have an idea . . ."

A slow grin spread over Shelby's face. "And that's why you wanted to call Barney? He's downstairs now."

I grinned back at her. "You've got it. He's been working in Philadelphia for years, and he must know plenty of people, particularly electricians. Maybe he can spread the word to his friends that the exhibit is sound? I'll go down and see if I can find him."

"Last I saw he was in the reading room with Felicity," Eric said.

I stood up. "Then let's go look for him."

Luckily Barney was still in the reading room, at a table spread with old documents, and Felicity was leaning over his shoulder. Barney looked up when he saw us approaching, and broke into a broad grin. "You're just in time to help me celebrate. This lady here has worked wonders and come up with just what I was looking for. Take a look!"

He pulled out a copy of an old black-and-white photograph. Shelby and I leaned over the table to look at it. "What is?" I asked.

"It's a team photo for the 1888 Philadelphia Quakers. And that there"—he jabbed a stubby finger at a face in the back row—"that's my great-great-grandpa. Looks just like me, or maybe I mean the other way around, don't you think?"

I looked, and maybe he was right, if you took away about forty years from Barney and removed the great-great's lush moustache. "I'm so happy for you, Barney. And great work, Felicity!"

"It's my job," she said, but I could tell she was blushing with pride. "Were you looking for us?"

"Actually I was looking for Barney," I said. "Can I steal you away for a moment?"

"Sure," he said, barely curious. It was interesting to see the impact that one discovery had made on him—one of the joys of research.

I led him to the small conference room under the stairs, with Shelby trailing behind. Once there, though, Shelby whispered, "Good luck," and headed to the elevators, leaving me alone with Barney. I realized I wasn't sure where to start, but after a beat or two, I took a deep breath and said, "Listen, Barney—didn't you tell me you knew Joe Murphy?"

"The guy who got killed at the museum? Yeah, sure. He was in the union. Course, he was a lot younger'n me, so we didn't exactly hang together. But I'd seen him around, worked with him on a job or two. He was a good guy." *Now* he was curious.

I tried to find a way to put my next question delicately. "From what you know, do you think he was a good electrician?"

Barney waited a moment before replying, and his expression became wary. "This have something to do with his death?"

"It could," I admitted.

His shoulders slumped. "I hate to speak ill of the dead, and he was always a help to me. But he was kind of sloppy, took too many shortcuts. I had some issues working with him on a coupla jobs. You saying that's what happened at the museum? He messed up?"

"It may be. Proving it is up to the police. But you think it's a real possibility?" I wasn't looking for evidence; I was looking for corroboration for Nolan's assessment of Joe's skills, or lack of them.

He hesitated, then nodded. "I do. I don't have to tell the police, do I? Because the guys in my union wouldn't be happy about it. He was one of ours, even if he was careless sometimes, and we always covered for him."

"No, I don't think it will come to that. There are other sources for that information."

"Is that what you wanted?" Barney asked.

"Actually, no. There was something else that I thought maybe you could help me with. Look, this exhibit is important to Let's Play, and I'd hate to see people—parents with children—stay away because they're worried it's not safe, all because of Joe's mistake. So I was wondering if there was some way you could spread the word among your friends and let people know the place is safe."

"Huh." Barney thought for a moment, and then his face lit up. "How about this? I'll talk with the other guys who worked on the show at the museum, and if they clear it, I've got a better idea. We've all got kids and grandkids. How about we get a bunch of us together and we can all go to the exhibit? Maybe spread it out over a few days, so the museum doesn't get swamped all at once?"

"Oh, Barney, could you do that?" I felt like clapping my hands. "That would be perfect. With half the electricians in Philadelphia there, no one could think there was a problem. And maybe we could get some good press for it. What do you think?"

"I can make it happen."

"I don't know how to thank you, Barney."

"Heck, you don't need to. I'm just happy to have found all the great records you have here, and it's terrific to know what my great-great-grandpa looked like, back in the day. I might never have known otherwise."

"Then I'll let you get back to your research. I hope we'll be seeing more of you around here—and I don't mean for the wiring."

"You can bet on it."

I trooped back to my office, where I found Shelby leaning against the doorjamb. "It all worked out well?" she asked.

"Indeed it did," I said. "And I believe in serendipity, and

justice, and good things happening to good people. Should I tell Arabella?"

"Maybe you should wait until you know if Barney can rally the electricians. You are going to the preview tomorrow, aren't you?"

It took me a moment to recall what she was talking about. "For the opening of the Let's Play exhibit? Of course."

"Tell Caitlin that Mrs. Carver says hi."

"I'll do that."

The rest of the day was peaceful, thank goodness. I was running on little sleep and food, and the excitement of the past few days was taking a toll. It was a good thing that I had no important business to take care of, because I would have made a mess of it. At five o'clock I stopped at Eric's desk and said, "I've had it. I'm heading home, but I'll be in early tomorrow."

"You take all the time you want, Nell. You did good work today, or last night, I guess. You know what I mean."

"I hope so. See you tomorrow."

I drove home in a foggy mood. Traffic was surprisingly heavy. Although there was little evidence left from the storm of the day before, the sky was overcast, and the light was gloomy. I arrived home later than usual and pottered around trying to cobble together a meal.

I was dozing on the couch when the phone rang. My watch said eleven. I answered it to find Shelby on the other end of the line. "Turn on your television, fast. Any network news."

I scrabbled for the remote and clicked on to the local ABC affiliate. The lead story was apparently about a major fire in Gladwyne. Still sluggish from my half sleep, it took me a moment to realize I recognized the house: Hadley's. "Shelby, you still there?"

"I am. You seeing what I'm seeing?"

"Hadley Eastman's house in flames." I realized that the scene I was looking at had taken place in daylight, probably a dozen hours earlier. "Was she there?"

"Nope, she was still at the police station. But I bet we'll be hearing from her on the morning news."

"I'd count on it. Thanks for the heads-up, Shelby. See you in the morning."

After I ended the call, I sat on the couch, dazed. Was this Joe the electrician's final revenge, from beyond the grave? Or had Hadley taken a little time to rig something up before she headed into the city this morning? One thing was clear: Hadley was going to get the publicity she had been looking for.

CHAPTER 34

Of course I turned on the news when I woke up the next morning, and was not surprised to see interviews with a tearful but brave Hadley, who was no doubt thrilled to be labeled "the well-known author of" et cetera. The whole timing of the fire made me suspicious, but Hadley had an airtight alibi, since she had been at police headquarters when the fire started.

It occurred to me that there was a small chance that the exhibit opening, or at least the upscale kickoff event, might be postponed due to Hadley's troubles, but I was willing to bet that Hadley—brave woman that she was—would find a way to soldier on. Somehow the news about Hadley's house fire had catapulted her back to the top headline, and Hadley's publicist had managed to twist the stories of Joe's unfortunate death and Hadley's tragedy together and suggest that poor Hadley was the unfortunate victim of circumstance. I'd bet that her book sales soared, at least for a day or two. When I called Arabella to check whether the reception was going forward this evening as planned, she said that Hadley had insisted that the show must go on, despite her personal tragedies. Why was I not surprised?

With the events of the previous day and night still swirling in my head, I made my way into work. I was pleased to find Eric already at his desk when I arrived. "Mornin', Nell. There's a message for you." He handed me a slip.

I took it into my office, and after hanging up my coat, I looked at it and was surprised to find that it was from James. "Eric, when did this come in?"

"This morning, early, before I got here. It was on voice mail."

That was curious—why would he be calling when he knew I wouldn't be at my desk? Or maybe he'd just missed me at home. I checked the number: from his office. There was only one way to find out what was going on, so I picked up the phone and called. He answered on the second ring.

"Hi," I said brightly if not intelligently. "You called?"

"Hi, Nell. Yes, I did. What are your plans for today? I've got something to talk over with you."

"Nothing on the calendar until five, when I was planning to go to the reception at Let's Play."

"Let's Play? Oh, for the new exhibit. How about I meet you at the reception, and maybe we can have dinner after?"

So it wasn't official business. "That sounds nice. Should I tell Arabella to expect you?"

"I think I can manage to wangle my own way in. See you then." He hung up.

Interesting. He'd told me nothing, and now I had to spend the day wondering what he wanted—the jerk.

And then I remembered that there was something I really needed to do. I left my office and went to stand in front of Eric's desk. He looked at me anxiously. "Everything all right?"

"What? Oh, the FBI call. Yes, no problems. Listen, Eric, I just realized that your probation period has ended. You still want the job?"

His expression morphed from anxious to hopeful. "I sure do. I really like it here."

"Then it's yours. You've been a big help, and I know you can be discreet. Welcome aboard. We can worry about the paperwork later."

He jumped to his feet, grabbed my hand, and shook it vigorously. "Thank you so much, Nell. You won't regret it. But could I maybe get a computer now?"

I laughed. "I'll work on that."

I muddled my way through the day. Midafternoon I went down to the reading room to have a word with Felicity, who was at her desk despite a nearly empty reading room. "Hi, Felicity. Thanks for helping Barney out—he seemed thrilled yesterday with what you'd found."

Was she blushing again? "It was fun. I love sports history, so it's a treat to have to dig into our collections for a patron. And he's a very nice man," she ended primly.

"I agree. I hope we'll be seeing more of him here." And I'd venture that Felicity hoped so, too.

At quarter to five I sent Eric home and took a cab over to Let's Play. I had to admit, as the cab approached the old building, that it looked surprisingly festive in the gathering dusk. There were strings of tiny lights attached almost everywhere possible. I paid the cab fare and walked through the front door: the tiny lights continued inside as well, making the shabby old industrial building look like a fairyland. Even Furzie sported some sparkling strings, plus a knit hat with a pom-pom.

An employee inside the door took my coat and spirited it away, and I turned to study the crowd. The exhibit was on the second floor, at the rear, and the party sprawled over both the first floor and the remaining space on the second. Even this early the place looked well filled, and there were a good number of children running around, excited. Young servers circulated with trays of hot hors d'oeuvres. I snagged a glass of white wine from the downstairs bar, helped myself to some of the yummy savories, and set about trying to find Arabella, Caitlin, and Hadley. Of course, my efforts were hampered because along the way I had to stop to greet and chat up the partygoers I knew or recognized—the work of a fundraiser, even a promoted one, never ceases. When I finally made it up the stairs, I found the key players all clustered together in an informal receiving line. Arabella looked radiant; Caitlin, at her side, looked relieved; and then there was Hadley, impeccably clad in a clinging red dress, holding forth in front of a small cluster of admirers. I caught snatches of her conversation.

"Oh, I'm completely devastated! My poor little cottage, gone! So many memories, and such lovely treasures. But I can only be happy that no one was at home when it happened."

I tuned her out and turned to Arabella, who threw her arms around me. I struggled to hang on to my glass without drenching her. "Oh, Nell, isn't it wonderful? Everyone came! And people were calling all day, asking if they could attend or bring a guest. And the head of the electricians' union is here, and he brought friends! Isn't that kind of him? That should really help with our PR. I was so worried!"

As I scanned the room, I could tell that Barney had done what he had promised—this went far beyond the usual society crowd. "It all looks terrific. I'm so happy for you. And for you, too, Caitlin—looks like you pulled it off. Congratulations."

Caitlin's face lit up. "Thanks! I'm really happy with how it turned out. Maybe I'll stop by and say hi one of these days. Excuse me." She was pulled away by someone with a question.

There was one of those curious lulls between waves of people, so I took the opportunity to pull Arabella aside. "She's doing well," I said—more statement than question.

"She is," Arabella agreed. "I'm so proud of her! I knew when I hired her that people might talk, but even with everything we've had to deal with, I know I made the right decision in having her handle this. She's blossoming!"

"What do you think about this thing with Hadley? The house?" I asked.

Arabella looked at me levelly. "You mean, do I think the timing is rather fortuitous? First Nolan says, in front of witnesses, that the wiring is a mess, and then Hadley's conveniently away from home when her house burns to the ground?"

"Yes. I did wonder about that."

She took my hand in hers. "Nell, the police are satisfied. I think we have to be, too. Joe's death was an accident, case closed. And Hadley's been amply punished for her poor choice in, uh, companions. I don't know if there'll be much of an investigation into the fire. So I think we have to accept things and move on. Don't you?"

"I do." It might be interesting to know how much insurance Hadley had carried on the house—and whether she had managed to sneak a few of her more treasured personal memorabilia away to a safe place, but it really was none of my business. The exhibit looked to be a success, thanks to

Barney's friends, if the children clustered there were any indication. Hadley stood a chance of reclaiming her stature as a children's writer—and might have a good excuse to retire Harriet and try something new. Let's Play would weather the storm. "Is Nolan still around?"

"Yes, he's here somewhere. After all the drama, there's no way he was going to miss seeing what it was all about. And he wanted to support Caitlin. Do you know, I'd built him up to be such an ogre! And I can see how Caitlin came to idolize him just to retaliate against me. I think seeing him now was good for both of us. I'm not angry at him anymore, and she's able to view him in a more balanced way. If she wants to go visit him, I can handle that. He's still her father."

Happy endings all around, then. "Well, I'll let you mingle, Arabella. It looks like your exhibit is a success, and you deserve it. When the dust settles, let's talk about that joint exhibit."

"That would be wonderful, Nell. And thank you for all your help."

She squeezed my arm, then turned to greet another guest, and I turned away, too, all but bumping into James. "I wondered where you were," I said. "Are you allergic to munchkins?"

"You mean all these knee-high creatures? Not at all. It looks like everyone is having a great time."

"Yes, and after all the mess!" I felt a sudden pang of doubt. "You aren't here to rain on anyone's parade, are you? Or arrest anyone?"

"Nope. The police are happy, and I'm not going to interfere. The case is closed, and our friend Detective Hrivnak has signed off on it." He smiled. "I'm here strictly as a civilian. And to see you. I've got a bit of good news for you—consider it a late Christmas present."

"Oh, lovely—I could use some! What is it?"

"We've found the person who purchased a lot of the items stolen from the Society over the last few years. As it turns out, he held on to most of them—he couldn't bear to part with them, so he kept the items in a secret room in his house. Not even his wife knew about them. Once the paperwork is done, you should be getting a lot of them back. I haven't told Marty yet—I thought you deserved to hear it first. You can give the good news to Marty and the board."

"That's *wonderful*!" Without thinking, I grabbed James and planted a kiss on him, then stepped back quickly, embarrassed. "Sorry—I got carried away."

"I, uh, guess I should try to bring you good news like that more often," he said, looking uncharacteristically flustered.

"It will be a real treat to have something good to tell the board." I leaned closer again. "Thank you. For everything. I get the feeling you were looking out for me even through this whole thing. I mean, really—terrorists, here?" I gestured around at the happy families amidst the twinkling lights.

His mouth twitched. "Does seem a bit hard to imagine, doesn't it? Are you ready for dinner?"

It was kind of a nonanswer, but it would do. "Certainly." I waved to Arabella, who was chatting happily with Caitlin, and even to Hadley, glowing with all the attention being paid to her. Would we ever know the real story? Maybe not, but at least Let's Play would survive, and I was glad for Arabella.

I took James's arm. "Let's go."